Reaper

Reaper

Book One of the West Baden Murders Trilogy

Patrick J. O'Brian

Writer's Showcase
New York Lincoln Shanghai

Reaper
Book One of the West Baden Murders Trilogy

Writer's Showcase
an imprint of iUniverse, Inc.

For information address:
iUniverse, Inc.
2021 Pine Lake Road, Suite 100
Lincoln, NE 68512
www.iuniverse.com

ISBN: 0-595-23260-4

Printed in the United States of America

This manuscript is dedicated to firefighters, police officers, emergency medical technicians and paramedics everywhere, who put their lives on the line every day.

I owe many thanks to Troy Smith, John Leach, Erica Cosgrove, Joey Oliver, and especially Troy Lobosky, because without their help, this book would not have the degree of accuracy I wanted it to.

Thanks also to Jim Lenox, Jennifer Sorrells, Troy Lobosky, Richard Cranor, and Rick Shellabarger for their time, and appearing on the cover.

As always, thanks to Kendrick at KLS for making a spectacular cover.
Check out KLS Digital at **www.kls.com** or and out the author's website at **www.pjobooks.com** to see the latest works by the author, where to purchase his books, and what's coming to print in the near future.

1

A stiff breeze darted across the open porch of a white Indiana farm-house as a bare foot stepped gingerly onto the cold wooden planks.

Leaves from several bushes along the house shivered, rustling as though a thunderstorm was coming, while the last flickers of a dying candle burned inside a jack-o-lantern.

Halloween night neared its end.

Angela Clouse picked the lid off the gutted vegetable, then put an end to the candle's fading existence with a quick puff of breath. Her nose took in the unpleasant combination of burnt wax and decaying pumpkin innards. For a moment, she stared at the single crooked tooth in the pumpkin her son had insisted on carving himself. Replacing the top, she suddenly felt uneasy, standing in the cold.

In the middle of nowhere.

Looking across the spacious yard, she could find nothing out of the ordinary. During daylight hours Angie could view what she called God's paintbrush, with all the leaves changing colors before their seesaw descent toward the ground.

Familiar smells of freshly-cut wood, horse manure, and apple cider from neighboring houses let her know she had escaped the confines of nearby Bloomington and the Indiana University campus.

Her car stood in front of the old barn, and the dogs were quietly within sight, reassuring her the property was safe. A chill ran from the bottom of her feet, into her bloodstream, telling her it was time to return to the warmth of the house.

A white paper ghost swinging freely from the top of the porch nearly struck her head as she turned around. Angie stepped inside, locking the doorknob and deadbolt immediately.

Trick-or-treat time was definitely over.

As midnight drew near, the selection of movies on television would be worse than the horror sections in the local video stores. Taking a seat in her comfortable plush chair, Angie flipped through the channels until she found the beginning of *Night of the Living Dead* on a local station.

She loved how the flickers and the black and white screen added to the dark effect of the movie. A familiar vehicle pulled into the cemetery as the opening credits rolled, and she knew what happened next. Johnny would always tease, then unwittingly die at the hands of the first zombie.

"They're coming to get you, Barbara," Angie said in her best Vincent Price voice as she stood, and darted to the kitchen, wanting some popcorn before the movie got to the good parts. She had the entire weekend to sleep in if she stayed up too late.

As she opened the bag of popcorn, one of the dogs barked from the back yard, catching her attention. Angie peered out the window, finding nothing out of the ordinary, and dismissed Spot, her husband's dalmatian, as paranoid schizophrenic.

"That dog barks at everything," she commented to herself, surprised he hadn't barked at her when she stepped outside.

She stuck the bag in the microwave, set the timer, and took a seat as the cordless phone rang beside her.

"Hello?" she answered, eyes glued to the screen as Barbara and Johnny emerged from their car, ready to place flowers on the grave site after a grueling drive.

"Hey, Ang, it's Margo," one of her friends said from the other end. "I figured you'd still be up."

"Are you tricked out too?"

"I spent half the night keeping the kids out of the candy and the other half getting them to bed. They wanted to watch some scary movie-thon on satellite."

"Oh, I know," Angie replied. "It took forever to get Zach to bed. We were out until eight-thirty, then I had kids coming out here until almost ten."

"It must be rough living in total isolation. At least you don't have neighbor kids screaming, crying, and hitting softballs through your window," Margo teased. "How is it alone these days?"

Angie stood to fetch her popcorn.

"I'm getting by. With Zach at preschool, I'm getting a lot more done with the business, and a lot of clients have called about my business software. Referrals are my best friends lately."

"I thought I was your best friend."

"You are, but you don't pay my bills."

Opening the microwave, Angie took out the bag, opened it, and let the steam filter out as she took a diet cola from the refrigerator. She took a moment to look in the mirror, noticing how much better her dark hair looked without a failed perm. Poofed hair always seemed to accent her already small nose, and most of her do-it-yourself hair jobs made her look like an '80s rocker.

She agreed with her mother that her hair looked much better without winding curls, which brought out the natural beauty her husband always said she had.

"Another couple of days and I'll be out with another software upgrade for returning clients, which will make them very happy," Angie said, sitting down to find Johnny and the zombie struggle as Barbara watched in horror.

"You still haven't really answered my question."

"What's that?"

"Has anything changed between you and Paul lately?"

Angie visualized a time when she could cuddle with her husband in front of a warm fire on cool nights like this. She missed the companionship, but things had changed between them recently.

"Nothing new between us. He's been busy with both jobs and I-"

A thumping noise from upstairs diverted her attention from both the movie and her conversation. She missed whatever question Margo had asked.

"Ang? You there?"

"Sorry. I just heard something from upstairs."

"Probably Zach feeling the effects of too much candy."

"Maybe," Angie said, standing up. "Let me go check on him and I'll call you right-"

A few abrupt clicks came over the phone line, cutting her sentence short, then a dead silence took the place of what normally might have been a dial tone.

"You there?" Angie asked, getting no response.

Her phone was completely dead.

Sounds of thunder in the distance offset the notion that it was anything but a storm downing the phone lines. Still, it was supposed to be a light rain, if anything, that evening.

Setting the phone on the coffee table, Angie looked up at the ceiling where the noise had originated. The spot above her was neither Zach's room, nor the bathroom. Her son had no reason to be rummaging through the spare bedroom, and after a full night in town, any four-year-old would probably be asleep soon after his head hit the pillow.

Darkness encumbered the den as she walked through it, sidestepping furniture on her way to the stairs. Since her husband had left, Angie seldom used the room, or the large fireplace inside it. It once served as a place where they once worked and played as a family. Now the house was segmented into seldom-used rooms, each with a particular purpose.

Angie paused, taking a moment to look outside one of the windows. There were no new vehicles in the driveway, and nothing else seemed different than a few minutes before, when she stepped onto the porch.

Once again she heard a thump, then a few footsteps. Zach was too small to make footsteps heard so easily. Now she was spooked, but her son was up there.

Like everything else in her life, the furniture in the den was very orderly and easily avoided. She reached the bottom of the stairs, took hold of the solid oak railing, and looked up, seeing only a slight flicker of light from above, off to the right.

A glow illuminated the lower half of the hallway wall, though the light was quite dim.

There were no candles upstairs, and Zach had no nightlight, leaving her curious where such an illumination might come from. Flipping the light switch beside her, Angie took in a cautious breath when the light above failed to come on.

Cautiously, she ascended the stairs, keeping her eyes focused on the flickers. Her son's bedroom door on the left appeared closed. The light source had to originate from the hallway, the bathroom, or the spare bedroom, where the noise had come from.

Something strange was going on, and she knew Zach would not play Halloween tricks at his age. He was too young to understand anything about the holiday besides candy.

Still, it was the witching holiday and she felt uneasy about what awaited her atop the stairs.

Feeling reasonably certain she had kept every door locked while she was out with Zach, Angie could not fathom how anyone might enter the residence without a key. An uneasy feeling Zach was not awake nagged at her, and none of the protective dogs were in the house. She had to check on her son and know everything was safe, before returning Margo's call.

Assuming, of course, the phone would work.

Clutching the hand rail, Angie reached the top of the stairs, slowly peering to the right, where the eerie orange glow appeared strongest. Her eyes widened, taking in the horror at the end of the hall, where the flicker of a candle's flame peered through the carved portions of a jack-o-lantern with a single, crooked tooth. Thinking it impossible, she looked closer to see if it was the one from the front porch.

One in the same.

Low light was not the reason visibility was so bad, but rather a large clump eclipsing the Halloween decoration. Squinting to see better, Angie was drawn to the object, focusing intently as she walked along the hallway floor, realizing, much to her horror, the object was a body and this was no prank.

Her eyes had adjusted enough to the darkness that she could make out shapes, even from the dim orange glow. On either side of the clump she could see tiny hands, rigidly contorted into a half fist. One leg buckled at the knee, sticking upward, leaving little doubt about exactly what she was viewing.

She dared not look at the head, feeling the evidence before her was compelling enough to warrant the numbing sensation creeping up her body.

Drawing her hand to her mouth in a gasp, Angie shrunk away from the sight, feeling nothing but utter shock that someone had violated her home, and taken away the most precious thing in her life.

Her child.

Instinctively, Angie reached for the door behind her, where Zach had gone to bed just hours before. After swiping at, and missing the knob, she turned to look for it, but heard a noise from the bathroom at the far end of the hall. The light from the jack-o-lantern was momentarily blocked, distracting her from Zach's room.

She turned to see a figure streak across the hallway toward her, then felt a sharp pain in her right shoulder as a sharp object gleamed in the low light before penetrating her skin.

Leaving her no time to react, or assess the danger she was in, the object swung back, then toward her again. Barely ducking from the blade's swing, Angie darted down the stairs, blood dripping from her wound, as the attacker yanked his weapon from the wall, taking chase.

As quickly as she descended the stairs, he seemed equally nimble. She reached the bottom of the staircase, cutting right as the blade struck the wall behind her, forcing an involuntary shriek from her mouth.

Her attacker spent a moment freeing his weapon, giving her an opportunity to reach the kitchen, then the freedom of the back door. So many times its solid wooden frame had given her freedom to the beauty and clean air of the country outside. Now it could provide freedom from certain death if she could just get it open.

Unlocking the doorknob, she tugged on the door, but it would not budge.

"Deadbolt," she stammered, nervously turning the lock.

Swinging the door open, she started for the porch, but felt a sharp, painful sensation rip through her back, as the breath was knocked from her body.

Paralyzed with pain and terror, Angie looked down at her chest, seeing the blade of a sickle, covered in her own blood, piercing her upper torso from behind.

Before she could contemplate escape, or the nature of her wound, the killer yanked the weapon, and her with it, back into the house. Her muffled screams went unheard through the vacant countryside as the killer went to work with his curved, deadly weapon.

2

A single brown cowboy boot with a gold tip on the toe stepped across the red *DANGER DO NOT ENTER* tape, followed by its counterpart as their owner stood a moment, hands firmly cupped on his waist, admiring his work. A photo of him at that moment would have mimicked any 20th century inventor beside his life's greatest accomplishment.

Naturally, the construction of the West Baden Springs Hotel was not Paul Clouse's own work, but he was a crucial part of the crew working on the restoration of the hotel to its previous glory. And to think, it was partly by accident he was working on one of the most interesting buildings in the world, right in his home state.

Standing at one of the four major entrances in the hotel's atrium, Clouse looked like the busy construction workers around him, wearing a hard hat as he stared at the glass dome two-hundred feet above him. Sunlight could stream through, during certain parts of the day, and the chandelier served as more of a centerpiece than a source of light during the evening hours. The thought of such a large, self-supported dome still awed him, considering it was built during an era when domes were rare, particularly in the States.

Before the National Preservation Society stepped in, the hotel had fallen to ruins, and one entire wall had literally fallen, prompting the group's action to define the hotel as a historical landmark, then begin funding its reconstruction.

Clouse recalled his early graduate work at Indiana University, majoring in architecture. He created a comprehensive blueprint of the hotel as part of the final project for one of his more challenging courses. At the time, the hotel lay in ruins with overgrown weeds and bushes, and Clouse had one of his friends on the county police department sneak him inside.

Beyond the faded paint, dust, and cobwebs, Clouse had found the beauty that drew visitors from around the world during the hotel's heyday. He took photos of various rooms, learned the layout, and discovered what held the hotel together.

That was the easy part.

Drawing six stories of floors in the building's unusual shape, complete with glass dome, proved much tougher. It took him another month and three more visits to complete a detailed blueprint.

He got an 'A' on the project, but memories of the blueprint and his studies in architecture faded after his appointment to the Bloomington Fire Department.

After a year-and-a-half on the fire department, he considered finishing work on his masters degree because it was so close to completion, but found an intriguing article in the newspaper about the restoration of the hotel, so he pursued it first. His love for historical landmarks, and an opportunity to see parts of the hotel few others could, prompted him to show his blueprints to David Landamere, the project leader, and the creative foreman for Kieffer Construction, the team contracted to remodel the hotel.

In a way, it was the perfect arrangement. Landamere hired Clouse as a part-time consultant, mostly for the use of his blueprints to save valuable time. It turned out the two had similar ideas, and knew how to save both time and money in the construction process. Clouse was getting paid for something he already loved.

"Morning, Paul," Landamere said from behind, patting Clouse on the back.

"Hey, Dave," Clouse replied, rubbing his chin, then the thick mustache above the smirk on his lips. "Ready to walk the grounds?"

Every week on Wednesday or Thursday, depending on his schedule at the fire department, Clouse met Landamere for a tour of the hotel grounds to see what areas needed immediate attention, and which rooms took priority in the restoration.

"It's a little nippy out there, Paul," Landamere commented. "They say it might snow today."

"This whole winter's supposed to be bad."

For a moment, both looked at the atrium where guests had once eaten dinner, danced, and listened to lavish entertainment night after night. Intricate, detailed paintings stood in sharp green, gold, and red colors along every wall and pillar. Every wall, ceiling, and floor had crafted designs that were beyond traditional American vision or make.

And they were exactly as they had been when the hotel was built in the early twentieth century.

Looking across the atrium was like staring at the opposite end of a football field. People could not simply walk across it without gazing at the designs above them on the walls, or imagine themselves on one of the balconies overlooking the very floor they stood on.

To Clouse, it was like stepping into a marvelous classic church, only more vast.

Marble parquet, a beautiful, shiny tile with intricate leaf and various Indian designs now covered less than half the floor. Part of it was being replaced by new carpet of similar designs in the next few months. The move was neither cost-effective, nor practical in keeping the hotel historically accurate, but it was necessary. Like several other items in the hotel, the marble tile had been imported almost a century prior, and could not be replicated. Carpet was the only realistic alternative in replacing the damaged areas.

Above him, Clouse could see five more floors before the beginning of the dome and the dozen dual metallic ribs that kept it towering above guests and rooms alike. Several rooms had small balconies where guests would be able to step out and see the activities in the atrium below. Along the walls of the round atrium were detailed paintings that matched the floor in both color and design.

After every third room stood a mammoth eggshell-colored pillar that almost gave the firefighter the impression he was back in church as a kid, with columns reaching for the sky and paintings of the Virgin Mary looking down on him.

Church scared him to death back then.

Restoration would give the hotel back its original look, hopefully attracting buyers who would finish the multi-million-dollar job. More than anything, Clouse wanted to see that dream become a reality and be around for the completion. Every day off, he visited the landmark to find something new on the grounds, or inside. He could envision the final product, and strangely enough, had an idea of how to make it happen.

"You know how much cheaper it would have been just to tear it down and build a new one?" Landamere asked, looking from the grand fireplace to his right, back to his designer.

"But then it's not restoration, is it?" Clouse replied with a grin, knowing exactly what specifications the NPS had laid before them.

Both men walked through the open entrance to the hotel lobby. Unlike the atrium they had just come from, the hallway was gutted and barren of decor. Much of the hotel was still skeletal in appearance, leaving only plasterboard, wood, and drywall framing on the upper floors where guest rooms once housed hundreds of visitors at a time. Only the atrium and selected primary rooms were being redone for the time being.

"So how are things going with you and the wife?" Landamere asked, knowing his favorite consultant appeared glum lately. "I haven't seen you together since the ball last month."

Landamere referred to a fund-raising ball held in mid-October. Tours and special events were a way to raise money for, what local residents hoped, would be a full restoration of the property. The ball was the last time Angie had agreed to be publically seen with Clouse before their separation. Both had remained quiet about their parting, and neither seemed to understand why they felt no more happy, or miserable, than they had together.

"It's been busy," Clouse replied as they entered Landamere's office, hating the truth of the situation.

He unzipped his brown leather jacket with its forest-green collar, then hung it behind the door. Now several years old, the jacket was probably out of style, but it was still his favorite. Clouse looked out the window, spying several leaves caught by the breeze as they fell from nearby trees, then took a seat beside Landamere's desk.

He wore a sweatshirt with fire department emblems on the front, and comfortable blue jeans. The sweatshirt hid his broad shoulders and powerful arms, which served him at work, and on the farm where he had resided until a few weeks prior. He currently found little use for a solid body in the one-room apartment he paid too much for in Bloomington.

Things had been going so well with their marriage that it seemed a shame to cut everything off. Angie was a beautiful business woman with a prospering self-made career, working out of the home. Clouse was a dedicated, handsome firefighter who had plenty of time at home for family before he started work at the hotel. In many ways, he seemed the ideal husband and family man.

Angie's notion of ideal differed from his own. She wanted a husband home most of the time, helping her by taking care of their son. With him working two jobs, she felt saddled with responsibility, raising their son while supporting their family, just as much as he did.

Working on the West Baden Springs Hotel was not the problem in his marriage, however, as Clouse's blue eyes, his smirk, and the nature of his career got him in trouble several times before their separation. Angie knew certain women adored firemen, and despite complete love and devotion from her husband, she always had a suspicious nature about his whereabouts, primarily spawned by rumors she heard, most of which he easily disproved.

In his early thirties, Clouse had the best of both worlds if only his marriage had worked. He was well on his way to some excellent jobs in architecture with Landamere, while under the protective umbrella of a city job and its benefits.

"You haven't missed much this week," Landamere commented, sitting behind his desk, looking around the bland office. Both the filing cabinet and desk were buried beneath blueprints and shuffled papers. "They found some more of the statues we thought were lost during the Jesuit era, and it appears one of the grave sites was disturbed last night," the foreman said, slowly shaking his head.

"Security didn't see anything?"

"No, it probably happened before they got here last night. Someone took a body out of there and it hasn't turned up yet."

Clouse disliked the thought of Jesuit bodies being dug up from the cemetery less than a quarter mile from the hotel. During an era after the second World War, Jesuit priests had control of the hotel and buried their dead in the nearby site.

After owning the grounds several decades, the Jesuits were entitled to bury their dead on the hill, but no one else received such special treatment. Clouse realized the historical significance of the dead buried there, but the priests had done so much to decimate the traditional appearance of the hotel, that he resented them in part.

After the second World War, the priests bought the grounds to use as a seminary, doing away with many of the statues, stained glass windows, and imported art Clouse and Landamere fought daily to recover. Through newspaper ads, radio, and even word of mouth, their construction company desperately sought anyone possessing the hotel's old treasures.

"If I find any of the boys dug it up for kicks I'll fire 'em," Landamere scoffed, speaking of the missing body. "That's plain unprofessional."

"I doubt any of them would," Clouse stated, kicking the corner of the desk with one of his boots.

Angie always hated him wearing them. She believed anything that didn't look upper-class, including her husband, hurt her chances of landing large clients.

"It's pointless to dig up a body with security here after hours," Clouse commented, finishing his thought. "And what the hell would you do with it?"

Landamere looked at his watch, seeing it was just past nine. The morning was wasting away, and they still had an inspection of the grounds to conduct.

"Take it on tour?" Landamere commented sarcastically, putting on his reading glasses to peruse the plans atop his desk.

Most of his hair had bypassed the gray state, turning a smoky color of white. With his glasses on, he reminded Clouse of his grandfather, who lived on a farm when he was a boy.

He was nearing retirement age, but appeared nowhere near it, despite the hair. Landamere could work all day, just like his crew, if necessary. A born leader, it showed whenever the man spoke or picked up a hammer.

"Well, grab your coat and let's get this started," he ordered Clouse.

As the two walked into the lobby toward the glass front doors, Clouse looked at the lobby area, taking note of the lights, the decor, and how incredibly good it looked in comparison to the start of the project.

Ordinarily, tourists poured through the doors after ten o'clock with their guides, in awe of what the hotel looked like. Some only made the trip once a year, and what a difference a year made in the reconstruction process. Clouse, like many of the construction workers, stayed clear of the tourist groups, though many would snap pictures of the workers in action.

Clouse thought someday the photos might be historically significant, and didn't mind being the subject of a photo every now and then, when he and Landamere toured the grounds. Occasionally, since he was more regularly dressed than the construction workers, he would eavesdrop on a tour to hear what tourists said about the hotel and how gorgeous it looked.

As they stepped outside, and down a long row of concrete steps, Clouse looked behind him at the looming hotel. From ground level, he could see the covered balcony, then traced the yellow walls with stark white trim up their six stories where the great rustic-red dome capped off its magnificence. Now four new towers, which did little more than beautify the landmark, had replaced the originals destroyed during the Jesuit era. They stood taller than the dome, adding to the complexity and mystery of the West Baden Springs Hotel.

"Any ideas what we should do with the storage barn yet?" Landamere asked as they crossed the sunken garden and the now-active water fountain, which displayed stone frogs propped at the edge spitting streams of water toward their turtle counterparts, sitting below the water surface in the center.

"We're obviously not wanting anything too permanent," Clouse said, knowing the building was a bowling alley in its day. "It's the right shape to house an indoor pool. But it's a little far from the hotel to be trudging barefoot with a towel. We could make it a bowling alley again, or just clean it out and leave it to a buyer's imagination."

"Maybe clean it, paint it a neutral color, and leave it," Landamere thought aloud.

To Clouse, Landamere was almost like an uncle. He was older, wiser, and always willing to see the good in people. He held no respect for laziness or what he called 'boneheaded' mistakes. His crew knew better than to cross him, and they worked hard or they wouldn't be working very long.

Landamere had a distinguished air about him that set him apart from his men. He seldom did manual labor himself, but no one, Clouse included, doubted his labor skills. More than once Clouse had witnessed him work wonders with a hammer or any number of saws in an instant. The man had nothing to prove around his crew.

Like Clouse, Landamere dressed better than the crew, which let tourists and volunteer workers know he was someone with clout. Though not arrogant, Landamere wanted people to know who he was, and he often wore his personality outright.

Clouse looked up at the overcast sky as they walked through the sunken garden, then toward the storage building, and the disturbed cemetery. It looked as though snow could spit from the sky at any moment, but it seemed far too soon for winter's arrival. Southern Indiana usually had a brief, mild winter after the holiday season, but rumor had it this year would be different.

"We need to get those fountains shut off and drained pretty soon if it's going to be this cold," Clouse noted aloud.

"Good point," Landamere replied as they walked up a small embankment toward the plain, white slabs serving as grave markers, and the single white cross behind them, nearly obscured by thick trees on the hillside.

A concrete stairway curved up the hill, surrounded on either side by impassible shrubs to the small cemetery, where two dozen graves sat to the left, another dozen to the right, and one single grave above those on the right side, completely cut off from the others by shrubs and the stairway.

There was no lack of space from what Clouse could ever see, since the graves were extremely close in proximity. He seemed to remember hearing a reason for the grave set by itself, but failed to recall the details of the legend at that moment.

It was that single grave on the right that appeared disturbed with small mounds of dirt on either side. In the cover of darkness, and with trees looming in every direction, Clouse figured it would be easy to dig up the grave undetected.

But why?

"Well, isn't this precious?" Landamere asked sarcastically, looking into the greatly deteriorated wooden box that once held a body.

Shreds of cloth and what Clouse hoped weren't pieces of skin tissue littered the casket. He could see dark tufts of hair at one end, and an eerie feeling shot through his body. They looked brittle, as though they might disintegrate to the touch. The stiff, frail nature of the hair reminded him of something familiar, but he could not recall exactly what.

"How long was that body in here?" he asked.

"I'm pretty sure it was Jesuit," Landamere replied. "The local library has some literature on these graves if you want to play detective."

Clouse shook his head.

"It's not that. It just seems quite preserved for being here four decades."

"It's a shady, cool spot. Strange things happen six feet under."

"More like three," Clouse said, noting how shallow the grave appeared.

"The priests had better things to do than dig graves all day."

"Yeah, it seems like they dug enough of them," Clouse replied, counting about three dozen stones. "Did they import their dead or what?"

Landamere chuckled, leading Clouse away from the grave, down the brick steps. He gave his designer another hearty pat on the back, reinforcing the uncle relationship Clouse rather enjoyed. Not that he and Landamere usually saw much of one another outside of work, but he liked knowing he was wanted, and there would always be a stable secondary income for him.

Most firefighters around him had second jobs, but most didn't like their work, or it was mandatory. To Clouse, working on the hotel was not necessary for income, or to fill his time. He simply enjoyed doing work that put his degree to use. A number of co-workers envied him for being so happy with both occupations.

As the two neared the bottom of the steps, two men in suits came into view from across the grounds. While Clouse figured they were businessmen wanting information about the hotel, Landamere guessed they were police detectives, there to look at the grave robbery he had phoned in that morning.

He was partly correct.

When they neared the two hotel designers, the men took out identification in the form of badges, and presented them.

"Detectives Kendle and Daniels, Bloomington Police Department," the first said, indicating he was Kendle. "Are you Paul Clouse?" he asked, looking to the firefighter.

"I am," Clouse answered, unsure of what to expect since the two were from Bloomington.

"I'm afraid we have some bad news for you, sir."

3

Even as he sat inside an interview room alone, Clouse had any number of things to ponder. The news of Angie's death had shocked him, and he felt any number of emotions coursing through his body, changing by the minute.

He was between interviews, and knew little, as they were asking him all the questions and leaking few details. Clouse knew his son was alive since Zach was the one who called 911 after finding his mother lying on the kitchen floor. They promised a reunion with Zach after the interviews, which irritated him.

He never imagined all the time spent teaching his son about distress calls would be used in such a way.

Stuck in a plain brown room that smelled faintly of smoke, with nothing but three chairs, a small table, and an unconvincing two-way mirror, Clouse was alone with his thoughts. Unfortunately, his thoughts were the worst possible companions he could have at the moment.

Both detectives found it difficult to believe he had heard nothing of his wife's death, considering he was working in Bloomington the night before. Angie's murder happened too late for the local newspaper to cover, and no one at the station had the television on that morning, so he had no way of knowing.

Refusing to mourn until he was alone, Clouse kept his irritation at the police, his grief over Angie's death, and his desperation to see his son to himself. He was outraged about being the prime suspect in Angie's death, and there were certainly more important things to worry about than clearing his name for a crime he would never dream of committing.

Clouse was horrified Zach had found his mother murdered, but relieved his son was fine. From what he understood, Zach had seen and heard nothing during the night. This neither hurt nor helped Clouse in clearing his name. The detectives seemed bent on extracting any piece of incriminating evidence from him, despite the firefighter already providing what he considered an airtight alibi.

He understood the importance in finding the killer, and eliminating suspects, but Clouse wanted to speak with friends and family, especially his son, before dealing with the law. Minutes seemed like hours until the door finally opened and Detective Larry Kendle stepped in.

"Just a few more questions for you, Mr. Clouse," he said, standing over the seated fireman. It was an empowering trick investigators used for leverage over interviewees, but Clouse was in no mood for games. "Rumor has it you and the misses were separated."

"We were," Clouse replied.

"She apparently made little secret of it, from what her friends tell us," Kendle noted. "You, on the other hand, weren't very open about it. Even when your boss asked you this morning, you dodged the question of your relationship with your wife."

Clouse said nothing, simply looking at the detective.

Kendle reminded him of a bulldog. His gray hair, lined with streaks of black, gave Clouse the idea he was nearing retirement age. He tended to show his teeth, whether in a sneering smile or with a curved lip to show his displeasure in how the interview went. His tie was perfectly straight, and his long-sleeved shirt was pressed, with no wrinkles. Kendle wore his firearm traditionally at his side, giving Clouse every indication he was of military background, and very regimented.

Clouse was somewhat surprised the detectives had interviewed so many people so quickly, but he knew most murder cases were solved within the first forty-eight hours or they often went unsolved. Many a night was spent watching the Discovery Channel at the firehouse.

Legwork was a must for any investigator in Indiana because forensic analysis had such a long turnaround time. Kendle knew he would have to put together a solid case with his own evidence, or risk losing a conviction if he made an arrest. Often it took months, even half a year, to receive results from the Indianapolis state police lab, unless a case was considered a major priority. Clouse, too, had knowledge of such things from his friends in police work.

"Were you simply too proud to admit your wife left you, Mr. Clouse? Or were you planning something much bigger, where public knowledge of your separation might hurt your chances of success?"

Clouse sighed aloud.

"Pressing my buttons won't get you any closer to solving this case, detective," he said. "You know full well I worked at Station 2 last night and any of the guys I worked with will tell you I never left the station."

"We'll be talking to them later, sir. Usually firefighters turn in early, don't they? I mean the murder occurred around midnight or later. And your house really isn't that far from the station."

"I see where this is going," Clouse said, notably disgusted. "Unless you're going to formally charge me with murder I want to see my son, and I would like to speak with my family about arrangements. I'd also like to get inside my house this afternoon and see for myself, since you people refuse to tell me any details about what happened last night."

"We were hoping you might tell us."

"No," Clouse said, standing from his chair, snatching his jacket from the table. "You were hoping for an easy way out."

Opening the door, Clouse stomped into the hallway, turning around after a few steps. "You really don't know a thing about me, detective!" he said angrily, edging dangerously close to the man. "I'm the kind of guy who enjoys boating, fishing, my family, occasionally going to church, and working my ass off to get where I want to be in life. I'm no murderer."

Daniels stepped from the viewing room area to join his partner, afraid Clouse's agitation might lead to violence.

"Where is my son?" he demanded of Kendle.

"Kelli Summers picked him up this morning after we questioned him," Daniels answered before his partner could say something irrational.

Just great, Clouse thought as he stormed out of the police station. His son had been subjected to the same inconsiderate detectives, and he was in the care of Angie's sister. Things were not improving in the least.

He understood why investigators might consider him the prime suspect, because no one else stood to gain what he did. To Clouse, the marriage was never irreconcilable and he could never consider taking such a drastic measure for financial gain. Still, he could think of no one else with a motive to kill Angie.

Perhaps that was how the detectives thought.

Climbing into his Chevy pickup, he let his emotions take over. He shut the door, feeling tears well in his eyes. Away from the detectives and the family he would soon have to confront, he let uncontrollable sobs run free for nearly ten minutes before starting the engine.

Clouse felt selfish for hoping the blame would not wrongfully fall on him, but longed for the opportunity to finish living the life he and Angie always wanted together. For six years, everything in their lives aimed toward one dream, and just as it had all came together, their relationship seemed to fall apart.

Angie finally saw profit in her business, they had a child, owned gorgeous property with everything they'd ever dreamed of, just outside of Bloomington, and Clouse had gotten a second job that finally made him happy while using his degree.

Perhaps it was his own happiness that caused the problems. Throughout their marriage, both had sacrificed, and both had conformed for one another. Clouse always thought he gave up more than she did, but never really minded. When they separated, he enjoyed the personal freedom, feeling more like his old self again. He grew tired of living for Angie, and perhaps she felt the same.

It was such a simple dilemma, yet so complex. Now it would never be resolved.

His tears settled as he saw the driveway full of cars only a block ahead. The notion of facing Angie's family alone distressed him, but he needed to see Zach. He expected mixed reactions from everyone there, hoping most knew him well enough to believe he was incapable of cold-blooded murder.

Pasty flakes of snow splattered on his truck's windshield as he pulled beside the drive, seeing a variety of family members inside the house, several shooting disparaging looks when they saw his truck. He felt like the devil arriving to fulfill their prophesy.

Even before he reached the side door, it opened, revealing Kelli Summers, his sister-in-law. She, more than most of the family, knew Clouse. He stared into a face of sadness, but found assurance that she believed he was unable to commit such an act on her sister.

Unlike her sister, Kelli kept her hair cut short. Her usually bright hazel eyes appeared misted, surrounded by flush skin from crying. Her petite figure attracted men every time she went out with Clouse or Angie, but somehow she remained single.

"Zach's been asking for you all morning," she said, pulling the door nearly shut behind her as they stood in the cold.

"How is everyone?" he asked.

"Holding up," she replied before looking to the ground. "The police haven't said much. They just asked us all a lot of questions. Mostly about you."

"No surprise there," Clouse noted with a hint of agitation. "Can I see Zach a minute?" he asked, not wanting to intrude.

"Sure," she replied with no hesitation. "Let me get him."

When Zach came the door, Clouse could see the close resemblance his son held to him, more than ever. From the chocolate-brown hair to the piercing blue eyes, Zach always looked more like Clouse than he did his mother. It was another thing that always seemed to irritate Angie when people saw their son.

"Daddy," he said, embracing Clouse, who was thrilled his son had not suffered so much as a scratch from the night before.

"How are you holding up, kid?" he asked, holding his son in front of him in a secure grip by the shoulders.

"Everyone keeps crying and telling me Mommy's gone," Zach said with youthful innocence and ignorance of the situation. "Why isn't she coming back?"

Clouse fought back a tear, pulling Zach into another hug.

"She just isn't, Zach," he said. "Mommy's in a better place now, and someday you'll see her again."

"But I want to see her now," Zach insisted, pushing against his father's broad shoulders, seeing the hurt in Clouse's eyes. For his son's sake, he fought back the urge to cry. "What's wrong, Daddy?"

"Everything will be okay, son," Clouse explained. "I'll be back for you later."

"But-"

"I know," Clouse cut Zach off with a foreboding finger. "I need you to stay with Aunt Kelli for a while longer. I'll be back tonight. Okay?"

"Okay," Zach reluctantly agreed.

"Roger wants to see you a second," Kelli said before taking Zach into the house.

Roger Summers, Angie's brother and a fellow firefighter on the department, had always been close to Angie and Clouse. He was the one person Clouse knew was incapable of murdering Angie, but he would also be one of the most hurt by her death.

At a time when Clouse was unsure of whether or not to approach Kieffer Construction about using his blueprints, it was Summers who insisted he talk to one of the general managers.

"Paul," he said coming to the door with a greeting nod. His eyes were puffy and red, displaying the hardship he shared with his family.

Dressed in sweat pants and a sweatshirt bearing fire department emblems, it was obvious Summers had been at work when the news came. He was barefoot, holding a steaming cup of coffee in his right hand as he stepped outside. His thicket of black hair appeared strewn like a wheat field after a thunderstorm.

"Rodge, how are you holding up?" Clouse asked uneasily.

"Doing okay, considering the police won't give us any details. My understanding is it'll probably be a closed casket service."

"Oh, God," Clouse said under his breath, only imagining how horrific the murder must have been.

"I got the news as I was getting off work this morning," Summers said with an involuntary sniffle. "Everyone's here helping with the arrangements."

"I'm sorry, Rodge," Clouse said, trying to excuse himself from the awkward situation. "I'll be back later to pick up Zach, but I can't imagine I'm going to be welcome here."

Summers thought a moment, then realized what his brother-in-law meant.

"Did the police question you?"

"They took it a step beyond that," Clouse replied. "I seem to be the extent of their search for suspects."

"That's not right!" Summers objected aloud, immediately realizing he could be heard inside. "You couldn't do anything like that, Paul. I know you'd never hurt Angie."

"Thanks, Rodge," Clouse said sincerely. "I'm glad someone thinks that."

"If you need *anything*, just call me. There's no sense in you going through this alone."

"Thanks. I'll be back later," Clouse said, drawing away from the house. "There are a few things I need to go check on with the police."

"Take care, Paul," Summers said, retreating to the warmth of the house and the comfort of loved ones.

Taking the lonely walk to his truck, Clouse opened the door, picking up the cellular phone from its charger as he climbed in. At the time he needed friends and allies the most, he was finding few, and one of his last chances to quickly find answers might lie in an old high school buddy.

He started the truck and pressed a button to automatically dial his friend's number on the cellular phone.

4

After contacting the only person who might help him find answers, Clouse stopped for a light lunch, then drove to his house, only to find a Bloomington officer guarding the end of his driveway. Seated in his patrol car, the officer worked diligently on a crossword puzzle. An unmarked car sat nearby, belonging to the officers conducting forensic tests inside.

Though the officer refused to give out much information, Clouse took a good look at the house and the yellow tape surrounding it. He could see what appeared to be blood spatters on the porch, but little else of significance. It would be the next day before he could get inside.

Now he pulled into the only place he felt comfortable. Even with dark clouds looming overhead, the hotel looked incredible to him. He was in no mood to speak with the crew, or even Landamere, but knew it would be impossible to simply brood alone on the grounds. Besides, Ken Kaiser, his old high school pal, would be dropping by shortly. Clouse hoped to find out anything about the murder from the Orange County police officer.

Both had graduated from Bloomington North High School the same year, then went separate ways soon thereafter. While Clouse attended Indiana University, Kaiser immediately pursued various law enforcement channels, first joining the Orleans Police Department in a small town several miles north of the hotel. When an opportunity to join the county police came, Kaiser jumped at the chance for a pay raise and a take home car with his first child on the way.

Fate brought the friends together again when Clouse began his design work, and Kaiser was one of three officers able to snatch up some part-time security work on the grounds after operating hours. He was the one person Clouse knew, who seemed to have contacts with every department in Southern Indiana. He could possibly shed some light on the fireman's unfortunate situation if he was privy to the information.

He would be granted no time alone as he stepped from his truck, only to be met by Rusty Cranor, Landamere's chief assistant on the project.

A working foreman, Rusty wore a yellow hard hat, and blue jeans tattered with dirt and a few minor tears. Nearly fifty-years-old, Rusty kept a red beard peppered with gray hairs. A year-round tan and several wrinkles under his eyes were the results of a career working outdoor labor in the worst of conditions.

"Hi, Paul," he said with his usual easy smile, obviously not knowing the bad news yet.

"Hey, Rusty. How goes the project?"

"That's what I wanted to ask you about," Rusty said, the smile fading. "Dave left this morning shortly after you did, and left me in charge. He hasn't come back yet."

"Everything's okay, isn't it?" Clouse asked, walking with the foreman toward the hotel's main entrance.

"Well, yeah, but I thought he was supposed to be right back. Do you know what he wanted us to do in the basement today?"

The basement held most of the tools, lumber, roofing supplies, and whatever else its gigantic locked door could keep behind it. It was several divided rooms within one large area, and an ideal spot to cut wood planks, hide from a foreman, or relax. Clouse often walked the basement to check the stability of the hotel, and create ideas, working from the ground up.

"I think he wanted some of the supplies moved from the first room to the roof," Clouse answered. "We need to get that trim work done before winter."

"I'll get down there and see what needs moving," Rusty said, beginning to walk away. He turned around after a few steps. "You know where Dave went?"

Clouse shrugged. "No. I'm sure he'll be back soon."

As Rusty walked into the hotel, the firefighter spied a county police car pulling through the gigantic yellow gates of the hotel, then up the brick walkway, parking next to several of the workers' vehicles.

"Good timing," Clouse said to himself, anxious to see his long-time friend.

"I'm sorry about the news," Ken Kaiser told Clouse as the two met on the walkway, quickly shaking hands. His friend was dressed for the weather, a nylon police jacket covering his uniform shirt and clip-on tie.

Kaiser was one of the very few people Clouse had talked to about his marital problems. The officer was simply biding time, doing security several nights a week, and turned out to be a good listener.

"It wasn't pretty," the officer said, walking with Clouse toward the front balcony area of the hotel. "The detective I talked to said there was blood everywhere in the kitchen, and multiple puncture wounds on the body."

"God," Clouse said, wiping beads of sweat from his forehead. All morning his body felt overly warm as he expelled nervous energy. All of the tension was wearing him down, possibly to sickness.

"They know it was a bladed weapon, but they won't know what until the autopsy is conducted. It occurred around midnight, and they're checking your house for every kind of DNA sample they can pick up."

Clouse noticed his friend had decided to shave his face clean again. He could never make up his mind how he wanted to look. This week it seemed he wanted the younger, former military look of the cops he worked with. His black hair was buzzed nearly to the point that his scalp was entirely visible. And just in time for winter, Clouse thought sarcastically.

To say Kaiser was impulsive or rash never quite covered it. He often bought items on the spur of the moment, and sometimes returned them the same day when his wife found out. Lately, the cop had an itching for a Harley-Davidson motorcycle, which Clouse's sensible advice had kept him from buying, at least to this point.

Clouse was amazed his high school buddy was still married with the stunts he pulled.

"Who would want to see Angie dead?" Clouse pondered aloud, stumped for an answer.

"The Bloomington Police think they know," Kaiser noted, shaking his head.

"That they do," Clouse replied. "And if they're looking at me, they're not looking for the right person, and he'll get away with it."

Both walked the front steps of the hotel up to the balcony, not saying a word. Taking a right turn atop the stairs, they stood on intricately designed concrete, surrounded by pillars along the hotel walls, and potted plants and trees on the outer rim of the walkway. Tourists were forbidden to walk this area for fear they might separate from their groups and take a personal tour of the hotel's off-limit rooms.

A terrible liability case if any accidents ever happened.

"I know you worked last night, Paul," Kaiser said in a hushed voice, making certain no construction workers overheard. "Is your alibi airtight?"

"It won't be, considering we went to bed fairly early last night," Clouse confided, speaking of his fellow firefighters. "They won't be able to vouch for certain whether or not I was there at the time of the murder."

Clouse and his fellow firefighters shared a common bunk area. If no one had woke up around midnight with insomnia, or to take a bathroom break, he had no sure alibi.

"How is Zach?"

"Confused. He doesn't really understand what's going on, and I know Angie's family is going to try keeping him from me."

"Do they think you did it?"

"Some do, I'm sure," Clouse replied. "Her parents turned on me when we separated. I think Roger and Kelli know me better than that." He sighed. "But it could get ugly."

Kaiser leaned against the balcony railing, feeling the wind whip around the circular walkway. He folded his arms, looking out to the grounds of the hotel, still littered with machinery and supplies, waiting their turn to contribute to the monumental project. Like Clouse, Kaiser shared a love for the hotel that went beyond working there. He knew the history of the land as well as any tour guide, sometimes noting quirky facts that annoyed his co-workers, sick of hearing him ramble about West Baden Springs.

"Just remember, Paul, they need concrete proof you were at the house to make a case. The DNA tests should lead them away from you as a suspect."

"But you know they're going to find my hair and skin samples in there, Ken," Clouse retorted. "It hasn't been that long since I lived there, remember?"

"I guess it hasn't," Kaiser concurred. "Then it can't hurt your case, either."

"But it won't help," Clouse said, trying to rub away the beginning of a headache from his forehead.

"There's no murder weapon," Kaiser said, recounting the facts. "There aren't any witnesses, and there are a ton of people Angie was in contact with."

Clouse let out a controlled chuckle. "You going to be my lawyer, Ken?"

"No, but I know what it takes to get a case to court, and they're not even close. Don't sweat it, Paul. We've got plenty of time to prove your innocence and get things back to normal."

"Normal? Here we are talking about my wife like she's a name on the eight o'clock news, and how to clear me, when I didn't do anything."

"It's not fair," Kaiser noted. "You're not supposed to worry about shit like that when your wife is, well, you know."

"Yeah, I know."

Clouse wondered what the 'normal' Kaiser spoke of would be from now on. It certainly made things clearer for him without Angie around, but he would now be a single parent. There was almost an entire family who would never dismiss his involvement in Angie's death because he stood the most to gain from her demise.

Life insurance was substantial on both he and Angie, and there was the property, the house, the boat, and everything else they worked so hard to own. Only now did Clouse realize how much he had sacrificed to get them there, and how nothing could ever be the same again. His situation was by no means good before, but he would take it over the mess he confronted now.

"You can't stay here and work," Kaiser said. "Take the day off. Go grab some coffee or something."

"I don't really have anywhere to go," Clouse confessed. "They've condemned my house, I'd go stir crazy in the apartment, and I can't pick up Zach until tonight. That is, if the family lets me have him."

"They can't deny you your son," Kaiser said vehemently.

"If they want to, they'll find a way."

Clouse was about to suggest they head inside when Rusty came out the front door, frantically looking in every direction until he spotted the two men talking on the balcony.

"Paul!" he called. "Paul! You've got to see what's downstairs! It's the damnedest thing I've ever seen."

Without saying a word, Clouse and Kaiser followed Rusty through the hotel, down to the basement where the first door stood open, its contents easily seen from a distance. To Clouse, nothing looked out of the usual, with various tiles, lumber, and boxes lining the room. As he drew closer, however, it became clear what the foreman was upset about.

Next to a sealed box, a mass of bone, decomposed dried skin, and small tufts of hair comprised what Clouse could only assume was the missing body from the cemetery on the hill. Most of the bones were still attached, but the body lay in a heap, as though thrown there. Small pieces of the dried skin and hair sat on the dirty concrete floor beside the body, thrown loose from the impact.

By no means did the body look peaceful with the jaw wide open, and the hands curved, as though he had died defending himself. Most of the bone was fully exposed, and dark gray in color. It seemed short and shriveled compared to how Clouse thought a decomposed body would look.

In no way did it appear at rest.

"Do you want the police?" Rusty asked of Clouse.

Rather than answer, the firefighter shot Rusty a questioning stare, then looked to Kaiser as an answer.

"Who has keys to this area?" Kaiser asked, taking control of the situation.

His friend and the foreman glanced at one another, then Clouse answered.

"We both do, and Dave Landamere."

Kaiser shook his head, knowing he could not be partial in such a bizarre affair.

"Yeah, you better call the police," he instructed Rusty.

Clouds still covered the skies as a stiff wind crossed the hotel grounds, causing various leaves to fall around Clouse, adding to the untended blanket along the landscape. He watched as Kaiser argued with a state trooper and the Bloomington detectives, who had shown up to possibly accuse him of more wrong doings.

Regardless, Clouse knew everyone's curiosity would be triggered, and rumors would fly abound. He was not the least bit interested in being part of a media circus. Performing either of his jobs would be difficult if the local papers got wind of his potential involvement in Angie's death, or the exhuming of Jesuit bodies.

He understood his friend's position, and there was little Kaiser could do to help him. Clouse would never ask him to lie, and there was nothing the county officer could do to provide an alibi. At this point, he needed witnesses to confirm his exact whereabouts from the night before to convince the detectives of his innocence, and they weren't forthcoming.

Because there were none.

Staring at his friend and the two police cars next to Kaiser's, he realized what a scene this had to be at the normally tranquil hotel. He looked behind him, taking notice of over a dozen eyes surveying the activity, avoiding their work a moment. Clouse could order them to return to work, but he was not their foreman, and Landamere was not around to back his authority.

After a few minutes, Kaiser returned to his friend, apparently unhappy with the result of his chat with fellow officers.

"Well?" Clouse asked.

"This body doesn't help your situation," Kaiser replied. "Their forensics people went through your house and found skin and bone tissue upstairs near a jack-o-lantern. By the looks of the fragments found at the house, there's reason to believe the body back there is the same tissue."

"This is insane!" Clouse fired back, realizing too late that others were listening.

"They also found some other things that don't help. There was no forced entry to the house, and the locks were all secured, except for the kitchen deadbolt, where the killer apparently left. Also, one of Angie's friends reported talking to her around midnight, and your firefighter buddies said you left your truck parked outside last night. They also said you usually leave it inside."

Clouse looked away from his friend, slowing shaking his head, knowing the entire story looked bleak, and he could disprove none of it.

If he had parked his truck inside the firehouse garage, starting it, or opening the bay doors to leave, would certainly have awoken at least one of his colleagues. It would certainly appear he left it outside with intent.

"They want to check your truck bed for traces of the DNA, Paul," Kaiser said in a tone that hinted it might not be in his friend's best interest.

Clouse agreed, but knew if he declined, the situation looked worse, and DNA lingered long periods of time wherever it settled. His choice was basically made for him, even if someone was going to great lengths to frame him.

"Let them."

Kaiser gave a questioning look, providing an opportunity to back out.

"No, do it," Clouse confirmed. "I've got nothing to hide, and nothing to lose at this point."

Kaiser looked as though he had just warranted his best friend to death as he dragged himself back to the officers. Clouse could not read exactly where his friend stood, or if Kaiser truly believed him, but it was in the hands of forensic science now.

He felt powerless, knowing everyone figured him guilty, with no way to prove otherwise. There was little he could do, because even he had no idea who might want Angie dead aside from himself. If he lost Kaiser's support, he would have no one to confide in, or ascertain answers from in a police perspective.

Clouse decided waiting around would do him no good, and decided to look for answers himself. As he walked toward the sunken garden, then the cemetery area, an officer with a bag carrying the exhumed body passed him. It was that body Clouse wanted to start with. If it was connected in any way to Angie's murder, which he suspected it was, he needed to know its significance.

Heading up the hill for the second time that day, Clouse paid closer attention to the white slabs atop the graves. He took notice of how each had a name and date, much like any ordinary marker, except for the open grave. It simply held the name "Ernest" inscribed on its cold, hard stone.

"No dates, no nothing," Clouse commented to himself. Suddenly the grave had a bit of meaning, or at least a distinct difference from the others.

He looked into the hole for anything overlooked, but saw nothing aside from the splinters of the casket, and pieces of the body. Picking up a bone fragment, Clouse could see the same dark patterns the entire body seemed to have. Thinking it looked dark, almost charred, he smelled it, but found no distinctive odor. After several decades of lying in the ground, he expected little else.

Landamere mentioned the library having historical materials concerning the hotel. Though he doubted much about the Jesuits or the cemetery would be documented, it would be worth a try, if it meant possibly clearing his name.

"You seem to have a morbid curiosity about that grave," a voice said from behind the firefighter.

"Detective Kendle," Clouse replied, standing to face the man he least wanted to see.

"Your friend says we have your blessing to check the back your truck?"

"Be my guest. I'm sure you'll come up with something to aid your narrowly-focused search."

Clouse started walking the brick steps down to the garden. The detective immediately followed, keeping a step behind.

"Do you have any guesses who might want your wife dead?"

"No," Clouse simply answered. "But I assure you, this is not the way I would do it."

"Oh, come on," the detective said with a light tone. "Blood everywhere, the body hacked to shreds, the boy left untouched? This has crime of passion written all over it."

Clouse stopped walking, turning to point a finger at the detective.

"*Now* you tell me this shit," he said angrily. "This morning you were all too vague because I was supposed to provide your clues, and now you're singing like a canary. Well, I don't have your answers, detective, and I am not capable of cold-blooded murder, much less dissecting a human body."

He started to walk off once more, but turned after another thought crossed his mind.

"Now I feel obligated to do your job for you, because you're looking at no one but me. For every minute you spend checking up on me, you're letting other leads drop. This is all I have to say to you."

Clouse stormed off, leaving Kendle to ponder the words a moment before he returned to his fellow officers.

*   *   *

"You want some ice cream, sport?" Clouse asked Zach from across his apartment that evening.

"No, Daddy."

After only a month of rental, the apartment truly looked like a bachelor pad. Sight alone could not determine whether the clothes hanging over various pieces of furniture were clean, or the cereal inside several boxes left on the counter would prove empty or stale.

The refrigerator held only a few staple goods, and even the freshness of those was in question.

A moderate one-bedroom apartment, it was enough for the fireman, who spent much of his life at work. He was anxious to clean the house and move back, knowing full well it would only make his character look worse. If Zach was staying with him, he would not keep them trapped inside an apartment, even if it meant moving back to a house that would haunt them both. Houses could be sold, and to an extent, the past left behind.

It was nearing both of their bedtimes, but neither was going to sleep. Clouse wanted his son to tire after the exhausting day, to sleep some of the emotional pain off later. His personal agony went far deeper because six years of his life were wiped out in one night.

Kelli was the only person Clouse saw when he picked Zach up. He sensed his presence was unwanted, but there was no objection to him keeping the four-year-old. Zach was the one thing keeping him sane through this whole ordeal, but only childhood ignorance kept his son from accusing him of murder as well.

"I'm just being paranoid," Clouse told himself as he pulled a bag of peanuts from the kitchen cupboard above the refrigerator.

"Do you miss Mommy?" Zach asked as Clouse entered the living room. He was lying on the couch, head heavily on a pair of pillows, watching an adventure on the Sci-Fi Channel with sleepy eyelids.

"Of course I do. Don't let anyone tell you any different, Zach."

"Are you going to leave me too?"

"No," Clouse said with more assurance than he felt. He could only hope the samples vacuumed from the bed of his truck would provide no further incriminating evidence against him. "You know I'd never leave you, son. And Mommy didn't want to leave either."

No answer.

Clouse took a blanket from the one chair his living room had and flipped it out, covering his son with it. Assured Zach was snug and warm, he checked the thermostat and went to bed, leaving his door open in case Zach awoke, and didn't want to be alone. For both, tomorrow would be a new day.

A day in which to start over.

6

"I can't believe you don't think he did it," Larry Kendle said to his partner, who calmly drew on a cigarette, feet propped on his desk in the detectives division office.

"What does he really have to gain, Larry?" Mark Daniels asked rhetorically, exhaling as he replied. "I mean they didn't have the house, the boat, or even their vehicles fully paid off, so there's not much property or financial gain. And if you're going to bump off the wife, why do it like that?"

"He was on his way to divorce. This way he gets the kid, keeps everything, and moves on with his life before she gets the chance to ruin it."

"I don't know about you, partner," Daniels said, fingering his tie. It was one of several nervous habits he couldn't break.

Daniels came from a different mold than his partner.

After earning a two-year degree from a local college in law enforcement, he had tested for the state police, and several local departments, before getting hired by the Bloomington Police Department. Most of the men he worked with barely had their high school diplomas, much less any further schooling, outside of their work.

Taller than his partner, Daniels had a naturally strong upper body, but he constantly worried more about his mind than his body. One common factor the partners shared was their obsession with neatness. Daniels wore his shirt wrinkle-free, and his tie clipped in just the right spot, so the strongest gale wind couldn't budge it.

His dirty-blond hair was cut short, though never buzzed like the younger officers on his department preferred theirs. Never much of a conformist, Daniels acted and looked as he pleased. He wore shined shoes, pressed pants, and a look that showed he was constantly thinking of something, though no one else ever knew exactly what.

Unless, of course, he chose to tell them.

Kendle picked a file up from his desk, waving it at his partner.

"This right here is the first step in putting Paul Clouse behind bars. Come on, there was no forced entry, there's a connection to this body at the hotel, and he has plenty of motive. He's the *only* one with motive."

Daniels crushed his cigarette in an ashtray, not sold on his partner's analysis. He looked outside the window to the parking lot below. The morning view, covered by fog, reminded him of how his brain felt after countless cups of coffee two nights before, when a new case came along.

"If I'm going to kill someone, I don't go through the trouble of digging up a body, I don't risk my career by getting caught skipping out of work, and I certainly wouldn't make a gigantic mess in my own house when a simple application of poison, or an overdose, would be difficult to detect and attract less attention."

Kendle slumped into his chair across from Daniels, settling in for a battle of words. It was the most effective way the partners established links and clues in their cases. By arguing, they brought up various view points and scenarios. Kendle naturally argued often, and did not particularly like being partnered with the rookie detective, which sometimes made him almost unbearable for Daniels.

"But it's a crime of passion," the older detective said, defending his view. "He couldn't help himself in mutilating her body once he started. He sneaks out of work, ten minute drive home, ten minutes to kill her, ten minutes to drive back. There weren't any fire dispatches recorded until almost five in the morning, so his risk paid off. He fakes some grief, sells the house, and moves on."

Daniels chuckled a few seconds at the notion.

"So he sneaks out of the station, sets up this whole sick scenario upstairs with the dead body and jack-o-lantern, then lies in wait, maybe making a noise to lure her up there, all when he's pressed for time?"

"Exactly!" Kendle said, as though his partner had fully solved the case. "It's pitch dark. The wife can't see what the body is, thinks it might be her kid, gets freaked out and distracted, so he's able to catch her off-guard and get in the first blow."

"Bullshit," Daniels countered, not giving in. "If you're that pressed for time, you don't set all that up. He'd have to be clinically insane to do that, and even *you* would agree he's not."

"But he's bright," Kendle noted. "The man has a degree, knows where he's going, and no one's going to keep him from getting there."

"Oh, like the wife who just gave him his freedom?" Daniels asked sarcastically.

Daniels could irritate Kendle to no end. He was younger than his partner, and certainly less experienced, but he always seemed to have answers, or at least thought he did. After only three years on the force, he was placed in the investigative division for a reason.

Though Kendle thought that reason was simply to agitate him, Daniels brought new perspectives to a clan of detectives long since stuck in their methods and beliefs.

Kendle hated the way his partner contradicted him, appearing unconcerned about whether he was correct or not. Daniels always spoke in a soft, mild-mannered voice that many mistook for arrogance, rather than his usual nature. He believed police officers needed to raise their voices only when necessary, and wasn't afraid to show people his true self.

"You know, kid, you're going to be wrong on this one," Kendle warned with a grin.

"We'll see. I just don't see a strong motive, and there are a lot of other people and places we can check out."

"You want to split up on this one?" Kendle asked, suggesting a tactic they sometimes used, where each would investigate certain facets of a case, then compare facts on a daily basis.

Since the two were obligated to work together during regular hours, the split often meant additional work outside their regular shift, which irritated Daniels, because he enjoyed time with his family. Still, he enjoyed proving Kendle wrong, and loved challenges.

"Yeah, you can dog Clouse all you want, but I think there's more to it. I'm not saying he's necessarily innocent, but if he did it, I don't think he was the one wielding the blade."

"Well, here's to violating Paul Clouse's civil rights," Kendle said as the two shook hands on the agreement, playing on his partner's words.

Daniels looked at the file a moment, somewhat puzzled. Attached to it was a plastic evidence bag. Holding it up, he looked at its contents, then to his partner.

"This shred of black cloth, Larry. What do you make of it?"

"It's silk, like a Halloween costume. Maybe one of those killer outfits from the slasher movies, or a witch's outfit," he guessed, attempting to explain the black coloration. "The kid might have worn it out that night."

"No," Daniels replied. "The kid went as an alien. Green costume. This snagged on a nail at the top of the staircase, but there wasn't any blood. And no respectable boy dresses as a witch, by the way."

Kendle grinned inwardly. They both knew blood testing for DNA would make for an open and shut case if the suspect's DNA matched. Murder cases never came that easy for them. He stood, stretched, and walked toward the door.

"Where are you going?" Daniels asked.

"I've got civil liberties to violate, partner."

*   *   *

In the numbing chairs near the magazine section of Indiana University's extensive library, four friends gathered on a quiet Sunday morning, talking amongst themselves, studying, and reading recent events in the Bloomington newspaper.

"Hey, did you read this story in the paper?" Tina Kindrick asked her friends after glancing through the local news.

"What?" Andy Smith asked, putting down his English homework.

As her three friends listened attentively, Tina paraphrased the article.

"It says here the body of a Jesuit priest at the West Baden Springs Hotel was dug up and removed from its plot yesterday," she began. "Little information is being released about the body or why it may have been exhumed, but police did say the marker simply read 'Ernest' and that the grave was some distance away from the others on the hill where the priests were buried."

Her friends simply stared at her, wondering how this was the least bit important.

"Don't you guys remember Professor Zanchas' story?" she probed. "The one about the mad priest at the hotel?"

Eli Zanchas was from the Middle-East where legends of pharaohs and pyramids were not uncommon. Yet he found a local legend in Southern Indiana most intriguing, and shared it with his class one day.

"Wasn't it something about the hotel being bought by the priests after the depression, and one of them going mad?" Nicole Brinkman asked.

"It went a lot further than that," Tina recalled, going into a story telling mode. "The hotel burned at the turn of the last century, and Father Ernest claimed to his fellow priests the dead spoke to him, though there were no reported deaths from the fire."

She paused a moment, trying to remember the details.

"Ernest was incensed that no one would listen to him, much less believe him. He slowly fell into his own world of darkness, trapped with the spirits some said, but alone nonetheless. Some said he went about preaching to anyone who would listen, when visiting the hotel, but what he preached seemed insane, and perhaps too dark for the others."

Tina could see the looks her friends gave as they recalled the story, but they failed to be equally captured in its meaning. Undaunted, she continued.

"The priests kept Father Ernest locked in a safe room most of the day when guests came to the hotel, telling no one about the maddened priest they harbored. Growing more disillusioned, Ernest began believing he was a reaper of souls as the dead told him, and believed in his power, telling those around him how he chose life or death, heaven or hell, for the souls he claimed. They say he dressed in dark attire and robes constantly, just to shadow himself from society and remain in his own world."

"Is this nearing the end?" Nicole asked, trying to be polite.

"Yes," Tina assured her. "They say in final days, Ernest went completely mad, ranting and raving in his tormented state, locked inside his room. One night he managed to find his way to the basement, where the priests stored the old statues they had removed from the hotel lobby and center court. The sight of these objects reminded Ernest of souls trapped without release, and it was there he took his own life, setting himself ablaze, dead before anyone could find his charred corpse."

"Touching," Smith noted. "So you think that's the same grave?"

"Why else would anyone dig it up?" Tina wondered aloud. "That is so cool that someone dug up the very same grave Professor Zanchas talked about. I would love to go see that place sometime," she said, sincerely excited about the idea.

"You've got a vivid imagination," Nicole said. "Maybe we can take you there some time and give you your own padded room."

"Thanks," Tina replied with the same sarcastic tone her friends used. "It's nice to know I'm loved," she added before flipping through more of the paper.

Though her story had failed to impress her friends, it caught the attention of the man seated behind them, reading some materials of his own, ironically related to the same topic.

Clouse could not help but overhear the story as he sifted through history books concerning the hotel, and the story gave him a faint glimmer of hope that perhaps the grave did hold some connection to the murder of his wife. His search could now be broadened.

He recalled the legend, but not the name associated with it. Now he realized why the grave would be apart from the others, with so little description. Somehow the idea of an insane priest setting himself on fire didn't seem realistic, but legends tended to deviate over time. He wondered if and how the tale might tie into his situation.

Most of the books he read held little information about the Jesuit era of the hotel. The priests spent most of their era hidden away from a public that tormented them for decimating their favorite historical landmark. After all, most of the statues were removed, and the baths removed from all rooms on the inner half, which Clouse himself now had the overwhelming task of restoring. Many of the changes during the Jesuit era posed the greatest challenges to the construction company throughout the reconstruction.

Few people entered the walls of the hotel during that era, much less documented the visits. The only noteworthy mass gathering of West Baden residents occurred during the funeral of Ed Ballard, the hotel's former owner, who had, in essence, handed his great property over to the Jesuits for no more than one dollar. It was one of the rare occasions outsiders were allowed onto the grounds, and for that reason, the Ernest legend could never be disproved or verified.

Clouse knew asking the police for a peek at the body would be a complete waste of time, but he wanted another look at it, just to see if it was indeed charred. Perhaps Kaiser could pull one last string for him.

With the advent of computerized library checkouts, Clouse had no idea who had read the books before him. Only dates were stamped on the slips of paper tucked in the back. His brain scrambled for a way to trace who might have perused the materials in recent weeks or months, but nothing came to mind.

Such information was confidential, hidden behind the help desks, but he was determined there had to be a way. If computers were the keepers of information, he knew access to them would be helpful, but he was no hacker, and knew few people with skill enough to dig into the files from an outside line.

He would save that thought for more desperate times.

In the meantime, there was a full day ahead of him that began with picking up his son from his parents' house, and searching for answers at the hotel. On a Sunday no one else would be there, and he held a master key, which strangely enough, the police could use against him. Clouse put the detectives out of his mind, ready to confront the truth.

No matter where it took him.

7

Before Clouse could visit the hotel, he needed to stop by the house to feed the animals. With a reluctant blessing from the Bloomington Police Department, the house was his again. He assumed every bit of vacuuming and photography possible had been done the day before, sent off to forensic labs for analysis.

Wasting little time, he phoned the cleaners, and despite being a Sunday, managed to get in touch with one for a Monday appointment. One more night in the apartment for Zach and himself would help them heal. They'd be away from Angie's family and the house where so many good memories were now covered in blood.

"You want to feed the cows?" Clouse asked his son as they stepped down from the truck.

"Sure," Zach said with little more than a shrug.

To Clouse, his son seemed apathetic to nearly everything he suggested. Zach needed time to recover from the loss of his mother. Clouse was patient enough to deal with that. He understood children dealt with pain differently, though Angie had always been more willing to wait than he was. Clouse had always wanted results from his job, his life, and his child much faster.

What he wanted came at a heavy price.

With Angie gone, there was little choice but to wait for Zach to recover at his own pace.

While Zach went into the barn, where he had helped feed livestock the past several months, Clouse retrieved some dog food from a shed behind the house, walked out to his two dogs, tied up

49

at their small dog houses, untangled their chains, and fed them. There was little time to pet them today. He would make it up to them when he and Zach settled back into the house.

Walking back from the dog houses, kept behind the house at the edge of one field, Clouse surveyed his property. Three sides of his property were open fields, giving his horse and two cows plenty of roaming room. Across from the house stood a full barn, partly converted into garage space, and beside it, a lean-to of equal size which sheltered sparsely-used farm equipment, hay, and occasionally, his truck.

Another such building stood at the beginning of the drive for a small tractor and several more pieces of farm equipment, owned by his father until the end of every summer when Clouse would suddenly be given custody of them, because only he had room enough to store the lot.

Stepping slowly up to the porch, Clouse felt a sense of apprehension before walking into the house, knowing what to expect, but not the extent. Scuffing his boots along the porch's wooden floor, he paced a moment, drawing in deep breaths. Lifting the yellow tape after a minute, he stepped inside his house, instantly feeling like an intruder.

"My God," Clouse stammered, seeing dried pools of blood across the kitchen floor, the largest nearly the size of his favorite recliner at the fire station. In spots, it almost looked like water color paint atop the linoleum floor, but there was quite a difference.

Walking into the family room, he noticed how empty and boring it looked without the usual family photos and furniture inside. Angie wasted little time in dispatching with his property once he left the house. Perhaps she had vented some frustration, or put him out of her mind by covering up his belongings.

Clouse walked through the room to the bottom of the stairs, looking at the drips of blood, which fell along each step during Angie's escape attempt. He knelt a moment, running his finger along one of the red spots, at the base of the stairs, finding it completely dry. Slowly lifting his head, he saw the darkness of the hallway above, wondering what horrors had unfolded upstairs. He stood up, hesitating a moment.

Clouse flipped on a light switch, illuminating the upstairs before he walked up. The light revealed more blood spots, and a notable gash in the wall at the bottom of the stairway. Clouse could already see a similar splintered area of the wall upstairs, but only damage and signs of death lingered.

Any traces of the jack-o-lantern and the crumpled body were gone, probably housed within police labs. In all, Clouse had inherited a house with blood stains, bad memories, and a spirit that could haunt him for eternity. He realized nothing good would come of his present situation.

He returned to the downstairs, anxiously heading outside to check on Zach, thankful his son hadn't come inside the house.

"Zach?" he called.

No answer.

"Zach?" he called again, more agitated this time. "Where are you?"

The next few seconds he ran toward the barn, throwing open the large sliding door where his boat was stored for the winter. Its white frame loomed above him, set upon the self-launching boat trailer Clouse had spent good money on when he had a family life.

"Zach, where are you?" Clouse yelled, pushing his way past the boat, toward the door leading to the stalls.

He threw open the door, finding a startled Zach staring up at him. Clouse dropped to one knee, putting his hands on Zach's shoulders.

"Thank God," he muttered to himself. "Why didn't you answer?"

"I didn't hear you, Daddy," Zach answered quietly. "I was thinking about Mommy."

Clouse pulled his son into a hug, knowing it would do little to ebb the pain. The least he could do was let Zach know he was there, and that he would never leave him.

At least he prayed that would hold true.

"Did you feed the cows?" Clouse asked, outwardly flashing a smile.

"Yeah, and Bucky too," Zach replied, making reference to the family horse.

Clouse hated the idea of anyone but himself feeding the horse with its unpredictable nature, but he said nothing for the moment, spying the horse grazing in the open field. It was part of the reason he was concerned for Zach's safety.

On several occasions Bucky had attempted to bite or kick Clouse, and the fireman knew that beast would think nothing of performing the same acts on a child. For some reason Zach was fond of the horse, which was part of the reason it remained.

He looked quickly to see if Zach had actually carried out the chores, which he had. Clouse needed to make certain the animals wouldn't go hungry.

Taking his son's hand, Clouse led him back to the truck, intentionally keeping a distance from the house. Zach made no comment about going inside, but simply climbed into the truck's cab, ready to go wherever his father decided next. He was too numb inside and confused to care. Clouse realized this, and how much more devotion and attention he needed to give his son. Zach was very susceptible to what other people said, and to wandering off for no reason.

Clouse started the truck, ready for over an hour's drive to West Baden. Today was his one chance to investigate without others around. And without the fear of being closely watched by police detectives. He planned to make every second count.

*   *   *

Heavy white I-beams intersected like railroad tracks overhead as the construction worker walked the outer level of the hotel on the sixth floor. Each of the bolts holding the beams steadily in place left small rust spots on the otherwise spotless metal.

The beams gave the West Baden Springs Hotel enough structural integrity to bring the walls and floors up to code, preventing them from eventually caving in. Nearing a century in age, the building needed several improvements. The beams were one of the first necessary restoration areas started on the hotel. Connected to brick and concrete supports, the beams were now part of the hotel's framework, ensuring no part of it would collapse again.

Though brick and concrete kept the building upright, it's primary makeup was a homely combination of plasterboard, tattered wallpaper, and the remains of oil-based paint that had long since faded and chipped. The unique blend of elements covering the walls probably gave any visitor to the gutted rooms the notion they were inside a condemned building.

Whistling to himself, the construction worker imagined he was a trolley following the tracks overhead, toward his destination. He wore tennis shoes, jeans, and a flannel shirt, indicative of what one might wear on his day off.

Brian Mathis was simply thankful to be inside the building, considering there was no work today, and security was tight to begin with. With the strange circumstances surrounding the exhuming of the Jesuit priest, work would be more trying the next several weeks. Luckily, the state trooper patrolling the outskirts of the hotel found sympathy in his plight, and unlocked the lobby door long enough for Mathis to get what he came for.

Walking into a numberless room, Mathis touched the door frame, finding it naked like every other room in the hotel. The rooms were gutted of plumbing, doors, and divider walls. Without doors, the hallway and vacant rooms seemed to mesh as one complete open space. Only skeletal wooded frames served as any sort of division between the old rooms. Occasionally the rooms had tubs or sink fixtures, depending on where they were located.

Rooms on the outside of the hotel were mostly bare of any content, while the inner rooms sometimes held remnants of furniture, or perhaps a mirror. They were considered more important, holding priority because of the better view. They faced the atrium, which was nearly complete in the restoration. From the atrium floor, the rooms usually appeared with a single light bulb inside, providing a hint to how empty they truly were.

Mathis pulled a plasterboard sheet from a wall where it appeared to have a perfect fit. It was the ideal hiding place for several of his smaller tools. Lugging them down five flights of stairs, or waiting for a turn on the elevator annoyed him, so he simply hid his tools where his co-workers would never look. Until remodeling began upstairs, he would have a useful secret, because some of his colleagues were not as trustworthy as himself.

For the past two weeks his wife had nagged at him to do some repairs around the house, including the eaves along the roof, and several divider walls she wanted installed in the closets. For such jobs, Mathis needed his cordless drill, which he usually left at work.

He was lucky the state trooper had let him in. The workers seldom had trouble getting into the building with any officers. After all, it was their job to be at the hotel too. Knowing no one was in the building, Mathis promised the officer he would get his tools and be right back.

Pulling a packed tool belt from the wall, Mathis snatched up what he needed, and replaced the belt, reaching for his drill case. Soon he would be putting it to use on his only day off. Working on his house would definitely pay off in the long run. Mathis and his wife were expecting their third child in a few months, which meant his current living situation would get crowded.

For the past two years Mathis had fought to make improvements on the roof, the interior, and the basement, raising the market value so he could sell it for far more than he paid. When that happened, he and his family could move into the country, build their dream home, and he could look forward to retirement once it was paid off. Of course his occupation allowed him to buy materials, and do labor himself, for fractions of contractor costs.

Before he finished assembling his collection for transport, a tapping noise from the hallway startled him.

"Who's there?" he called, thinking it sounded like a rock skipping off the concrete floor.

No answer came, and Mathis carefully set his tools in a pile before stepping outside the barren room to look. His range of vision was limited by the curvature of the hallway. He saw very little either way because the hallway was circular. He was ready to dismiss the noise when the tap came again to his right, just out of sight.

Cautiously, Mathis stepped to his right, cocking his head to the left for a better view, before he rounded the corner. The hallway came into sight, revealing nothing. He passed the first door to his right, seeing nothing inside. An eerie darkness encompassed the rooms, because the hazy day allowed little light to peer through the plastic sheets covering the windows on the other side of the hall from the outside.

Mathis wondered if the trooper had put someone up to playing a prank on him. Any of his co-workers would happily give the construction worker a scare if they happened to be there. Even on days they worked, most had fun at the expense of others, several times per shift.

Drawing near the second door, Mathis glanced outside, seeing little but tree tops and the gray sky that seemed a permanent fixture in the Southern Indiana sky. He turned his head back too late as the scythe was already coming toward him.

He drew back as the weapon cut into his abdomen, immediately drawing blood as it pierced several organs. Mathis grunted as his back hit the wall, but he was not mortally wounded. Grabbing the wooden handle of the scythe, he shoved it out and away from his body, taking flight down the hallway, stumbling as he went.

A quick loss of blood and the gash in his stomach forced him to clutch his lower torso as he ran, dripping blood along the dusty concrete floor. He stood little chance, unless the elevator was open and ready to go. Mathis would need to fight off the killer long enough to shut the large door and take the elevator car down to safety, and he knew it.

His faceless killer, donning a black cloak, took chase, walking briskly behind his damaged victim. Mathis felt the warmth on his side, feeling his life ebb a bit further with every desperate step. Survival instincts took over, leaving him no choice but to run, because he was incapable of defending himself in a lengthy confrontation.

Feeling a great loss of energy and warmth, Mathis slumped against the wall for support, still stumbling toward the elevator. He was unaware of how slow he had become, or that this was now a game of cat and mouse.

When the elevator drew near, Mathis made one final push toward it, only to have his legs tripped up by the killer's scythe. The construction worker collapsed to the ground, his shins lacerated and his side still dripping blood. Rolling himself over slowly, in pain, he could only lie still and breathe, waiting for the killer to decide his fate as he looked up in a semiconscious haze.

Helplessly on the ground, leaking blood into a pool beside him, Mathis watched as the killer stared at him from above, as though deciding exactly what to do. Behind the hood, cold eyes stared through a mask of pure black, revealing none of the killer's features from behind the shroud of death he wore.

In fact, the costume was that of the grim reaper. He held the scythe above Mathis in judgment, studying his victim before he decided what fate to place on the construction worker. Mathis could only groan slightly as his fingers twitched, displaying what little mobility he now possessed.

Mathis actually wondered in his disoriented state if death itself had come for him. He felt positive the next world awaited him as his consciousness wavered. As the killer grabbed hold of his foot, dragging him toward the elevator, Mathis knew his final destiny awaited, wherever this reaper decided.

*   *   *

In Landamere's office downstairs, Clouse shuffled several papers together, placing them in a folder. Earlier that morning Rusty Cranor had phoned him, informing him that Landamere was nowhere to be found, and he could not be reached. The assistant foreman had orders from Dr. Martin Smith, the hotel's current owner and driving force behind the restoration, to place Clouse in charge of the project if he was willing and able, with all the turbulent events occurring in his life.

Clouse looked around the office, making certain he had the essentials to take over the project he had reluctantly agreed to. Though Rusty knew far more about construction than Clouse, the man refused to take a true leadership position over the men he worked side by side with every day. Clouse didn't mind overseeing the construction, because he and Landamere shared similar taste and ideas. Besides, unbeknownst to the workers, the next month's work was fully planned.

"You ready, Zach?" Clouse asked, taking one final look around.

"Sure."

Things were getting no better for the firefighter as his wife's calling hours took place the following day, and it would look worse with him taking time off at the fire department only to work at the hotel. Of course, the chief had actually requested he and Roger Summers both take the week off.

Clouse cared less about how others thought, but wondered if keeping his emotions held in, and missing so much time with family at a time when he needed others, might lead him to a breakdown. Eventually everything would catch up to him, emotionally and physically, if he continued to work nonstop.

As he and Zach stepped from the office, Clouse locked the door, hearing a noise from down the hall. From the loud metallic thud, he assumed the elevator had reached the bottom floor. The officer outside had informed him Brian Mathis was upstairs, and ordinarily Clouse would have stepped over to say hello.

But not today.

Taking Zach by the hand, he headed for the lobby door, anxious to get home before anything else bad happened in his life. He worried about Landamere's whereabouts, realizing a number of strange occurrences were taking place around him the past few days. How everything went from being nearly picture perfect to completely disastrous was beyond him. Clouse could only take life one day at a time and put the shattered pieces back in a dysfunctional jigsaw puzzle.

He walked outside, giving wave goodbye and a forced grin to the uniformed trooper before helping Zach into the truck, then leaving the hotel with the hope Landamere might return to handle the affairs by Monday morning. Clouse needed personal space before his emotions exploded. His truck pulled through the arched entrance gate as he gave the great structure one last glance, hoping his luck improved by the next time he visited.

*   *   *

Nearly an hour passed before trooper Jason Brinkman noticed Mathis' truck parked along the brick path that led to the hotel entrance. He had walked the grounds both outside and along the first floor of the structure, losing track of time, assuming the construction worker was long since finished retrieving his tools.

"Damn it," Brinkman said under his breath, followed by a sigh.

A dark sky rumbled overhead as clouds shuffled into position for a thunderstorm. To the officer, the weather seemed too cold for anything but snow, but distant thunder and black clouds made him a believer.

He was in no mood to search for Mathis, but standing outside with the cold and wind was about his only other option. The only lighting inside on a Sunday would be auxiliary lights, usually atop posts, or mounted to walls. Brinkman knew turning on additional lights was impossible, because there were none until the electricians rewired the building.

Removing his flashlight from his gun belt, the trooper unlocked the front door, stepping inside from the unfavorable weather. The sound of the glass door closing behind him echoed through the entire hotel as he turned the flashlight on, heading for the elevator.

He knew Mathis and his group were working on the sixth floor, gutting several rooms and redoing plumbing fixtures. Brinkman also knew the sixth floor had absolutely no lighting, or power, unless extension cords were present from the lower levels. He wondered what would keep Mathis so long, praying no accident had occurred.

He could see the word "liability" hung over his neck like an albatross, after losing his job, if anything happened to the laborer. No one except the foremen were technically allowed to enter the hotel on days off, but security officers were usually kind enough to let police colleagues look around, or construction workers fetch their belongings. For his sake, he hoped his kindness hadn't forsaken him.

During the elevator ride up, Brinkman shined his flashlight around the metallic box, finding nothing except white paint, peppered rust, and what, at first, he considered to be more rust spots on the gray floor plate. Kneeling down, he found what appeared to be partially dried specks of blood, possibly from a small wound. He imagined cuts were common for construction workers in their line of work.

When the elevator drew to a stop, the trooper opened the solid door, greeted by a pool of blood soaking into the concrete floor. Shining his light, he saw a red trail leading around a corner along the hallway wall.

"Holy mother of God," he stammered, knowing all too well this was no prank.

Carefully stepping forward, away from the reddish trail, the trooper shined his light around the corner, the beam glimmering off the liquid.

Finally, it led into the fifth room where Brinkman shined the light inside with his left hand while the other clasped the Beretta nine-millimeter at his side, his thumb undoing the holster latch. The blood went further than this room, but he noticed a prominent pool outside this particular door.

Carefully stepping around the blood, Brinkman slid around the doorway, finding nothing but an arranged pile of tools in the corner, ready for transport, but lacking an owner. The lightning flashed outside the window, startling the trooper, while highlighting just how much blood was on the floor outside the room.

"Oh, shit," the trooper said, taking his two-way radio from his duty belt. He needed backup immediately.

8

Brinkman waited outside the hotel, wearing a rain slicker as the thunderstorm unleashed its fury on the town of West Baden. His Smokey the Bear hat, covered in protective plastic, was not enough to keep his head dry as rain spattered up from his shoulders, soaking him thoroughly down his shirt collar.

When red and blue lights pierced the dense rainfall at the edge of the drive, the trooper breathed a sigh of relief to see Ken Kaiser's patrol car. Kaiser often spent his Sunday afternoons watching the hotel, but a schedule change kept him on patrol this week.

"What's the matter?" Kaiser asked, stepping from the car, protected only by his departmental jacket. Wearing no hat, the county officer was drenched by the freezing rain within seconds of stepping from the vehicle. "You sounded spooked on the radio."

Brinkman's hands were animated as he answered.

"Ken, there's a huge puddle of blood upstairs and the construction worker I let in to get his tools has been gone over an hour."

Remaining calm, Kaiser took the lead toward the hotel.

"There has to be some explanation," he stated. "Maybe the guy cut himself getting at his things. It's dark up there, you know."

When the elevator reached the sixth floor, Kaiser's expression matched that of Brinkman's initial response.

"That's some cut," the county cop said in awe, staring at the trail of blood illuminated by his flashlight.

"It leads back to a room where I found some tools. I think they're his," Brinkman said, referring to Mathis. He took a moment to show Kaiser the specks of blood along the elevator's bare floor.

Kaiser walked alongside the trail to its sudden end where he found a large spatter of red on the wall where the initial strike from the scythe had occurred. Now he knew where the blood began, but not where it ended.

"Well?" Brinkman almost demanded the older officer's opinion.

"He made it to the elevator, but I don't know where he went from there."

"It could be any floor," Brinkman hypothesized.

"I don't think so," Kaiser said with some thought. "If he was bleeding that bad, he didn't get very far on his own. Someone probably dragged him into that elevator, possibly using a sheet or a tarp. There isn't much blood in the elevator itself."

"Would they take him to a different floor?"

"Hard telling, especially without any light around here."

Kaiser led the way back to the elevator, formulating a plan.

"Let's check the ground floor first, then work our way back up if necessary."

Several flashes of lightning greeted the officers when the elevator door opened on the ground floor. Kaiser ignored the power of Mother Nature, shining his flashlight beam toward the tile floor, kneeling for a closer look. If Mathis was placed on plastic, as he suspected, drops of blood would occasionally trickle off, but they would be scarce, and difficult to spot.

"Anything?" Brinkman asked.

"Not yet," Kaiser replied, straining to see any variances in the dark patterns along the floor. The tile had its own shimmering effect, making detection of blood drops highly difficult.

Rubbing his hand along the tile, the county officer felt a slight wetness graze one of his fingers. Unsure if it was the water they had tracked in, or more blood, he shined his light beam over his palm, finding traces of red.

"Oh, no," he said, realizing the direction in which the blood was found led toward a back entrance.

Brinkman noted the blood under the light as well, looking down the dark hallway. There were only a few ways Mathis could have been dragged. The most likely would have been out the back door, which led to a nearby path visitors might want to travel along the hotel grounds.

Kaiser threw open the back door, unhappy about being in the pouring rain again. The trooper followed a pace behind, like a puppy anxious to learn a new trick. He was nervous and excited at the same time. Brinkman was new enough to have never seen a dead body, and his curiosity got the better of his professionalism.

Once both were on the back lawn, consisting of mowed grass and clumps of dirt awaiting a use, Kaiser pointed to his right.

"Check over there around the truck entrance," he ordered.

While Brinkman investigated the secondary entrance, Kaiser looked around the lawn, finding nothing out of place, nor a dead body as he expected. He looked up the hill where flower beds would be planted in the spring, seeing little through the thickets of trees that encumbered the hillside.

He trudged up the hill, collecting mud on his treaded boots with every step. The trees seemed to amplify the amount of precipitation hammering him from above as he walked along the hill, looking for any disturbances in the muddy embankment. Shining the light to his left, the officer thought he spied a glimpse of color in the otherwise dark terrain.

Drawing closer to the object, he could see a blur that looked like flesh, then a leg emerging from the murky ground. His jaw dropped when he saw ripped blue jeans gripping the leg of a person he assumed to be Brian Mathis. Before approaching the body, he yelled urgently through the rainfall for Brinkman, hoping the trooper would hear.

He was about to radio the trooper when he whirled to confront a noise behind him. Kaiser let out a sigh of relief when he found Brinkman had already arrived.

"Up here," Kaiser led the way, wondering what remained of Mathis.

Both stared into a makeshift grave which left an arm and a leg of its victim lying out, the dirt barely covering most the head and torso. Half afraid to touch the body, fearing evidence contamination, Kaiser could only stare, noticing several areas along the muddy grave where a plastic painter's tarp pierced the surface. He heard distinct tapping sounds as the rain drops smacked its synthetic edges.

Crouching beside the horrific grave, Kaiser stared up to the dark sky, allowing the moisture to strike him squarely in the face. He wondered what possessed someone to murder a family man, simply at the hotel a few minutes to gather some tools.

Standing up, he plucked his radio from the left side of his gun belt, ready to call for the necessary authorities to close a homicide, when he saw Brinkman look more intently at the grave, as though something possessed his attention.

"I think he's still breathing," the trooper said with awe, staring for further evidence to support his claim. It came a few seconds later with a heave of Mathis' barely exposed abdomen where blood seemed to encompass the man's skin and clothing.

"You sure?" Kaiser asked almost defiantly as the trooper began to claw dirt away from the construction worker, convinced what he witnessed was true.

"Yes, now help me get him out of here!" Brinkman yelled, still pawing dirt behind him like a crazed dog getting close to his prized bone.

Reluctantly, Kaiser knelt down, helping the trooper, hoping Brinkman was right, praying they weren't disturbing evidence of a homicide. He knew of few quicker or more severe ways to be reprimanded by any police department, than to tamper with evidence at a crime scene.

*   *   *

"He's damn lucky to be alive," a doctor told the two officers standing across the hall from the room Mathis was resting in. "He lost a tremendous amount of blood."

"Has he said anything?" Kaiser inquired.

"He hasn't regained consciousness yet, but he keeps muttering something about a reaper, or grim reaper, and gets agitated when he sleeps. The next forty-eight hours will determine whether or not he makes it."

Kaiser nearly missed the last of what the doctor said, realizing the reaper statement from Mathis fit the coroner's findings of a curved blade used to kill Angie Clouse. He wondered how well a sickle served as a murder weapon, and if someone was using a grim reaper gimmick to kill in serial fashion.

As the doctor entered Mathis' room, Kaiser stared down the hall at Larry Kendle. The detective read a Sunday paper, sitting patiently on a cushioned bench, waiting for a crack at either officer, or Brian Mathis, if he regained consciousness.

Kaiser felt for the man's family, who paced the Bloomington Hospital surgical waiting room, hoping for good news that might never come. The officer had written Mathis off, but whoever buried the construction worker packed dirt tightly over the tarp covering Mathis' wound. This act put just enough pressure on the gouge to prevent fatal bleeding, whether it was intentional or not.

To Kaiser, Kendle was like a bulldog, fighting and tearing his way toward answers, but the officer felt the detective was barking up the wrong tree. He knew Kendle wanted to pin Angie's murder on his friend, but he knew there wasn't much evidence supporting Clouse either.

Taking a look at the clock down the hall, Kaiser found midnight a lot closer than he expected. Mathis' surgery took over nine hours with several surgeons trading off. Shock had kept him alive through cold rain and a partial burial, but he had yet to wake from the ordeal. Now two hours removed from the cutting table, time would tell.

While Kaiser waited patiently at the hospital, Brinkman had finished his shift at the hotel, gone home, and changed clothes before making the trip to Bloomington. Kaiser had comforted Mathis' family, while the trooper gathered what information he could from surgeons as they left the operating room. Until now, the two had barely spoken a word to one another, since finding Mathis behind the hotel.

"Was anyone else there this morning?" Kaiser asked Brinkman in a hushed voice, staring down at Kendle, who perused the sports section.

Taking notice of the stare, the trooper turned Kaiser away from the detective before answering, knowing how his answer would impact the county officer.

"Your buddy Paul Clouse stopped by with his son for a few minutes just after Mathis went inside," the trooper replied.

Kaiser closed his eyes dejectedly. He rubbed his cheeks and chin with both hands, nervously searching for any positive thoughts that might separate Clouse from this tragedy. It seemed ridiculous that the firefighter was around every time blood was spilled, or bodies popped up, but even he could not overlook the coincidence.

"How long was he there?"

"About ten minutes or so," Brinkman replied, trying to clearly recall. "He came out carrying a briefcase, acting normal as could be."

"And Zach?"

The trooper shot a questioning look.

"His son," Kaiser clarified.

"Oh, he acted pretty down, but certainly not worried or scared."

Kaiser considered the attempted murder situation momentarily, realizing no one could commit such an act and leave the scene without some trace evidence on him. Blood, dirt, or DNA would have to be present on Clouse's clothes, or in his truck. The plastic would be checked for prints, which he imagined would turn up nothing, indicating the killer had used gloves.

Given the circumstances, Kaiser seriously doubted his friend would have time to settle Zach, don gloves, go up the elevator, commit murder, partially bury Mathis, dispose of evidence properly, and leave the scene while he and Zach acted perfectly calm and collected. He wanted Kendle to immediately check his friend for evidence, but shared Clouse's fear.

Someone could be setting him up.

"Did Dave Landamere show up today?" Kaiser asked curiously.

"No," Brinkman answered. "Why?"

"Nothing, really. He's been gone since Friday when all of this mess started."

"You think something's up with him?"

"Hard telling," Kaiser said, discontent. "This whole weekend has been one big shitball. I'd probably take off too."

He started down the hall, wanting to find Clouse before the police did, even if it was getting late.

"Where are you going?" Brinkman called.

"To see a friend," the county officer replied without breaking stride. "You can fill Detective Kendle in on everything," he added, shooting the detective a cold stare as he passed the bench.

*   *   *

Two hours ago Clouse had been ready to return to his apartment. That was before Zach fell asleep on Kelli Summers' couch and Clouse found all sorts of topics to discuss with Kelli about the next day's calling hours, memories with Angie, and several secrets he never knew.

"So Angie didn't plan to get back with me," he replied more to himself than Kelli, who had led into such an unfortunate statement with several others that softened the blow.

"She still loved you very much, Paul, but Angie saw how much you both flourished when you were apart."

"That doesn't sound like her, and that's not how I looked at it," Clouse stated calmly, carefully adjusting how he sat on the love seat in the dimly-lit living room. He looked at his son, sleeping peacefully beside him, head in his lap, oblivious to the adult conversation filling the room. "It was always rewarding when I got home to see this little one and Ang waiting for me."

Kelli took a sip from her sweetened tea, looking at the nephew she always enjoyed caring for. While Angie found love early, her younger sister waited patiently for the right partner, learning from her sister's trials and tribulations in marriage.

"He sleeps so soundly," Kelli noted, quickly changing subjects. "Most kids fuss, or they toss and turn, but Zach always goes right to sleep."

"This has been so rough on him. I think sleep is his only escape right now."

"And you?"

"Work," Clouse answered. "It's the only thing that keeps me going."

"You need time off to be with him, Paul," Kelli advised. "Zach needs you more than ever right now."

"I know, but I'm not left with any choice. The head foreman at the hotel took a hiatus without telling anyone. I'm the only one who can fill in."

Kelli threw her arms up in disgust.

"Screw the hotel, Paul. It can wait, or they can build it without you. You've got yourself and your son to worry about. This was part of the reason Ang was always pissed at you. You always made work your number one priority and got to family matters when you had time."

Such a statement could have angered Clouse, but it was too true for him to argue against.

"I know." He took a drink from the warm beer can beside him. It was only his second of the night. There was no arguing the point. As happy as his family life appeared, and actually was, the joyous moments seemed scattered over six years of marriage, never consistent. "So I won't cause any waves at the calling hours tomorrow?"

Kelli thought several seconds, taking note of a police car turning onto her street a block away.

"Mom and Dad aren't thrilled about you being there, but they don't have a choice, and I don't think anyone here yesterday truly considered you capable of murder. Hard as this has been, I know in my heart you would never hurt my sister, Paul."

"Thanks," he said with a sincere nod of appreciation. "You're about the only one who thinks that."

"Roger's been your biggest advocate," Kelli admitted. "He told everyone to leave you alone the next few days, and that the breakup with Angie didn't mean a thing."

It meant a great deal to Clouse, now more than ever. He had no idea she intended their separation to be so permanent, or that her personal ambition had made him an obstacle. If what Kelli said was true, Angie still loved him, but lost use for him as part of her life. Being used and discarded did not suit Clouse, and now a serious emotional dilemma haunted him.

Roger Summers, his brother-in-law, had been as much of a close friend as anyone the last several years. Summers was a groomsman at his wedding, helped him land his job at the fire department, and often took Clouse boating with him on Lake Monroe during the summer. Strangely, he took Clouse's side in the separation, telling his sister she was insane for even considering parting ways.

In some ways he was like the older brother Clouse never had.

Before he could wallow further into the implications of a dissolving marriage, or the notion that he permanently solved his problems through murder, a knock came at the front door, which failed to stir Zach from using his father's leg as a pillow.

"I'll get it," Kelli said, opening the door to find Ken Kaiser standing outside, a look of concern across his face.

"Ken," Clouse said with an air of surprise. Carefully replacing his leg with a real pillow, Clouse let Zach slumber as he stepped past Kelli. "I'll be back in a minute," he told her, closing the door behind him, leaving the two friends in the cold silence of the night.

"Were you at the hotel today?" Kaiser asked before Clouse could inquire how his friend had found his current whereabouts.

"Yeah. Why?"

"Someone tried to kill Brian Mathis, and they still might have."

"What?" Clouse asked, genuinely shocked.

"He got cut up pretty good, dragged to the elevator, went six floors down, then the prick buried him in a shallow grave out back," Kaiser abridged the story. "You arrived a few minutes after he did and left a few minutes later."

"Ken, I couldn't have-"

"I know. Kendle's going to have a field day when he finds out you were there. He'll want to check your truck and your clothes for DNA again."

"Let him."

"That's what I say. We've got to get some evidence in your favor, Paul. Sometimes a lack of evidence can be just as good as an alibi."

"Damn it," Clouse said, caressing his forehead. "Is someone setting me up, Ken? I mean this whole thing is going too far."

"You still wearing the same clothes you were this morning?" Kaiser asked, ready to help however he could, but avoiding the question.

Clouse looked at his jeans and shirt, then to the tan, lizard-skin cowboy boots. Everything was the same. He nodded an affirmative to Kaiser.

"Let's go to the hospital, have Brinkman identify what you're wearing, and get this over with so Kendle can't bitch that you're evading him," the county officer suggested.

"Okay," Clouse agreed, thinking of something he'd prefer to give Kendle, like a broken jaw. "Let me tell Kelli what's going on, so she can keep Zach tonight."

Kaiser stared at the frost forming on the lawn in the quiet Bloomington neighborhood, as Clouse walked inside. He wondered if his efforts would be enough to keep Kendle from crucifying the firefighter, as he had so many others. The detective had a reputation for tenaciously pursuing suspects, sometimes ignoring important facts. Several cases had been overturned in appeals with evidence Kendle never presented to the court. The detective had been accused of creating his own verdict and leaving no room for opinion in court hearings.

Kaiser respected Kendle's abilities, but not his methods. He understood most homicide cases were open and shut with obvious motive or overwhelming evidence, but sometimes the easiest solution was not the most accurate. Kaiser regretted having to protect his friend's name by playing a trial game with the detective. He hoped Kendle was open to all possibilities, but he would push the envelope to make certain the detective remained impartial.

Clouse returned in a moment with a look on his face Kaiser could not read. The firefighter looked worn, almost defeated, yet hopeful deep down that this could be resolved. He had never seen his friend so dejected, so Kaiser felt more certain than ever Clouse was innocent.

"Ready?" he asked.

"Let's do it," Clouse answered as they walked toward his truck.

9

Monday morning and afternoon came and went quickly for Clouse. Landamere failed to show up for work at the hotel again, but Clouse left Rusty in charge, taking a full day off for the calling hours, and time with his son.

Rusty informed him Landamere's wife had considered involving the police by listing her husband as a missing person. Strangely, no sign of the man's car, wallet, or anything he left the hotel with on Friday had turned up. Clouse found it odd the project manager would up and leave without notice, but imagined it might simply be a self-made vacation. With all the strange events surrounding the hotel and his life, he hoped that was all it might be.

Under ordinary circumstances Landamere's wife, Joan, probably would involve the police, but Clouse knew, from what Rusty told him, that theirs was a marriage of convenience where either partner could leave at any time and sleep around as they pleased. Clouse found the situation odd, but he knew this was not the first time Landamere had taken unexpected time off. It was the first time he had left without informing his crew though.

As he drove toward the funeral home, Zach in the passenger seat beside him, Clouse thought of how much he had learned for such an inactive day. Keeping an eye on the red taillights in front of his truck, he let his memory wander.

Kaiser's helpful idea turned out to be less useful than Clouse expected. For every piece of evidence the county officer told Kendle he needed, the detective came up with a counter to how Clouse might have hidden or discarded it.

No trace of the Jesuit priest's remains turned up in the bed of the fireman's truck, but Kendle noted a large plastic sack or trunk of some sort could have been used for transporting the body. Kaiser insisted a hair or dried flesh sample would have appeared somewhere, but Kendle would not hear of it.

From the partial autopsy done on Angie's body, it was determined a scythe was indeed the murder weapon, and that it was several years old. Tiny rustic flakes were found in the body, but the weapon's exact age could not be determined. Though Clouse had never owned a sickle, or needed to, Kendle decided it might have come from anywhere, such as a neighbor's farm, or a friend who had leant it.

Kendle's reasoning for Clouse taking so little time in the hotel was that he could have attempted murder on Mathis, left the body a few minutes, and returned in the back where security would probably not have seen him, to bury the construction worker in the shallow grave.

"What about the muddy footprints we found around the grave?" Kaiser had questioned, knowing they would not match Clouse's cowboy boots.

Kendle countered, saying Clouse could have easily changed to a more practical treaded construction boot for burying the body, then replaced it, possibly in the hotel, where no one might think to look. A careful change of footwear before reentering the hotel would have prevented any muddy tracks on the tile floors inside. The detective went on to criticize Kaiser for treading on the crime scene himself, despite saving a life.

Kaiser countered by asking how Clouse could pull off any kind of attack with Zach present, but Kendle explained how easily children were amused, and that Zach, in a state of mild shock from his mother's death, likely sat in the office for a few minutes without question.

Clouse left halfway through the discussion, disgusted at Kendle's lack of effort on the case. Kaiser later filled him in on the missing details, including the fact it was verified the Jesuit body was indeed in the upstairs of his house. There was no reason Clouse could imagine why it would be placed up there, unless to implicate him. Even so, it seemed highly unlikely, and hardly feasible, that he would risk taking nearly three hours to leave the fire station, dig up a body, kill Angie, then hide the Jesuit body until morning.

Firefighters were never allowed to leave the station, unless they ran an errand assigned by an officer, or they were dispatched on an emergency run. Getting caught in such a situation out of the station typically provided a stiff punishment from the chief's office and almost certainly implicate him in the murder. To Clouse, it made little sense that someone might set him up that way.

He wondered if Kendle realized there was nothing but circumstantial evidence on him. Otherwise the detective would charge him with murder, Clouse decided. He realized the evidence was weak, if not too bizarre for him to have killed Angie. He wished the police would begin drawing some of the same conclusions.

"You okay, sport?" he asked Zach as the truck pulled into the funeral home parking lot.

"I'm okay."

Clouse noticed the cars of his in-laws, Roger Summers, and Kelli already there. It would be an open casket wake because the funeral home director announced he was able to create a presentable look for Angie once the coroner's office was done.

Both he and Zach dressed in gray suits, and Clouse made a point of wearing shined black shoes, which he typically wore only when working at the fire station. He felt the knots tying inside his stomach as he stepped from the truck, knowing his discomfort would either intensify or lessen once he dealt with Angie's parents.

Clouse hoped the open casket would help Zach put some closure on his mother's death. He debated the entire morning about the effects on Zach if he attended, but Kelli talked him into bringing the boy. She agreed with Clouse that actually seeing his mother dead would hurt tremendously in the beginning, but make the healing process smoother in the long run.

Four-years-old was too young to lose a loved one, Clouse thought, especially a parent. In the past, he had played the reverse scenario in his head, knowing it was always possible he might go into a fire and never come out. He always thought Zach would be protected, and taken care of financially, but never truly considered the emotional scars. Now, being Zach's only parent, Clouse needed to change his outlook at work, and his reasons for making it home after every shift.

Stepping through the front door, Clouse drew the attention of everyone present, including Angie's parents. He said an uncomfortable hello to Ralph and Susan Summers, then to Kelli and Roger, suspecting it would be a long two hours.

It turned out he was right.

Clouse spent the calling hours accepting condolences from his fellow firefighters, most having no knowledge of his separation. A good number of Angie's family avoided him, while his own family seemed to be there to take his side. It was the first time Clouse had seen his own parents in over a week. He barely found time to speak with his mother about Angie's incident the morning he found out.

"You okay?" Ken Kaiser asked toward the end of the ceremony, walking up to Clouse with Tim Niemeyer, another close friend from high school.

A thick man with conditioned arms and a waistline as robust as his chest, Niemeyer had played football, and run around with both the cop and the firefighter during their teenage years. Eventually he went his own way after high school, working construction for other people, while drawing a steady paycheck, but feeling something was missing from his life.

He realized how much better he could do working for himself, finally having time for his own family, if he removed some of life's obstacles. Each year as a business owner he saw less of his friends, but made himself available when Kaiser informed him of Clouse's trouble.

"I'm getting by," Clouse said to Kaiser's inquiry. "Good to see you, Tim," he said, shaking hands with Niemeyer.

"I'm sorry, Paul. Truly I am."

"Thanks."

"Anything we can do?" Kaiser asked.

Clouse hesitated. He wanted to tell them not to leave, or to make things right again, but asking the impossible did no good. His friends would think him crazy if he suddenly became dependent on them, or asked them for a night on the town to forget his troubles.

That would be selfish.

In truth, he wanted to be alone and have the people he cared about all around him at the same time. A river of emotions traveled through his body simultaneously, leaving him emotionally torn.

"Thanks, guys, but I just need time alone," he finally answered the appropriate response.

After his friends moved on, every passing second felt more uncomfortable, and the urge to leave intensified. When it drew to a close, Clouse barely recalled who was there or what they had said. Guilt overwhelmed him, but he could not help but think of the investigation against him, or how much different things were.

To some, the funeral was closure, but Clouse considered it just another step in piecing his life together. He needed to know who killed his wife, or he would never live comfortably again.

As the last few guests walked out the front door, Clouse approached his parents. Before he could say a word, his mother's arms were around him, gripping him in a hug. Helen Clouse wanted to be with her son much more, but his schedule made it nearly impossible.

"How are you doing?" she asked.

"Fine, Mom," he replied. "I guess the worst of it's over."

"Are you getting the third degree?" John Clouse asked his son, looking in the direction of Angie's family.

"It could be worse."

He paused, afraid to ask a favor after neglecting his parents for so long, even if it could not be helped.

"Can you two keep Zach for the night? I could use some time alone."

Helen saw the pain in his face as he said those words. Even the strong-willed needed to mourn in their own way. She knew from personal experience he needed the evening to himself. Zach would feel the same, regardless of where he went. Her son, however, was too strong to show emotion in public. He would deal with Angie's death his own way and move on.

"We'll keep him," she replied. "You do what you have to."

*   *   *

When Clouse opened his front door, he was already partly undressed, barely holding back the flood of emotions knocking at his mental dam. He pulled the dangling tie from around his neck, flinging it over the apartment's kitchen table. Undoing the last few buttons on his dress shirt, he tossed it as well. He felt tears well up in his eyes as the night's events flashed before him, accompanied by all the good times he realized were gone, never to be relived.

He slumped against a wall, his bare back sliding down until he was seated on the carpet, tears of mourning once again slipping through. He quit fighting his emotion, letting it run free as he remembered his honeymoon with Angie in Florida.

Clouse recalled them running on the beach, carefree of life or anything in Bloomington. He envisioned himself grasping the gritty sand atop the beach as they made love every evening for two weeks at sunset. He could hear the waves caressing the sand while they lay across the beach, staring at the stars, their feet massaged by the tide. Occasionally they would giggle for no apparent reason, and he rather enjoyed Angie letting go of her serious nature, if even just for a little while.

After the memories of Florida, his mind ventured to visions of the wedding day itself. Clouse remembered the photos before the wedding, how uncomfortable the tux was, and how he disliked breaking the tradition of seeing the bride before the ceremony.

Her practical nature won him over, and they were able to attend the reception immediately following, instead of putting it off for pictures. It was the first of many concessions he recalled making for Angie. At that point, it was the happiest day of his life.

His memory turned to riding horses at her parents' farm during summers past, Angie's hair blowing gently in the wind. She smiled so much then, and so little toward the end. He remembered her laughing just for fun as they rode through open fields and tamed woods. One year they went through the effort of having a picnic at her favorite clearing, and she talked of her adventures growing up on the farm. He felt so close to her, hearing such personal details of her childhood that she never shared with anyone else.

As he sniffled, the memories of boating at Lake Monroe returned. Many of these were with Zach and other family members, but there were several nights he and Angie escaped the world together, boating until they found a secluded area of the lake. After setting anchor, they would talk or frolic, then sleep under the stars. He savored the evenings they had alone because so many obstacles kept them apart.

Clouse rubbed his eyes, realizing how much they hurt from crying. Despite keeping his emotions checked in public, he could no longer hold back the pain. Nor could he let Zach see him mourn. It would only add to his son's confusion and added to the loss. He realized he could not keep pawning Zach off on others, or he risked losing everything he held dear.

Standing up, Clouse kicked off his shoes, then undid his belt, when a knock came to the apartment door. Rubbing the moisture from his eyes, he quickly located the shirt and answered the door after putting it back on, surprised at who was visiting him.

"Kelli?"

"I'm sorry, Paul," Kelli Summers said, gently holding her hands at her waist.

She looked beautiful in the flowery dress covering her slender form. With her hair let down, Kelli looked similar to Angie when Clouse first met her. In some ways, she was like a younger sister to him. Clouse often gave her advice on her house, or ran errands for her when a truck was necessary. In the dress she looked young and innocent, like he felt a younger sister should.

He realized he was standing in complete darkness and flipped on a light.

"Were you going to bed?" she asked, as though interrupting something.

"No," he answered quickly. "Come on in."

Kelli stepped inside, surveying the apartment and its bachelor-like qualities. He knew she had seen the redness of his eyes, and probably assumed she could help him through the loss. Clouse wondered how she was so strong through all of this.

"It's not easy, is it?" she asked.

"No."

"I did all of my crying the morning I found out," Kelli admitted, as though knowing what his thoughts were. "Tomorrow will be tough when they-"

"I know," Clouse nodded in understanding, knowing Angie would be buried in the morning.

He planned to attend unceremoniously, since her parents made all the arrangements. Clouse actually preferred it that way, letting them have a sense of finality with Angie's death, knowing they came as close to what she wanted as they could.

"My parents don't really hate you like you think," she said as he led her to the small living room.

"They don't?" he asked skeptically, taking a seat on the couch as she picked the recliner.

"This hasn't been easy on anyone," Kelli noted, "but they just want whoever did this to pay."

"And I do too," Clouse said, wondering what his sister-in-law was getting at.

"I would like to go through Angie's things with you, Paul, if I could. Maybe if we get into her computer files something will pop up."

"Maybe," he said reluctantly, wondering how sincere the offer was. He became more paranoid about people incriminating him further, with every passing day. Clouse had to suspect everyone else to keep his objective perfectly clear.

"I'll leave you alone," Kelli said, apparently realizing they both needed time to themselves.

He walked her to the door, unable to say much more. His mind felt numb, and he felt saying nothing would prove better than saying something regrettable.

"See you tomorrow, Paul," she said, giving him a kiss on the cheek.

"Good night, Kelli," he replied before shutting the door, suddenly feeling awkward about the entire evening.

He headed for the bedroom, figuring sleep might do him more good than he realized.

10

Most of the funeral was like Clouse envisioned it would be. Again, he numbly waited it out, letting the images of the casket and its descent into the ground burn into his mind. He could not believe it was over, but the book of his life as he knew it closed.

While he traveled to the hotel for a routine inspection of the grounds, he left Zach with Kelli, promising she could go to the house with him afterward to look through Angie's belongings. The cleaners had called Monday afternoon to inform him the house was cleaned and, what he assumed was a sizable receipt, had been left on the table.

Looking over the grounds, Clouse noticed most of the workers steadily carrying items or hammering on various areas of the hotel. From the front, one could see and hear nearly everything going on. He was disappointed in Landamere for failing to show another day, refusing to believe it was anything but the manager dodging the circumstances surrounding the priest's body, or the Mathis incident.

An unannounced vacation was still a feasible possibility, but Landamere informed no one of his intentions, leading Clouse to think foul play might be involved in his disappearance.

"You hear about Mathis?" Rusty Cranor asked, approaching the firefighter from behind.

"What about him?"

"Died this morning. It's been all over the radio. Now everyone's going to think this place is spooked."

Clouse's eyes widened.

"You mean they let the public know about the attack here?"

"Yeah," the foreman replied. "It's absolutely everywhere, Paul. That, and the priest's body, isn't going to help our publicity campaign in the least."

Funded primarily by local residents, Dr. Martin Smith, and the occasional anonymous donation, the hotel needed community support and tourism to flourish in the remodel. If police encumbered the grounds, more rumors would fly, and charitable dollars would begin to dwindle. People might balk at helping restore a historical site littered with murders and strange hauntings. Clouse foresaw immeasurable peril if the media made a circus out of the latest events.

"We've already had police around here this morning looking for any clues they missed, I suppose," Rusty added.

"I'm sure the hired help won't get any boost in morale when they see a blood-soaked floor up there, or that grave out back," Clouse said.

Rusty drew close to Landamere's designer, looking around cautiously.

"I heard you were here that day."

"I was," Clouse replied. "Just to get some papers. I've already talked to the police and cleared everything up."

"Maybe you were lucky."

"How so?"

"Here you were that close to the killer and walked out. It could have been you, if you'd gone upstairs," the foreman noted.

Somehow Clouse doubted that. If he was being set up for these murders, it made no sense to harm him. He could not imagine being caught off guard enough to allow a scythe to slice him open anyhow. Lately he was on edge wherever he walked.

Walking toward the sunken garden, Clouse took note of the fountains. Water still spat from the frog statues, reminding him of what winter weather could do to them. Though today was moderately warm, he knew a cold snap might hit Indiana and remain there through the entire winter.

"Rusty, please make sure those fountains are shut off and drained by tomorrow," he told the foreman. "The last thing we need is for those to freeze up and bust."

"Sure thing, Paul."

From the garden, Clouse spied activity on the graveyard hill. The old grounds keeper, known only as Vern, dug the barren grave even deeper to prevent further mishap. Beside him lay the bagged, bony remains of what everyone claimed was Father Ernest.

The police were done with the corpse, but Clouse felt an undying urge to know if the body was actually burned or not. He put little stock in the legend of Father Ernest's fiery death, or the notion that a priest considered himself some dark angel, without knowing the truth about the body. He needed to speak with Kaiser about any forensic findings.

Clouse disliked the grounds keeper. He considered Vern more of a local drunk, given a job out of sympathy, than anything else. The man's job was basically to clean up after the construction workers and keep the hotel property from getting cluttered.

I want to see that body, Clouse thought to himself, wishing the old stubborn man would leave his post a moment to sneak a drink. Before he realized it, he had stepped several paces toward the cemetery, away from Rusty. He was drawn to the body, becoming obsessed with the truth.

"Paul?" Rusty called.

"Yeah?"

"You okay?"

Clouse turned around, finding the foreman busily studying the layout of the garden, but attentive enough to monitor him. It seemed a lot of people were looking out for him lately.

"I'm fine," Clouse said, realizing he would not receive a chance to examine the body as Vern began shoveling dirt atop the shallow grave.

"Good. Let's get back inside," Rusty said, shooting a suspicious look back toward the grounds keeper, as though Vern's work efforts didn't meet his specifications.

Walking with Rusty toward the hotel, Clouse thought of lengths he might need to go to find the truth. He could not picture himself digging up bodies at midnight to disprove local legends, or combing through his house for samples he had no chance of analyzing. He could, however, begin rummaging through Angie's belongings and her computer for clues about who might have a grudge against her, or Clouse himself, for that matter.

Nearing the hotel, Clouse looked to the top of the towering building, despite the rare appearance by the sun nearly blinding him. He could see several workers walking without fear along the top of the dome, even as dark clouds moved closer, threatening to storm. Despite his work as a firefighter, he maintained a controlled reverence for heights.

Some of the workers could walk all day six stories above solid ground and take it for granted the materials beneath their feet would never collapse, or that an accident would never take them tumbling off the side. Clouse took no such thing for granted.

As his eyes panned down the hotel, something on the third floor caught his attention, keeping his eyes focused on the windows along the gutted rooms. He nearly dismissed it as glare from the sun when a dark streak crossed another window, then another. As Rusty started up the stairs toward the main lobby, Clouse stared, this time seeing more clearly a dark-cloaked figure scurrying along the floor where he knew several workers were clearing the remains of the gutted rooms for disposal.

"Oh, shit," he said to himself, rushing up the stairs past Rusty.

"What's wrong, Paul?"

"Get to the third floor as quick as you can," he ordered the foreman, darting quickly up the rest of the stairs, Rusty following several paces behind.

Avoiding the elevator, Clouse took a direct route of stairs up to the third floor, standing at the doorway to the dreary floor before cautiously stepping into the hallway. He had lost Rusty a few floors back as the older foreman grew winded.

Walking quickly along the bare, exposed hall, the firefighter peered in each room as he passed it, finding nothing out of the ordinary.

Door after door passed without incident. As he neared a bend in the hallway, Clouse heard Rusty reach the top of the stairs behind him. He turned to look without breaking stride, and hit a solid object as he rounded the bend in the hallway.

Startled, Clouse stumbled back, finding one of the workers in front of him, wearing dark clothes as he carried several worn boards, probably for disposal.

"Stevens," he said the man's last name, catching his breath. He was thankful to run into a live human being. "Who's up here with you?"

"It's just me and Felding, Mr. Clouse. Did you need something?" he asked as Rusty approached Clouse from behind.

"You haven't seen anyone else?" Clouse asked for clarification.

"Nope. We've been the only two people up here all morning."

"Thanks," Clouse said, turning away, ignoring the shocked look on the foreman's face.

Rusty waited until they were several steps away from Stevens to rip into Clouse's strange behavior.

"What in the hell was that about?"

"I thought I saw someone up here that didn't belong."

Rusty shot a puzzled look.

"You drag my old ass up three flights of stairs for that? You may be the boss right now, but I'm worried about your state of mind, Paul."

"I'm starting to worry too," Clouse replied, wondering if his imagination and the recent talk of scythes and reapers were getting to him.

"Take the rest of the day off, Paul," Rusty suggested. "I can handle it."

Clouse gave a weak grin, knowing how the foreman must have felt about his crazy actions. He could accomplish more at home than the hotel anyhow.

"You win, Rusty. I'll probably see you tomorrow."

As Clouse walked down the hallway to leave, the foreman wondered just what demons ran through the mind of Paul Clouse, and if they would ever be exorcized.

*   *   *

Atop an electric pole behind the hotel, Robert Bennett put the finishing touches on the new wiring that would bring the facility into the current decade. Part of the reason so few lights were on could be blamed on old, faulty wiring, which Bennett was subcontracted to correct. Owning his own company, he was thankful for the business, and the notoriety that went with helping restore one of the greatest historical monuments in the country.

After checking the transformer sitting atop the ground, behind the hotel, Bennett realized his problem stood a bit further back in the wiring connected to the nearest pole. The closest power company workers were often more than an hour away, and seldom did they rush to check wire connections.

He knew from experience they usually sat around drinking coffee unless something urgent, like a downed power line, or a sparking transformer, was called in.

Bennett decided it would be in his best interest to climb the pole and probe around to save time.

Supported only by a line belt and correct placement of his feet, Bennett finished securing the wire to its connection points, checked it and the brackets holding it in place, and began his descent. As he slowly climbed down, the electrician looked over to the grand dome, loving the view from such a high vantage point.

He would see more of it in the coming weeks once he set to work on the backup generators in the basement, and installed new wiring along each floor. Several relatives had nagged him for photos of the hotel's interior. Diehard fans of the West Baden Springs Hotel always wanted to see what the unaccessible rooms looked like. He promised to take pictures of whatever he could, in the hope his traditionally poor photography skills might be enough to get some decent pictures.

From above the grounds, he had taken some shots using his telephoto lens the week before. Outdoor shots were easy, but without a good flash for his old Canon camera, photos inside might prove more difficult.

He had received the camera in high school as a gift when he took a photography class just to get into the newspaper class a semester later. It was top-of-the-line then, and he had refused to upgrade since. Little had his parents known his interest in journalism was merely to be around his girlfriend in a few more classes.

Eventually he married her, eventually they divorced, and in between had a daughter who was now going on eight years.

Owning a business kept Bennett too busy to see his daughter more than once or twice a month. He made it a point to schedule time in for her, because he could work every waking day if he wished. Electrical work was always plentiful, but his employees also needed time for their families, so he carefully planned blocks of days off for them.

Bennett removed the spurs from the underside of his boots when his feet touched the unfinished landscape behind the hotel. He then took off his tool belt, setting his equipment on the soil while he peeled his sweaty shirt away from his chest.

Dirt clumps and piles were everywhere, and would be until the layout of the hotel's lavish grounds was complete. He didn't care about it. After all, his work would be above the grounds, or in the hotel basement below.

Whistling to himself, Bennett carried his gear over to the white van with his business name painted along both sides in red lettering. He swung the back door open, tossing his gear inside. The gleam of his Canon camera caught his attention from behind some wire bales. Taking up the object, he removed the telephoto lens, replacing it with a regular lens. He had time for a few shots inside the hotel before returning to the shop.

He checked the counter, reassuring himself there was film still inside. He saw a high number of shots left, so he set it on a rapid shot setting, hoping for some artistic shots along the balcony as he walked it. Holding it up, he looked through the viewfinder, seeing nothing but pitch black inside the van.

Bennett lowered the camera, turned around, and saw a dark streak hurl toward him as his insides ripped apart. Pain jolted through all of his nerves simultaneously, causing his finger to lodge on the camera's shooting button.

A scythe remained lodged in his abdomen while someone covered in a black robe, with no visible face, pushed him back with the object against his van. The camera dropped from Bennett's hand, shooting off two more pictures before it, and its automatic winding system, fell to the ground just behind the dying electrician, under the bumper.

Bennett groaned as the killer propped a foot against his van's rear bumper, using it for leverage as he freed the sharp instrument of death from the mass of pink innards bulging from Bennett's abdomen. It tangled on part of his large intestine, pulling the stringy organ halfway out before the blade gave release. The scythe dripped blood as the killer stood a moment, watching Bennett slumped against his own vehicle, clutching his stomach. The mortally wounded man could only look at the killer with blank eyes, as though to ask 'Why?'

Picking Bennett up by his belt, the killer propped him against the van, watching him suffer, leaking blood a moment more. The electrician could only watch helplessly in his weakened state as the killer drew the scythe back and let it swing toward his throat, finishing the job.

Taking a quick glance around him, the killer was relieved to see no one had seen his deed, and no one would probably miss a utility man on the renovation project. He loaded the body of Robert Bennett into the van, scuffling dirt over the blood pools and specks around the scene. His load intact, the killer climbed into the driver's seat, heading out the back entrance where no one would see him. He had plans for the body and the van, so he needed to be extra careful.

Leaving a trail of gravel dust behind it, the van departed the hotel grounds, barely missing several blood specks on a tiny mound beside a partly obscured camera, hidden beneath a thin layer of kicked dirt.

11

Steam rose from the pot atop Clouse's stove as he and Zach stared down at the noodles in the boiling water. Macaroni and cheese was not the father's idea of a hearty supper, but Angie had left little in her cupboards but boxed items and health dishes. The refrigerator and freezer held surprisingly less.

Signs of a happy homecoming were scarce.

Thanks to the firehouse, Clouse's cooking skills were above average. The food he found available was inadequate to test his ability. Angie often preferred to eat out when they were together as a family. This upset Clouse because he never wanted Zach to believe eating out was healthy, or economically sound.

"You want peanut butter and jelly or bologna?" Clouse offered Zach the only two choices available.

"Jelly," Zach answered, climbing down from the chair that gave him a vantage point into the boiling pot.

He walked to the kitchen window, staring at the field past the back yard, illuminated by intense orange light from the late afternoon sun. Clouse looked at his son while draining the water from the pot, noting how well Zach took to being in the house again, despite the tragedy only days before.

Zach's reaction to his mother lying in a coffin was less animated than Clouse expected. True, the boy cried, but he was by no means hysterical. Perhaps getting over Angie's death wouldn't prove as hard as Clouse anticipated for Zach.

Clouse quickly finished his son's late lunch and placed it on the table as Kelli pulled into his driveway, in her small beige Toyota. He was thankful for the company to sort through Angie's belongings, but felt a need to check everything himself, just to be certain nothing was overlooked or misplaced.

Zach continued to nibble on his food while Clouse walked outside, greeting Kelli as she stepped from her car.

"Hello," he said, giving her a hug as she approached. "I appreciate you doing this."

"I'm happy to help," Kelli replied, refusing to release her end of the hug just yet. "I want to know who did this as much as you do."

"The police went through everything," Clouse said, having already glanced over the boxes. "We probably know more than they do about Angie's stuff, so maybe we'll find something they missed."

"Have you checked out her office?"

"I started with the cabinets. The desk and computer will probably give the most clues, so I'm saving them for last."

As they entered the kitchen, Clouse noticed Zach barely touching any of his lunch.

"Is it that bad, Zach?" he asked.

"I'm not hungry."

"It's okay. You want to play outside with the dogs awhile?"

"Yeah," Zach answered, hopping down from the chair. He darted out the front door, ready to enjoy one of the last decent afternoons before winter cold fronts moved in.

"No playing with Bucky!" Clouse called.

Kelli smiled as Clouse turned to face her.

"You're so lucky, Paul," she said, looking out to Zach, who was now running circles around the dogs.

"I know. He's been a real trooper through all of this."

Clouse led the way to the family room where a line of boxes awaited them. To the right, he had Angie's office open with all of the lights on. Both the boxes and office were a mess after police had sifted through them a full day, apparently finding little or nothing of use.

"I'm going to start with the cabinets in there," Clouse said, nodding toward the office. "The boxes have a lot of personal stuff Ang stored away. Some of it will be wedding stuff, her old business books, and whatever else."

"Okay," Kelli said, digging into the first boxes of papers and tiny bins.

Clouse opened the large storage cabinet in Angie's office, finding little but manuals, software boxes with instructions, and a few tax books. As he expected, it was organized specifically for her business.

As he sifted through the desk, he found little more of use. Several pictures had been put away, most with him in them. She had several personal letters from out-of-state friends in the second drawer. He set them aside for reading later. He also set aside an address book that contained both personal friends and business associates.

Little else besides envelopes, a change pouch, and other staple items a desk required, could be found inside the drawers. As Clouse finished his search, he turned the computer on, suspecting it might hold more answers than anything else. He left one desk drawer for searching once he finished with the computer.

Angie worked quite a bit over the internet and kept most of her business dealings in the memory chips of her computer. She once told him it was the heart and soul of her business. Clouse hoped an autopsy might reveal everything it held to him.

"You finding anything?" he called to Kelli.

"Nothing helpful," she replied. "I've been looking at some of your wedding photos."

Clouse rolled his eyes, but he knew he would probably do the same thing if he were looking through the boxes. In fact, he would probably have Zach look through them with him, so his son realized he would not let Angie's memory fade easily.

As he looked over the top of the desk, an envelope caught his attention next to the stack of important books and documents he planned to review later. Clouse picked up the envelope, recognizing the Florida address in the top left corner. He pulled out the letter from the already opened envelope, saw it was dated three weeks prior, and read it to himself.

Dear Paul & Angie,

We're looking forward to having you down to the ranch after the holidays. Our company just expanded in St. Louis and Kansas City so we've been busy traveling. I still love keeping my hands on the business.

Just put out six new albums and printed over a dozen books last month. The online business has been phenomenal and we're looking at expanding there too. Maybe we can get Angie to help us develop our website.

Concerning the hotel property in West Baden you sent me information on, Paul, it looks very promising for some projects I've got in mind, and I'll be talking it over with my partners at our next meeting. I'll be in touch with you once I have some more information. If you're working on the restoration I'm certain it will be a major success.

We'll be talking to you both soon.

Michael Hathaway

Clouse put the letter and envelope on the desk, contemplating what opportunity he might have missed by not seeing it three weeks prior. The Hathaways were a couple he and Angie had met in Florida during their honeymoon. Michael Hathaway owned Trident Enterprises, a company that worked in music and print media. A shrewd businessman, Hathaway had made an impact with his books and music labels years before, then dabbled in business properties for sport.

About a month before he and Angie separated, Clouse had sent Hathaway a packet of information concerning his work on the hotel and what solid potential the hotel had if the businessman was interested. He explained the renovation was partial, and that the new owner would have limited creative control over the project's completion.

He wondered if Hathaway had called during the separation. The invitation was to the couple's ranch in Texas, where they spent part of the year. Angie certainly would have turned them down, and possibly explained the circumstances surrounding the separation. If she hadn't, Clouse would certainly have to decline the offer to vacation with them.

Clouse hoped the man was considering buying the property. He easily had the financial resources and a genuine love for historic properties. Though persuasive writing was not his forte, Clouse had tried to sell Hathaway on the idea of buying the property as best he could. If Hathaway passed, the hotel might not sell for years, or the restoration might come to a standstill. Clouse also liked the idea of having a free pass to the property at any time, which he felt sure the businessman would give him.

Smith technically owned the property, but wanted to sell to a worthy buyer, who would not tarnish everything they had worked so hard to restore.

Valued at millions, Hathaway would get West Baden Springs at a bargain if he generated the funds with his partners. The only conditions the National Preservation Society made clear to potential buyers were that the property would need its renovation finished, and that no major changes could be made, keeping the original design of the historical building intact.

Of course certain updates were necessary to keep the building within modern code, but the remaining visible portions of the building were required to appear as they did when the hotel opened a century earlier.

Using the mouse beside the computer, Clouse clicked on a business program where Angie often kept her financial records, as well as information on her clients. While the program loaded, he checked the last desk drawer, finding telephone statements, carbon copies of her business checks, and several other opened envelopes. He set them on the desk with the other items he wanted to examine more closely later.

Clouse clicked on the client information box, calling up a list of Angie's software buyers from the time she began her business to the present. He skimmed the list of names and addresses, finding a high number of people in her life he knew nothing about. Most of the clients lived within Indiana, but Clouse knew only a handful of the names.

He printed a copy of the list to place with the stack atop the desk. Clouse then called up Angie's internet server and found her user name in place, but the program called for a password before he could log on to look for anything.

"I'll be damned," he said to himself, typing in several notions of what her password might be, with no success.

He tried simple words like Zach's name, various animal names on his property, her friends' names, and even a nickname he gave her when they were first married. Nothing worked, then he recalled a message the server sometimes gave when he logged off his own computer about creating a password with a mixture of letters and numbers to prevent unwanted entry. Angie was quite practical, and that was something she would certainly do to keep Clouse and Zach away from her business files.

"I'll never get in there like that," he told himself. He needed to gain access to her online information, but it would take someone who knew how to hack passwords.

Clouse had someone in mind.

"I'm not finding anything in these boxes," Kelli called from the family room. "You having any luck?"

"Not much. I've got a lot of papers to look through later."

Clouse suddenly thought of something concerning Hathaway's letter. Whatever Kelli said from the next room went ignored as he picked the letter up, looking at its date.

"Damn her," he said under his breath.

After the separation, Angie had agreed to make one last appearance with Clouse, knowing how important the fund-raising ball was to his work with Landamere. The ball raised thousands for the restoration of the hotel, while providing a gathering for many of the financial elite in Southern Indiana. Clouse would not have missed the event for anything, and virtually pleaded with Angie to get her to attend.

From the date on the letter, it was in Angie's possession, and more than likely opened, before the ball took place. Throughout the entire party, they gave the appearance of a perfectly happy couple. Angie never strayed a moment from her charade, even to tell him about the letter. She looked beautiful in her dress, and he remembered disliking his rented tuxedo, even though it gave him a distinguished look he seldom got to enjoy.

Perhaps things were going so well, she forgot about the letter, or meant to tell him later. Perhaps Angie saw Clouse looking happy, living out the notion they were still happily married. To him, there never was a problem, but now he wondered just what Angie might have hidden from him.

Did she intentionally keep the letter's contents from him, perhaps for personal gain?

"Did you hear me?" Kelli asked, standing at the door of the office.

"Sorry, Kelli. I was just thinking."

He stood from the chair, suddenly uncomfortable being in the office.

"I've got to go. Roger wants the family over for drinks while everyone's in town. He said you were invited."

"I can't," Clouse refused softly, looking out toward Zach, still playing with the dogs. "If you and Roger get a chance to drop by later, we'd love the company."

Before turning to leave, Kelli dropped an unexpected kiss on Clouse's lips, surprising him, though it came and went equally quick. He wondered if she had missed her mark, but it was over so quickly he couldn't react.

"Take care, Paul," Kelli said without any comment on the kiss as she turned to go. "We'll be by later."

It wasn't uncommon for Kelli to kiss him before she left, but usually they were pecks on the cheek. Clouse often thought of her as his own little sister, and thought the feeling was mutual. Perhaps the kiss was innocent, but emotions were running high in the family lately, and he certainly didn't want a replacement for Angie, even if it was her sister.

Still shocked by Kelli's kiss placement, Clouse slowly turned to the desk. He looked over the stack of papers atop the desk, shook his head, and walked into the family room. Several boxes of photos, both wedding, and Zach's early childhood, caught his attention. It was time to call Zach inside and recall some better days.

12

Most of the afternoon built up to one large thunderstorm in West Baden until the dark clouds cut loose at dusk.

Even the hotel's elegant lamp posts were barely visible through the downpour of rain, as thunder rolled in the distance. Occasionally, lightning struck behind the huge, rounded hotel, making it appear like a castle, daring would-be travelers to step inside for shelter.

Sean Timmons threw back a clump of hard dirt with a vengeance before thrusting his shovel into the ground once more. It was bad enough digging the grave of an alleged nutcase, but doing so in the middle of the pouring rain seemed even more absurd.

"You know, you could have avoided this by getting here a little sooner," Vern, the grounds keeper, said from behind Timmons, startling the teenager.

"There is such a thing as school, you know," Timmons replied.

"Not that I'd imagine you attend much," Vern retorted, keeping himself dry beneath an old umbrella as he took a swig from his flask.

His raspy sentences, often framed with audible exhaling, sent shivers through Timmons' body whenever he heard the man speak.

"I can think of worse fates than digging that hole, boy."

"I can't."

"It beats me reporting you for firing your little gun on the hotel grounds, doesn't it?"

Timmons merely grumbled to himself as the grounds keeper walked away, whistling cheerfully to himself as he went, probably to distract the security guard.

Only the day before, his life had seemed much better, never having met the grounds keeper. Timmons always made it a point to carefully check around before firing the gun. Either Vern had outsmarted him, or happened to be lucky enough to hear him this time.

Unfortunately, after several months of using the woods behind the hotel for a target practice area, Timmons was caught by the snoopy Vern.

He had only fired his .22 pistol on the grounds because there were no other areas available, but the keeper refused to hear his testimony. Instead, he set the young man to doing his dirty work. Though he hated the notion of being blackmailed, the teen had little choice but to comply, or his parents would surely ground him and take away his firearm.

Vern had not dug the grave deep enough to suit Rusty Cranor. The foreman wanted to ensure no one else could disturb Father Ernest's resting place, and caught the grounds keeper just before his shift ended, stating he wanted the job done before the construction crew arrived the next morning.

Timmons dug a few more minutes before his arms began to ache. The rain pounded his head and back as he threw the heavy, soaked chunks of dirt up behind him. Sighing aloud, he wiped a combination of sweat and cool rain from his forehead, pulling himself out from the grave.

His arm brushed against the canvas bag containing the bony remains of Ernest. A hand grayed with age, still containing traces of flaky skin, emerged from the open end of the bag, it's fingers curled as though summoning someone to it.

Timmons made a disgusted noise to himself, jerking his arm back as he stood beside the grave a moment.

Leaving the shovel beside the open hole, he wandered down the hill in search of where Vern might have gone. He called the man's name several times through the dense rain, seeing and hearing nothing.

"Damn," he said, turning to the brick path beside him to ascend the stairs toward the grave.

His parents would begin to wonder exactly where he was on a school night. His driver's license was less than a month old, and easily taken away if they suspected he was out doing no good.

When he returned to the grave site, Timmons noticed the shovel missing. He searched wildly around the area, knowing he was gone only a moment. In the dense rain, only the white of the tombstones along the hill was easily visible. The thought of being on a hill filled with corpses, completely alone, without shovel, frightened him.

Desperately looking around for Vern, the teenager stepped back a few feet. As the rain impaired his vision and hearing, Timmons never saw the blade of a scythe rise from the hole he had just added depth to a moment prior.

He cried out as the curved blade lodged its sharp end into the back of his leg's calve muscle, tripping him as it yanked back.

Timmons hit the ground face-first, clawing at the dirt for an escape as the killer attempted to pull him back, using the weapon as a pulley. Several seconds into the process the scythe slipped out, forcing the killer to rise from the grave, cloaked in black, as the teen scrambled to regain his footing.

Unable to escape very quickly on the slick ground, Timmons opted to pull his .22 pistol from beneath his jacket, flipping to his backside for a better aim at the reaper stalking him. Still attempting to further himself from the killer with his left hand, peddling his body down the hill like a fiddler crab, Timmons fired the gun into the chest of the reaper, only several feet from him.

No damage.

Not even a flinch.

He fired again and again into the chest, seeing no reaction from the killer as he walked ominously toward his victim. Frozen in terror, his gun empty, Timmons could only stare upward as the killer loomed over him.

With one swift action the reaper swung the weapon like an axe, lodging it in the teenager's thigh muscle, causing another scream, this one longer due to the intense pain coursing through his leg.

"No! Please!" Timmons pleaded as the killer dragged him toward the grave, screaming, and kicking with his free leg, clawing at the hard soil for any way possible to slow or stop the killer from finishing the job.

Using the scythe for leverage, the killer swung Timmons into the grave, letting the weapon's blade release with an upward jerk. As the teenager fell hard into the rectangular opening, the reaper reached for the shovel hidden behind the dirt pile, scooping dirt into the occupied grave.

Refusing to be buried alive, Timmons leaped to his feet, despite the agony of his crippled leg, clasping the killer by his ankle, tripping him up. As the reaper lost his footing, Timmons began to scale the other side of the large opening, attempting an escape.

Before he could raise his second leg over the ledge, he felt something tug him back. The killer had entered the grave to stop him. After pulling him back, the killer whirled Timmons around, allowing the teenager to claw at his mask.

Timmons' attempt to unmask the killer only resulted in him receiving a swift knife to, and through, his abdomen, as it stuck in the dirt wall behind him. He felt the hollow void death would soon leave within the confines of his stomach, as the knife twisted around his guts, knocking part of the dirt behind him loose.

Groaning his last few sounds, the teenager smelled the stench of stomach acid and the remainder of his lunch intertwined as his intestines split open, assuring his death would come momentarily. He slumped to the ground, tasting a few drops of rain as they belted his lips, becoming the last things he would feel or taste in life.

*   *   *

As Zach lie asleep on the couch, Clouse looked through the last of the papers from the desk. If there was crucial information in any of the papers, he would never have recognized it. Angie's clients stretched from coast to coast, and most were probably contacts established through her online accounts.

Clouse felt helpless, knowing her business life never included him. She was independent in her business, constantly working alone. Many of the people and businesses listed in her manifests sounded powerful and well-established.

Clouse wondered if Angie had intentionally hidden the letter from him, trying to attain her own buyer for the hotel her husband worked so hard to rebuild. That would be downright hateful, and he never pictured her acting that way.

He never imagined Angie being so bitter. She would never be that vengeful toward him, or undermine his work. After all, she was the one who wanted the separation.

Then why did she not tell him about the letter?

Clouse picked up an album full of wedding photos taken by friends and relatives, remembering it as his favorite. Some of the pictures were a tad embarrassing after the alcohol wore off, and the honeymoon was over, but he didn't mind. He figured receptions were meant to be fun, and he certainly enjoyed himself, though most of the events were hazy in retrospect.

Brief thunderstorms gave way to a cool, overcast evening surrounding the house. As a blaze finally grew in the fireplace, Clouse turned on a floor lamp, opened the photo album, and peered at the memories he once held precious.

A thousand or more photos had snapped that day, but one of his favorites was taken by Roger Summers, when they stepped to the first dance at the reception, and he got them to smile once the professional photographer had taken his shots.

It was at that moment Clouse remembered being the happiest he had ever felt. At that point, everything seemed perfect.

Zach had looked through several albums with him, but lost interest and grew sleepy from his adventures outside. Clouse was happy his son could be a kid again, and begin moving on. The happier Zach became, the easier being a father would be for Clouse.

Before he could get too far into the album, headlights flooded the window in the office, catching his attention. Clouse walked to the kitchen, opening the door to greet his guests without waking Zach.

"Hey," he said happily after stepping outside, seeing Roger Summers approach, Kelli a few steps behind.

Kelli gave a smile that left him uneasy. He could not help but wonder what her kiss that afternoon meant, if anything. Clouse focused on Summers as Kelli stepped past him, into the house.

"Get some clothes on," Summers ordered in a tone of voice indicating he had something mischievous in mind.

"Why?" Clouse asked, perfectly content with a pair of sweat pants.

"We're going out for awhile."

"Out?"

"The family had its time together, so I figure its time you get your mind off this ordeal. Even if it's just tonight."

Clouse shot a suspicious look.

"Where are we going?"

"Get dressed," Summers said. "You'll see."

"And my kid?"

"Kelli volunteered to stay with him as long as we want," Clouse's brother-in-law replied. "We're covered, so get ready."

Reluctant, but with nothing else to do, Clouse stepped inside to get dressed.

*   *   *

Two hours later the two sat inside the Sport's Fanatic, a sports bar just outside city limits. From his bar stool beside Summers, Clouse took in the sights. Several cardboard cutouts of race car drivers and country singers stood along different walls. Three pool tables were active around the corner, while the bar's jukebox blared out a Clint Black song.

A smoky smell carried through the bar, dispersed only by the odor of onion rings, steaks, and seasoned fries. Dim lights provided obscurity for everyone in the bar, making it difficult to be recognized, or find someone suitable to take home. Three television sets were mounted above the bar at even intervals. Each carried a different sports program via satellite, but Clouse did not find the college basketball game above him the least bit interesting.

In the back corner a band took down their equipment after playing several sets. Clouse considered it odd that a band would play any time except the weekend, but ignored the feeling as he tipped the beer bottle to his lips. It was his seventh, and he felt better than he had all day.

"You okay, Paul?" Summers asked, noticing how much Clouse took in the view, his eyes possibly a bit more glazed than he realized.

"Fine."

Clouse found a growing number of people paying cover charge, filling the bar. He usually felt uncomfortable around large groups to begin with. This place was loud, and potentially hostile, based on what he had overheard at some of the pool tables. Only the numbing effects of the alcohol kept him calm.

"Kelli said you guys looked through Angie's things this afternoon?"

"Didn't get far. We kept getting stuck on old pictures."

"Understandable," Summers said, finishing his beer with a deep gulp. He motioned to the female bartender for another, leaving another sizable tip on the bar when the bottle arrived.

He seemed to know her pretty well from the way both had acted when the two firemen entered the bar.

Summers flirted with the bartender several minutes, making it obvious to Clouse he was a regular at the bar. Clouse knew it was unusual for his brother-in-law to be openly coy in public. Since Angie's death, Summers had acted strangely, trying to channel his emotions toward other people.

"Is Dierker pretty good with computers?" Clouse asked, quickly moving on, once the bartender left.

"Tony? Yeah, he's always getting into city files he shouldn't be. The dumb son-of-a-bitch is going to get caught one of these days," Summers said with a laugh. "Why you asking?"

"Angie's online files are password protected and I can't break it. I'm hoping Tony can get me by the code."

Tony Dierker worked with both men on the fire department, often bringing a laptop computer into work. He spent most of his downtime creating small programs, or improving his computer's configurations. Clouse seemed to recall the man once challenging him to create a password, only for Dierker's self-made program to crack it within ten minutes.

"What else are you thinking, brother?" Summers inquired, motioning for the bartender to bring Clouse another drink. Summers often referred to Clouse as his brother, and with everything the two had been through, it seemed fitting.

"I keep wondering how I'm going to raise Zach myself."

"You'll do okay," Summers encouraged him, obviously feeling better after several drinks. "You keeping the house?"

"I don't think I can," Clouse admitted. "But it'll be awhile before I can think about looking for another place. Zach doesn't seem to mind, and it's stupid to live anywhere else with all of our stuff there."

He looked to the back of the bar where the four members of the Paradise Band packed up their equipment. Never heard of them, Clouse thought as he started on the new beer.

"So how are *you* holding up?" he asked Summers.

"Okay. It's actually tough being around the family like this. I needed to get away from them awhile, and I felt so bad for you, Paul. You don't have anyone to talk to."

"My parents want to help, but with the police involvement, I hate dragging them into it."

Summers stared at the basketball game on the television screen above the bar. As the channel went to commercial he took a swig from his beer bottle, then slapped Clouse on the shoulder as he stood from his bar stool.

"Let's go throw some darts."

Questioning his brother-in-law's sobriety, Clouse gave a brief stare, then stood, grabbing his leather jacket and beer bottle. He followed Summers through a sea of people who danced, or simply crossed the wooden dance floor like themselves.

Clouse favored the bar stools to the dart boards, which he considered dangerously close to the pool tables where several bikers were arguing about who won which game. They were obviously more affected by alcohol than he and Summers were, and showed little regard for whoever knew it.

While Summers fed the electronic dartboard a few quarters, bringing it to life, Clouse set his beer on a ledge and his jacket on a nearby stool, as far from the pool tables as he could. All night he had been fighting the urge to tell Summers about Kelli's sudden kiss. He was extremely curious why Kelli would plant a kiss on him like that, but decided against talking about it. Summers had enough on his mind without hearing about his other sister.

"You go first," Summers said, dumping the darts into Clouse's hands.

Taking relatively careful aim, Clouse hit the eighteen point mark twice, then missed the board completely on his third shot.

"You a bit tipsy, Paul?" Summers teased.

"Not at all," Clouse said, placing a hand against the wall for support while his fellow firefighter shot.

After barely being bested, Clouse took up the darts again, trying to find the right spot to stand. He suddenly felt conscious about the angle of his darts, realizing the beers were thinking for him. Ordinarily, he could care less about bar sports, but Summers had accomplished his mission. Clouse was thinking about everything except Angie.

Whether he backed into the man, or the biker shooting pool behind him shifted for better position, Clouse would never know, but their bodies connected. Clouse felt an elbow or a pool stick jab his back, causing him to jerk forward, turning around as he did.

"You ruined my shot, asshole!" the man verbally charged Clouse, gaining the attention of the entire bar.

The biker smelled of cigar smoke and hard liquor with a build somewhat larger and bulkier than Clouse's.

Clouse attempted a quick apology, but a fist striking his jaw prevented the words from forming. Summers quickly stepped in, as Clouse toppled backwards to the floor. His brother-in-law said something he could not make out, but it sounded defensive. With blood dripping from his lip, Clouse felt anything but sympathetic now.

In a flash, the firefighter stood, elbowed Summers aside, and threw a thunderous right hand that floored the biker, rendering him unconscious, or close to it. Regaining his composure, Summers quickly directed Clouse toward the front door. He grabbed their belongings as he nudged Clouse in the right direction.

"Let's get out of here before you do any more damage, slugger," he said.

"Did I knock him out?" Clouse asked with glassy eyes as they reached the front door, attempting to get his arm into his jacket sleeve with a degree of trouble.

Summers looked back, seeing several people on the floor beside the semiconscious biker, who would surely be unruly when he came to.

"I think you had an assist from the fifth of Vodka he downed earlier, brother."

"Can I drive?" Clouse asked, finding the last sleeve in his jacket, pulling it up as the two stepped outside.

The cold air hit them both like a midnight lake swim.

"I think I better drive, Mike Tyson. We need to get back in one piece."

Both climbed into Summers' truck, shut the doors, and stared back at the bar. Apparently no one took too much exception to Clouse clocking a loudmouth biker. It was the first time the fireman had struck anyone since junior high, when he won a parking lot fist fight with a high school bully.

Nearly a mile away from Clouse's house, Summers turned to ask a question, finding Clouse passed out beside him. He hated carrying his own kids into the house, much less a family member who weighed as much as himself.

"Good thing you didn't drive," Summers said more to himself than the unconscious Clouse as he pulled into the driveway.

13

Daylight broke over the garden of the West Baden Springs Hotel as Rusty Cranor walked along the outside balcony, parallel to the first floor of the building. He was up early, checking the grounds for necessary winter preparation, figuring neither Clouse, nor Landamere, would show up for work.

He hated being in command.

Usually Landamere or another manager was there to give creative direction while Rusty oversaw the work of the men. Now he had to do both, and it was frustrating to plan upcoming stages of renovation while keeping an eye on the workers. He knew additional breaks would be snuck past him, or the work might go slower than he hoped, but it was to be expected.

None of the construction workers were at the hotel yet, and some were probably still in bed. It wasn't uncommon for many to come in and work until dark, especially with winter weather arriving early. Rusty had any number of rooms, buildings, and garden areas that needed securing or protecting from frigid weather.

As the foreman inspected some of the stained glass windows along the building's side, he failed to notice someone approaching along the balcony behind him.

"You the man in charge?" Mark Daniels asked, startling the foreman.

"Holy shit," Rusty replied, catching his breath as his left hand clasped his chest. "I'm the only one left, so don't scare me like that." He looked the detective over. "You're the one who interviewed everyone the day we found that body," he said, recognizing Daniels.

"Sorry," the detective replied in his quiet tone, causing Rusty to question his sincerity. "Mark Daniels," he said, extending his hand.

"Rusty Cranor," the foreman replied, shaking it. "Awful early to be out here, isn't it, detective?"

"I wanted to get a look around the grounds after I ask you a few questions. You know, before the workers arrive."

"I think your partner did most the talking the last time you were here," Rusty recalled.

Daniels grinned.

"He usually does. I wanted to talk to you about several issues that have come up concerning the murder of Angela Clouse, and the body you found here."

Rusty's look explained his confusion, but he needed to ask.

"Are the body and the murder related?"

"I think so," Daniels replied. "Before we get into this, can you call Paul Clouse and have him come down here? I think he's going to want to hear some of what I've got to say."

"I can certainly try. It's tough getting anyone in charge out here these days."

*   *   *

On the third ring, Clouse finally heard his phone, groaned, and rolled over to answer it, impeded by a warm body. Stretching over the body, his mind not thinking clearly, he picked up the cordless phone from a night stand. He pressed the talk button, falling back into his sleeping area.

"Hello?"

"Paul, this is Rusty. I've got Detective Mark Daniels here at the hotel. He wants to talk to you."

"What time is it, Rusty?" Clouse asked, his head throbbing with pain in every direction from a hangover.

"A little after six."

"You're at the hotel this early?"

"Someone has to be. So you coming down?"

"I'll be there as soon as I can."

"He's going to look around the grounds after he's done with me, so don't drive like a maniac or anything."

"I won't," Clouse said, pressing the button to hang up, still sitting on the edge of the bed.

For a moment his mind had lapsed into the past, thinking Angie was in bed beside him. He let the phone fall from his hand to the floor, barely able to think past the pain inside his head. Vague images of the night before came and went through his mind, and the last thing he recalled was being shoved during a game of darts.

His eyes twitched open as he turned to see who was sleeping beside him.

"Shit!" he said, clambering away from the bed, standing up to see Kelli lying there.

"What?" she asked from the under the covers, covered by a bathrobe from what he could see.

Clouse tried to recall the prior evening with every ounce of mental power he could muster, but the bookmark stood at the bar in the story of his life. All the makings of a good hangover loomed inside his skull, adding to the already awkward start of his day.

"Did we?" he left the question open, hoping his fun was limited to the bar.

"No, Paul," Kelli answered. "Rodge carried you in when you guys got back. I helped him tuck you in."

"I was pretty far gone, wasn't I?"

"I'd say," Kelli said, sitting up with a smile. "Knocking out a biker isn't part of your usual routine."

"My God," Clouse said, suddenly remembering the incident. "I did do it," he added, putting his hand against his aching forehead. "It wasn't a dream."

"I stayed to keep Zach company. Zach wanted to sleep on the couch and I wasn't about to sleep upstairs alone. Roger's going to pick me up later."

Clouse picked up the phone from the floor, realizing underwear was the only thing keeping Kelli from seeing all of him. He instantly felt uneasy.

"I've got to talk to a detective at the hotel. Can you keep Zach until I get back?"

"No problem," Kelli answered, pulling the covers over her. "You weren't hoping we'd fooled around, were you?" she kidded.

Clouse simply grunted, walking to the bathroom for a shower and some aspirin.

*   *   *

"So you believe Paul is innocent?" Rusty asked the detective as they walked around the grounds.

Daniels drew on a cigarette, looking at the ground as he walked alongside the foreman.

"I just find this whole thing kind of bizarre. There was no reason for him to come over here, dig up a body, and leave it in the upstairs of his house."

"But you said you've pieced together a likely scenario of what happened," Rusty urged for information.

Stopping at the edge of the brick path where the dirt-covered back entrance began, the detective took a final drag from his cigarette, crushing it under his shoe as he stared pensively at the clear sky beyond the hotel grounds.

"I have a scenario, but that's what I want to talk to Clouse about. In the meantime, I want you to tell me everything you know about the weird events happening *here* lately."

Rusty thought a moment, trying to think of where it all began.

"First thing I remember is Dave Landamere coming to work on Friday, bitching about the empty grave on the hill and how he'd fire any of us who dug it up. The boys have some strange ways of having fun, but I doubt any of them would ever do that."

"I doubt any of them did," Daniels commented.

"So anyway, we found the body later that day, then Dave disappeared."

"That's part of what I wanted to talk with you about. Dave Landamere hasn't been seen or heard from since Friday?"

Rusty chuckled, indicating he knew something about Landamere others would not.

"Dave doesn't much care for the press, and he probably feared a media swarm around this place after that body popped up. He left me in charge, said he would be back, but never said when. I just assumed he meant later that day."

"But he didn't tell Clouse, didn't tell his wife, and there's no trace of the man."

"That's the thing about Dave, detective, is he'll sometimes take a break from it all without telling a soul. It's not against his contract with Kieffer Construction, and he could care less if his wife knew or not."

Daniels smirked.

"Marriage of convenience?"

"Anymore, yes it is," the foreman said, a strange look crossing his face as he patted himself down.

"Lose something?"

"I'm always setting my damn keys down and forgetting them," Rusty replied, not finding them in his pockets, or hanging from his belt loop.

Taking a few steps to his right, Rusty looked along the balcony, spying his key ring shimmering atop the railing, close to the main entrance. While examining some of the windows earlier, he had set them down to use a tape measure.

Daniels wondered how often Rusty misplaced his keys, and if anyone else had access to them while they were missing. A copy of one certain key might give the wrong people access to the hotel. No one had mentioned Rusty's forgetfulness in earlier interviews, either because they found it irrelevant, or wanted to protect him.

Deciding not to press the issue, Daniels viewed the hotel's exterior, noting how the golden paint with white trim looked similar to the scheme used on Mexican villas he saw on the Discovery Channel. He wondered what inspired such a look at the turn of the last century when the hotel was built.

"So what do you know of Brian Mathis?" he asked Rusty.

"Good worker, good kid," the foreman summed it up. "He was one of the few I trusted to get a job done quick. One of the first in, usually the last to leave. Was kind of a shame with his family and all."

"Did he have anyone who didn't like him?"

"No. He was always quiet, but he'd joke around with the guys. Everyone here liked him."

"What about Paul Clouse?"

"I'm not sure they really knew each other," Rusty replied with a look of thought. "How does his death tie into all of this?"

"He was killed with the same weapon that murdered Angela Clouse," Daniels revealed, figuring it would be public knowledge soon enough. "I'm trying to figure out how all of this ties in myself. There's not even a remote link between the two killings, the priest's body, and Landamere's disappearance."

"Well, I already told you my view on Dave's disappearance, but there might be a little something between the murders."

"How so?" Daniels asked, fishing in his shirt breast pocket for another cigarette.

"Someone told me Mathis was mumbling something about a reaper before he died. This true?" The detective nodded an affirmative before lighting up. "Do you know whose body was dug up?"

"Father Ernest. No last name given," Daniels said slowly, making certain he remembered correctly.

"And that doesn't ring a bell for you?" Rusty asked, forgetting how young the detective was in relevance to what he asked.

"Not particularly."

"You never heard the legend of Father Ernest, the one all the Jesuits kept locked up because he went mad, believing he was the taker of souls?"

Daniels' face showed his amazement as the connection hit him.

"The one who dressed in dark robes and eventually set himself on fire?"

"The one," Rusty confirmed.

"But that's just a myth I heard as a kid. It's not true, is it?"

Rusty shrugged his shoulders, unable to prove or disprove the myth.

"So someone could be using the legend as a coverup for these murders," the detective told himself. "But what's the motive? And why two completely different settings?"

Daniels found an entirely new set of circumstances to ponder. He berated himself for not realizing the connection earlier, but felt assured new answers would come from this information. He knew the central figure in the entire mess was Paul Clouse, but refused to believe the man would be so obvious in committing murder.

But if he wasn't behind the killings, who was? And why?

"Care if I take a walk around the grounds?" Daniels asked Rusty, who was anxious to finish his rounds.

"Go right ahead. I'll be around if you need anything."

Smoking as he walked the brick walkways surrounding the building, Daniels felt an eerie calm around him. For so long the hotel had stood vacated, and in the morning, before construction workers filed in, everything about the building appeared tranquil, as though the hotel was meant to remain this way.

The detective wondered what the fate of the great building would ultimately be, and if it was meant to have human companionship again.

He found it odd that a foreman would misplace his keys on a regular basis. It would give someone ample opportunity to copy important keys if Rusty left them in the open. From what he gathered, the foreman knew his business, but seemed oblivious to most everything else. Perhaps he was one of the chosen few, whose work was his life.

Daniels knew the feeling, wondering why he was working before most of his fellow detectives even heard the shrill of their alarm clocks.

A free trip across the grounds would have meant more to him, if not for the bizarre circumstances drawing him in. He sensed the connection between Angie Clouse's death and that of Brian Mathis, and possibly the disappearance of Dave Landamere.

Several newspapers were beginning to surmise the theory of a Father Ernest tie-in, which angered the detective. Local murders were not fair game for sensationalism in his eyes. He also felt irritated they had seen the connection to the legend before he had.

Such notions probably played into the hands of the killer, raising public attention to the possibility of a supernatural involvement. He knew if they fell for it, panic would grow in the West Baden community if more murders occurred. It seemed an easy way to place a dark cloud over the hotel and keep people away, but for what purpose?

His mind raced in a thousand directions, seeking answers from every piece of information or physical evidence he knew of. Daniels took pride in the fact that he sought more than one solution, unlike his partner, but chided himself for not finding anything more concrete than Kendle had.

Daniels found himself in the back of the building, about to turn back when he decided to explore, knowing that Mathis was dragged through part of the area and buried in back. The construction entrance was also an area where people might be able to come and go without attention. He felt the security of the gate would be worth checking, if nothing else.

As he crossed the grounds, Daniels noticed the morning fog lifting as the sun raised more prominently in the sky. He heard several birds from nearby trees as the stiff, cold breeze lessened in intensity.

A thick chain and padlock kept the back gate closed, not surprising him. It was adequate security in the evening, but he wondered how secure it was during the day. Few trucks came in and out of the gate during work hours, so he wondered if it was locked, and who had access to it.

Whoever was responsible for the murders probably had access to the hotel grounds, and the number of people involved with the restoration was more than met the eye. He knew over two dozen people had access to the grounds any time of day because of their position in a historical group, the restoration crew, or hotel ownership.

Growing frustrated with the thought of investigating so many people, Daniels kicked a small clump of dirt on his return to the formal walking path.

"Damn it," he said, looking to see how much dust his shoe collected from the kick. He hated polishing them any more than necessary, and cursed himself for losing his temper.

His eyes caught a glimmer from something different than the black leather of his shoes as the sun reflected off an object several feet ahead of him. His face twisted to a puzzled stare as the detective walked toward a fallen camera, half buried, and plucked it from its resting spot.

A quick examination showed nothing wrong with the piece. Daniels was familiar with all sorts of photography equipment from various surveillance details.

Kneeling down, he found nothing else around the camera except several dried, darkened spots atop the dirt which he dismissed as remnants from the recent rain. He stood a moment later, dusting off the camera, hoping Rusty Cranor agreed with his philosophy of finders keepers.

14

Clouse drove up the hotel's lengthy driveway to find Mark Daniels and Rusty outside, talking on the grand staircase which led to the hotel's second entrance. He parked in front of the hotel, feeling it was allowed since the helm was his to command.

When he ascended the stairs, it looked as though he might have interrupted a discussion between the two men, but Daniels nodded to Rusty, allowing the foreman to return to his work.

"Thanks," Daniels said as the foreman walked toward the inside, holding the camera over his head.

Daniels sauntered down the steps toward Clouse, carefully placing the camera's strap around his neck where it rested upon his sport coat's collar.

"Rusty showering you with gifts?" Clouse asked.

"Not quite. Found this out back. Said I could have it if the film didn't reveal who the owner was."

Clouse stared at it a moment, noting the dusty coating.

"Yours?" Daniels inquired, thinking he knew something about it.

"Nope. So what brings you here, detective?"

Both descended the stairs, walking toward the open garden area.

"It's unusual for someone in my position to speak openly with the primary suspect in a murder case, but that's what I'm here for."

"So you believe I'm innocent?"

"I can't say with any certainty, but that's my gut feeling."

Daniels led the way along the garden paths where dying flowers shriveled beside the red brick walkway.

"I've been doing some investigation of my own," Clouse remarked.

"Getting anywhere?"

"Nothing concrete, but once I break the code to Angie's computer, it might give me more information about her clients and contacts."

"It doesn't look good for you, living in the house and all," Daniels noted.

"I don't have much choice. My son is *not* spending another day without me, and we're not going to be crammed in some apartment. Once everything settles down, I'll sell and move on. Zach is young enough to put this behind him."

Daniels stopped in front of the fountain, staring at the cemetery atop the hill, some distance away.

"I've got a little one of my own," the detective confessed. "They become your whole world the day they're born."

Clouse grinned, agreeing fully, but knowing his entire world was rocked by Angie's death. Every day following came just a bit easier, despite the murderer label hanging around his neck like an albatross.

"So what can I do to help you?" the blueprint designer asked, drawing Daniels' attention from the graves.

"Tell me who might have motive to kill your wife."

"I don't know," Clouse answered emphatically. "But the more I think about it, the more it occurs to me that Angie might not be the focus of this whole ordeal."

"You're talking about the hotel, and the Father Ernest deal?"

"I did some research at the library and checked out that story, and it all ties in. Father Ernest apparently thought he was some sort of soul reaper toward the end, and burned himself alive, which created the legend we all heard growing up."

"It may be nothing more than legend," Daniels supposed aloud. "Someone could be using that angle for the murders, but what purpose would it serve?"

"I'm not sure. It would scare away the local population, or at least tarnish their memories of this landmark, but it's not under sole ownership, so there wouldn't be financial gain, except maybe lowering the selling price."

"And even at that, there's lots of work to be done, correct?"

"Yeah," Clouse said, pointing to the upper floors. "All those rooms are completely gutted to concrete, plaster, and steel. You're talking millions more in work."

Daniels sighed.

"I can check into potential buyers," he said, pulling a notepad from his coat pocket to write himself a reminder. "Oh, can you take me to Landamere's office?"

As they walked inside the hotel a moment later, Clouse finished explaining how he had contacted a potential buyer for the hotel and never received an answer, until finding a letter from Michael Hathaway among Angie's things.

"And she never told you?"

"No," Clouse replied. "And she had an opportunity at the ball. Maybe things just slipped her mind or she was going to surprise me with the news later."

Clouse unlocked the door to Landamere's office, flipping on the fluorescent lights before either entered.

Instantly the room sprang to life as a floor to ceiling bookcase loomed behind Landamere's desk, filled with family photos, clipboards, several notepads, and a miniature model of the hotel and its grounds.

As Daniels took a seat in the swivel chair, surveying the mildly cluttered area around the desk, Clouse looked at the filing cabinet in one corner and several folding chairs set randomly in areas of the room, often used for impromptu meetings with foremen or various renovation leaders.

"Care if I take a look?" Daniels asked, pointing to the desk.

Clouse looked around, as though expecting Landamere to catch them in his office any second, then thought more rationally.

"Go ahead."

While the detective rummaged through several drawers, Clouse walked to the restroom down the hall. He loved the way both restrooms were done to match the rest of the hotel's interior. Beautiful gold and green tile covered both the walls and floor of each room.

In the men's room, stalls and urinal dividers were painted a dark, rich green to accent the trim on the wall tiles. It was a touch of class compared to the closet-sized rooms he and the construction workers were forced to use when the project first began.

"Feel better?" Daniels asked when Clouse returned to the office.

"Much."

"I don't suppose your boss informed you about this?" the detective asked, holding up a letter, which Clouse took and unfolded.

He skimmed the contents, learning that Michael Hathaway had sent a letter of inquiry to Dr. Smith and copies to Landamere and several other project board members. From the look on Clouse's face, Daniels knew the answer.

"Landamere didn't tell you about this?"

"He didn't," Clouse replied.

"I get the impression several people were keeping it from you for a reason."

"If they were trying to surprise me, it wouldn't exactly have shocked me. Unless Michael wanted to tell me himself."

Daniels replaced the letter, closing the desk drawers. The two men left the room, Clouse locking the door behind him.

"Has your friend contacted you about his interest in the property?"

"I haven't exactly been home the last month," Clouse admitted. "Knowing him, he probably wants to surprise me if he buys it."

"My main reason for coming here was to share my theory about your wife's murder with you," the detective said as they walked outside the hotel.

"And?"

"Unlike my partner, I don't think you had the time to pull it off. That doesn't mean you didn't have motive, but it seems odd that you would dig up a body *here*, transport it almost an hour away, and leave it upstairs for your wife to find."

"Why the body at all?"

"It's small enough that in the darkness, Angela may have thought it was your son and panicked, leading her right into the killer. We found your upstairs light unscrewed, so it wouldn't have come on when she flipped the switch."

"Did someone choose that body with reason?"

"Probably the Father Ernest connection. Using a scythe to kill? Come on, it fits perfectly," Daniels said. "Every killer wants an angle. Whoever's doing this is carrying out some fantasy, but killing with a deeper intent than just random selection. The hotel is definitely tied in somehow."

As Clouse walked Daniels to his car, the detective found few encouraging words in parting.

"If you aren't responsible for any of this, someone close to you probably is," Daniels advised him. "It's awfully convenient that every time something bad happens around here, you're nearby," he added, opening the door to his Honda.

Though several years old, it was a car much like him, practical and efficient. With one child, and another on the way, Daniels watched every penny and worked every bit of overtime he could, to save for his future and that of his family.

"If I were you, Mr. Clouse, I would keep a close eye on my friends, my family, and everyone at this place," Daniels said, waving a hand across the span of the hotel grounds. "And if it turns out you're in any way responsible for all this, damn me for believing you."

"Don't worry, you've got me sized up okay," Clouse assured him.

"I hope so," Daniel said, climbing into his car.

"Can you do me a favor during the course of your investigation?"

"What would that be?"

"I'd like you to check out the gardener here. His name is Vern, but I don't know much more than that. He's just kind of an odd guy."

"No harm in checking," Daniels said with a shrug. "Watch your back."

Clouse watched as the maroon car rolled down the brick drive toward the roads of West Baden.

A long day awaited him, and a good breakfast might do him good. Rusty would be around until he got back.

*   *   *

Larry Kendle's morning had consisted of little more than reviewing photos and evidence from the Angela Clouse murder. The wedge between he and Daniels grew because of their varying opinions.

Though he would never admit it, he liked having a partner who thought differently, but he wanted to bring Daniels along slowly. The man was new to the investigative division, and needed to be completely objective, letting the evidence guide him, rather than his opinions and wild theories. Without evidence, opinions were useless in court.

Despite his reputation, Kendle played by the rules. He followed the evidence trail like a bloodhound, sniffing for the clues of his predetermined quarry.

He was concerned about Daniels' train of thought, and how he strayed from his veteran partner. Kendle had kept their temporary separation from his sergeant. Things would have to get completely out of hand before Kendle would say anything to their division leader, because the investigators prided themselves on being independent and capable.

Things had been much harder when he started investigating years before. The advances in forensic science made a world of difference, but Kendle knew the aspects of an investigation driven by detectives themselves made all the difference.

He could interview with the best, do surveillance, and comb a crime scene for evidence most officers missed, or stepped on. Kendle wanted to pass the torch to Daniels, but he feared the young detective might be too rash, and easily influenced, to be effective.

Daniels would need to learn self-control before he could gain the respect of his fellow investigators. He had much more to learn than he realized.

But time was on his side.

One of only two detectives seated in the office, Kendle scooped up the phone on its first ring, hoping for something to distract him from the case for a few minutes.

"Detectives," he answered in short.

"Larry Kendle or Mark Daniels, please," the voice said.

"This is Kendle."

"Hi, Larry. This is Ed Miller from the state police."

Kendle remembered the state trooper from several cases they had worked together. Miller was now the second-in-command of the Bloomington post.

"Hello, Ed. What can I do for you?"

"Actually, I might have something for you. A conservation officer found a car at Mounds Park in Anderson. He ran the plates, and they came back registered to one David Landamere, whom I understand you wish to speak with."

"Word travels fast."

"Your case is all over the news," Miller added. "They haven't touched the car yet. You want a crack at it?"

"Definitely," Kendle said immediately. "Can you have one of your technicians meet me at the park in two hours?" he asked, knowing it would take that long to reach the city of Anderson.

"You got it."

"Thanks, Ed. I owe you one."

*   *   *

Everything in the town of West Baden seemed to have a historical ring to it, which nearly drove Clouse insane. He grew tired of seeing 'historical landmark' posted on every other building, and inside the others. He considered himself a visitor, and wondered if residents simply ignored the signs defacing their buildings, or if they were raised to love them.

When Clouse walked into the B.B. Café, few heads turned. He was as close to a regular customer as the small restaurant could get. It was also the only place relatively close to the hotel that served all three meals. Many of the construction workers took their lunch breaks at the café or stopped in for morning coffee.

The restaurant's ownership would see no decline in sales for at least a year while the construction continued.

Sliding into a stool at the bar, Clouse took up the menu he had practically memorized, scanning it for what sounded the most appetizing. He figured an order of eggs and bacon would cure his grumbling stomach, and informed Kayla, the waitress, of such.

While he waited for his meal to fry, the waitress brought him some buttered toast as an attractive woman with notably long, brown hair slid into the stool beside his. Her light complexion and soft skin, along with her attire, gave him the impression she was not a regular to the café, or the small town of West Baden.

Seated among a pool of truckers and construction workers, she added color to the otherwise bleak setting.

Dressed in dark slacks and a light blouse which accented her shapely figure, the woman reminded Clouse of Angie in several ways. She was pretty, appeared intelligent and self-assured, and commanded the attention of everyone in the building, himself included.

"Don't I know you?" she asked, returning Clouse's unintentional stare.

"Sorry," he quickly apologized, turning to the less exciting view of bottles behind the bar.

"No," she said with a laugh. "I meant don't I recognize you from the hotel?"

Clouse gave a curious stare, wondering what this lady of evident importance had to do with the hotel.

"I give tours there once or twice a week," she explained, unable to break the perplexed look from Clouse. "My mother lives down here, and I visit from Bloomington."

"Paul Clouse," the fireman said, extending his hand, finally gaining some understanding of the situation.

"Jane Brooks," she replied, gently shaking it. "I see you at the hotel fairly often, so I gather you're part of the renovation?"

"I'm a designer for Dave Landamere, the project manager, when I'm not working for the City of Bloomington," Clouse explained.

"City job?"

"I'm a firefighter."

Jane smiled, apparently understanding why he wasn't visible on a daily basis.

"I run the Northway Medical Clinic in Bloomington," she informed Clouse.

"Doctor?" Clouse asked, raising an eyebrow. "And you share a love for the hotel with the rest of us?"

She laughed easily, not uptight like Angie. Clouse already enjoyed company who took the time to smile without thought.

"My mother brought me up to love the hotel. I can't count how many times she told me stories about the Jesuits, the college era, and how she and my father would sneak into the grounds when it was abandoned, just for a peek. I guess I'm just a sap for it now, so I volunteer on my days off."

"I'll bet your mother is proud."

"Oh, yes," Jane said with a grin. "She occasionally surprises me by showing up in one of my tours."

Clouse turned his attention briefly to the plate of scrambled eggs and crispy bacon laid before him as Jane placed her order for orange juice and wheat toast.

"So, do I get a mention in your tours now?" Clouse asked, chuckling.

"Only if you happen to be outside," she said, appearing serious. "You'd be surprised how many people want to know every little aspect of the grounds, including the people working on them."

For the next fifteen minutes the two talked about their lives away from work, and what they enjoyed most about the West Baden Springs Hotel. Clouse finished his meal, left money for the bill, and a tip, and stood.

"I guess I'll see you on some of your tours today," he told Jane. "We'll be working on some details inside the atrium."

"Would you like to talk some more during lunch?" Jane asked. "I'll have breaks at eleven and two."

"I'd like that," Clouse said with a smirk. "I'm easy to find."

"We'll talk later then," Jane confirmed.

Clouse nodded an affirmative before leaving the café for a full day's work.

*   *   *

At noon Clouse found himself seated in a lawn chair beside Jane. They were behind the hotel where several other employees and tour guides ate lunch. Several large trees provided shade over a couple picnic tables and folding chairs. Most everyone brought their own lunch, since the town had very few fast food or carry-out restaurants.

The day became uncommonly warm, allowing everyone to eat outside one last time before the next cold front arrived, bringing the onset of winter.

"I keep noticing your wedding band," Jane commented between sips of iced tea. "Are you the one who-?"

"My wife was killed last week," Clouse said, finishing the sentence. "And you shouldn't believe too much about what the papers are saying."

"I don't put much stock in them."

"So, what's your status?"

"Divorced with a daughter of my own," Jane answered. "It's not been easy, but we all cope."

Clouse took a bite of his ham sandwich.

"You probably wonder why I'm working here so soon after Angie's death."

"It's not uncommon. Lots of people throw themselves into their work to avoid mourning a loved one."

Staring at his wedding band, the fireman wondered if and when the grief would end. He hadn't given up hope while she was alive concerning their relationship, making it tougher to put the ring away.

"I feel bad, like I'm not dealing with this right. My son is confused, and I feel powerless to explain this to him, or even console him," Clouse said, staring above the tree line toward the clear sky. "It's tough to even be around him right now, and it's not fair to Zach."

"You're being too hard on yourself, Paul. You need time and space. Everyone does. With everything going on around this place, I'm surprised you can keep your sanity."

Clouse forced a grin.

"Are you referring to the Father Ernest stories in the papers?"

"Was it really his body?" Jane asked with a squeamish look.

"Unfortunately, yes."

Several people turned to see a county police car pulling into the drive. Clouse recognized the driver as Kaiser.

"Looks like I've got to run," he said, standing.

Jane jotted something on a piece of paper, handing it to him.

"A few of my friends are meeting me at this pub later. If you want to stop by and talk, I promise to be a good listener."

"I appreciate that," Clouse said with a smile. "I'm probably going to spend some time with Zach tonight. Short of a major disaster, maybe I'll stop in before I pick him up."

"If not, I know where to find you," Jane replied.

"It's my life," Clouse stated, looking up the hotel's six story walls. "Take care."

Tossing the remains of his lunch into a nearby trash can, Clouse approached his friend, who wore a grim expression. Kaiser was out of uniform, meaning he made a personal trip to the hotel, which he seldom did.

"What's the matter, Ken?"

"It seems we've had a disappearance, and it might be related to this place," the county officer stated, steering Clouse away from the workers on break.

"What happened?"

"Robert Bennett, an electrician who owns his own business, was subcontracted to do some electrical work out here," Kaiser explained. "A couple days ago he came out to do some wiring, was seen heading out the back gate around dark, and hasn't been heard from since."

Clouse remembered who he was. He and Landamere had given the man a brief tour of the grounds, so the electrician knew where to start. He kept wanting to talk to Clouse about unions and how they helped the working man, so Clouse quickly made an excuse to leave Bennett in Landamere's hands.

"But he left the grounds?" Clouse inquired, finding it hard to believe the man simply disappeared.

"His van was seen leaving, but no one could positively ID him as the driver."

"Not good," Clouse said. "No one's heard from him?"

"No. Two of his employees said he didn't show up for work yesterday or today. They claim it's extremely out of character for him to miss work, and if he does, they say he always calls."

"Are you handling it?"

Kaiser's expression soured.

"No, and my captain doesn't want me out here in any official capacity until this thing gets resolved. He doesn't want me around you either, because the department might get some bad publicity, or some bullshit like that. *And* he doesn't want me to do security detail here either, but he can't really stop me from that."

Clouse led his friend further from the others, toward the main steps.

"You say that electrician left around dark?"

Kaiser nodded.

"I was here until dark the other night, Ken."

"So?"

"Doesn't it seem a little coincidental that every single time something goes wrong around here I seem to be near it?"

"I suppose," Kaiser answered slowly, treading carefully around his friend's line of questioning.

"Maybe I need to stay away from this place."

"But if you're being set up, we won't be able to catch whoever's doing it."

"But maybe no one else will die or disappear," Clouse deduced aloud.

"I can help you nab whoever's doing this if we play our cards right," Kaiser suggested.

"You said it yourself. Your captain doesn't want you near here or me. Somehow I'm going to have to handle this myself."

"Running from it isn't the answer," Kaiser said emphatically. "I've never known you to back down from a challenge."

"Lives are at stake, Ken. I can't risk the killer framing me for all of this. I've got a son to look out for. Besides, if I leave maybe all this will cease."

Kaiser shook his head negatively.

"You're being rash, Paul. I hope you aren't thinking of resigning your position over this?"

"Maybe I am, Ken. If that's what it takes, maybe I am."

The county officer made certain no one else was within earshot before handing out his next batch of bad news.

"There's a kid named Timmons who disappeared too," Kaiser almost whispered to his friend.

"A kid?"

"Teenager. Not exactly your model citizen, but he was an okay kid."

"Surely that's not related."

"Might be nothing," Kaiser said with a shrug. "Wouldn't really surprise me if he ran away from home. Kind of the mischievous type, if you get my drift. I pulled him over a few times for-"

"I hate all this," Clouse interrupted. "Life used to be so much easier."

"It might be again if you let me help you figure out who's behind all this."

"I may not have much choice, Ken. But at the same time I don't want to see you walk into a trap, either."

Kaiser grinned.

"It'll take more than this guy to knock me off, buddy. Just hang in there," the cop said, walking toward his car. "I'll call you later."

Clouse gave a wave before turning to see almost two dozen eyes quickly disperse in every direction but his.

Life was not getting any easier.

*   *   *

When Kendle stepped from his unmarked car alone, he found the conservation officer and a forensics expert waiting for him beside a white Cadillac parked awkwardly at the edge of a small parking lot.

The lot, used exclusively for one particular exhibit, had only two other vehicles parked on it, leading Kendle to believe the car could have sat for a day or two without really being noticed. The Department of Natural Resources employees seldom checked such a small parking lot.

Snapping a latex glove over each hand, Kendle walked carefully around the car, looking for damage or anything unusual. He saw tufts of grass stuck to the tires and in between the fiberglass and chrome areas of the fenders. Around the front he saw the driver's side of the windshield spider-webbed with speckles of blood where something might have hit it.

Amazingly, the keys were in the ignition and the doors unlocked. Both the state police technician and the officer stood by while Kendle silently went about his initial investigation. He looked at the door handle for traces of blood or stains, but found none.

"Start dusting here, please," he said to the technician. "I'm going to get inside and see if there's anything useful."

Kendle got inside, finding no rips or tears along the seats, and nothing unusual on the floor mats, but his flashlight helped him spot several dark stains on the driver's seat, near the head and shoulder area for most drivers. He asked the technician to swab the seat, and the cotton swab picked up relatively fresh blood from the surface.

Knowing how slow state police labs could be, usually due to an extensive backlog, the detective asked for a second swab to send to a friend at Indiana University in Bloomington. If he found a DNA sample from David Landamere, they could determine whether or not this was Landamere's blood on the seat.

"I can comb the vehicle for fingerprints, and vacuum for hair and fiber samples," the technician said when he assumed Kendle was finished, nearly half an hour later.

"Go ahead. I'll see about getting some comparison samples for you."

The technician pulled a card out from one of his pockets, handing it over to the investigator. Kendle did the same.

"Let me know if you find anything," Kendle urged. "It concerns several ongoing homicides, and we don't have any thorough leads yet."

The technician grimaced.

"I'll put a rush on it, but you know how things go in the lab."

"I know. But I'd appreciate any help," Kendle said before getting into his car.

He wondered if his list of murder suspects was narrowing, or expanding. Kendle started the car and prepared for his two-hour trip home. A trip in which he could think about the new evidence he might have.

Evidence that might put him closer to the truth.

*   *   *

Most of the workers pulled away from the hotel grounds as the sun began to set in the late afternoon. Rusty had a tendency to send people home early, especially when he felt nervous about something. Lately he had plenty to be nervous about.

As the foreman spoke with one of the workers about the hotel's winter preparation, Clouse walked to the back of the hotel where he spotted several clusters of construction workers talking or joking before heading out for the day. He was finishing up an exterior inspection of the hotel before heading to Bloomington.

His body felt exhausted from walking all day, but his mind felt worse. The more he pondered the situation, the more he felt resigning his position would be for the best. If it saved lives, he had no reservations about leaving.

He also thought about what Mark Daniels had said concerning who the killer might be. Who around him could be a murderer? Clouse chose his friends carefully, and felt no one in his family was capable of murder, much less framing him for it.

Motive seemed to be the missing element. He wondered what hidden motive someone had for linking several deaths and disappearances to the hotel. It had to be there, just not openly. Clouse felt helpless, knowing he was the only person who could help himself out of this predicament.

What Kaiser said was true, in that Clouse did not back away from challenges, but this appeared to be a no-win situation if he fought it. There was no way to find the killer by himself at the hotel, and maybe if he took the time to carefully search Angie's things and crack her computer code, he could find more answers.

Finishing his rounds, the temporary project manager looked to the brick road behind the hotel where several workers continued talking before they headed out. He crossed the lawn between them and the hotel, looking up at the great structure, seeing something unusual streak across a third story window.

Clouse stopped, looking for it again.

"No," he murmured, seeing a darkly-clothed figure cross another window.

Sprinting directly toward the hotel's main entrance, Clouse passed Rusty, calling the foreman's name. After gaining Rusty's attention, he continued toward the entrance, unsure if the older man would follow this time.

*   *   *

On the third floor, Scott Beaman finished caulking the last of the windows on the building's west side. It had taken most of the day, but his side of the hotel would be ready for winter. Now he knelt, putting his equipment in a box for another crew to use the next day.

Most everyone else was out of the building, leaving him alone. He hated working by himself to begin with, and the strange occurrences around the hotel left him feeling more insecure. Beaman just wanted to pack up and get out.

An eerie calm overtook the hotel, and for a moment, Beaman heard no one talking outside, or any vehicles starting. A sensation he was completely alone panicked him enough that he walked to a window for a look outside. Seeing several men talking amongst themselves, he realized he was overreacting and went back to his equipment.

"Calm down, Scott," he told himself, thinking the barren walls of the hotel might close in on him at any moment.

He needed the money, or he would have left in search of another job, which sometimes took days or weeks to find. His employers didn't seem overly concerned with the safety of their men, which surprised him. Construction companies hated liability, and here they were leaving an inexperienced designer and a foreman with little backbone in charge.

The men respected Rusty Cranor, but he wasn't the tested general Landamere was. He could not bark out orders, or stay on top of everything well enough to keep the project moving along as it had been.

Exhaling deeply to calm himself, Beaman packed up the caulk gun, the remaining tubes, and several hand tools before closing the box he knelt beside.

Quickly standing to leave, Beaman turned around, hearing a swoosh sound as a large curved blade tore through his abdomen, piercing his backside, cracking the window behind him.

Workers below heard the noise of the splintered glass, much like the sound in an automobile accident, looking up to the window where a spider web formed in the glass from the impact, highlighted in red mist. They saw Beaman's back against the stained window, knowing instantly what they viewed was no joke.

Mortally wounded, the construction worker could not defend himself as the killer pried the scythe from his body, threw it to the floor, then took hold of his flannel shirt collar, launching him out the already weakened window. Shattered glass rained on the ground three stories down, followed by Beaman's body, which landed backside first, accompanied by cracking and popping sounds as nature finished the job the killer had begun.

"No!" Clouse screamed from a gutted room's frame, too far away to have prevented Beaman's death, but able to see through the skeletal framework almost two rooms away.

Taking up the weapon, the killer darted off in the opposite direction. Clouse delayed the chase just a few seconds to peer out a nearby window, seeing Beaman's mangled body on the ground, while several workers noticed his stare. Much like in the fire service, his concern for a colleague had initially overtaken a desire to catch the killer, but one look at Beaman's mangled body gave Clouse the green light to commence his hunt.

"Fuck!" the fireman said as he broke himself away from the gruesome view, pursuing the killer through the rooms devoid of any walls. He carefully leapt over structural frames, boxes, and piles of rubble as he gave chase.

Any number of staircases were available to the killer, and the two nearby elevators were in working order, meaning he could take them, or lead Clouse to think he had. The fireman rounded a corner, pulling to a stop before he looked down the staircase, finding nothing except winding flights of stairs. He stood, intently listening, hearing nothing except the commotion in the back yard where Beaman had landed.

"Damn," he said to himself, continuing down the same hall, allowing the killer to slip from behind a partial wall once he was in the clear, and descend the stairs for a clean escape.

Walking along the hallway, Clouse knew the sound of his boots would give him away, but he refused to stop looking. He could also not afford to walk in socks with so many potential hazards on the floor just waiting to puncture human flesh. He approached a bend in the hallway and picked up his pace.

Clouse let out a yell as he impacted with another person around the bend. He stepped back, realizing the foreman had followed him upstairs again.

"I saw you from the stairs, Paul," Rusty said quickly. "I know you didn't do it."

"But whoever did got away," Clouse replied angrily, upset with himself for not stopping the killer, or finding him afterward.

"There was nothing you could have done, Paul," the foreman said, clutching Clouse's arm, trying to settle him down. "Let's go call the police before you get yourself killed."

Clouse took a few deep breaths, realizing how out of hand things had become. No one would want to be around the hotel, or him for that matter. A sense of responsibility overtook his sense of reason, even if he had no direct hand in the murders.

"Okay, let's call the police," Clouse finally said, ready to put the matter where it belonged.

15

Both Clouse and Zach sat on the couch watching the television as the boy flipped through several channels, finding little of interest to watch.

Clouse didn't really care what was on. His mind stuck on the events almost four hours prior, and how Detective Larry Kendle refused to believe he was innocent of the murders at the hotel, and the one inside his own house.

Rusty's testimony of seeing Clouse too far from the murder spot failed to convince Kendle, because Rusty never actually saw the murderer from his vantage point. Even Daniels, who struggled to be impartial, had to ask why it was only Clouse who saw this dark figure on the upper floors twice.

Clouse had to question why they were so far out of their jurisdiction, working on a case two counties away from their own, probably sounding more defensive than he recalled. They said the killer had used the same weapon in all of the murders, tying the hotel murders in with Angie's, thus leaving him, or someone around him, a prime suspect.

Kendle went so far as to imply Clouse had a partner, and set up the scenario to prove his innocence to the police. There seemed to be nothing the firefighter could do to convince Kendle otherwise. He grew tired of the accusations and the senseless death surrounding him, yet Rusty's testimony seemed to shed some light on his innocence, to those who would listen.

"This okay?" Zach asked permission, stopping on a movie of the week.

"Sure," Clouse answered before picking up another of Angie's printouts, studying it for any names or addresses that might seem suspicious.

He had gone through her papers several times, finding little of significance. It now seemed more logical that someone who knew the hotel well, and knew Clouse's habits, was setting him up. He needed to look closer to home, or perhaps his workplace.

Still, he arranged for Tony Dierker to come over and look at Angie's computer. If anyone could bypass the code, it would be him. Dierker had the next day off from the fire department, and Clouse took advantage of it. He knew the man could not resist a challenge, so he invited him over to break the password.

While Zach watched the movie, Clouse pondered the day's events, wishing his life wasn't such a disaster. Things were so peaceful when he and Angie were married.

He remembered when there was time for days away from it all, just taking Zach to the park, or working around the house. It seemed they had become too busy for one another as a couple, and drifted apart. Before Clouse could reconcile the differences, however, his life was changed forever.

Damned perhaps.

As though he wasn't spooked enough with the week's events, Clouse heard a bump from outside the house, as though something had hit the siding. He sprang from the couch, looking back to see if Zach had noticed.

He hadn't.

With his son engrossed in the movie, Clouse stepped outside to see where the noise had come from, and whether it warranted further investigation.

It had come from the corner of the house, away from the porch. As he drew closer to the corner, the light from behind him grew less intense, leaving almost no visibility as he neared the origin of the noise.

He cautiously approached the area, looking around as he saw a large rock lying beside the foundation. No sounds emerged from the darkness, and no one could be seen in the shadows. None of his dogs had barked, leading him to believe maybe the rock had been there quite some time, and the noise was just a fluke.

Clouse returned to the house to find Zach calmly watching the movie. He wondered if his son sensed any of the danger that plagued him. As much as he tried to shield his concern, he felt certain some of it leaked through the facade.

He had just sat down again when something different caught his attention from the outside.

Headlights beamed through the family room window, and Clouse found it odd for a visit after dark. Expecting no one in particular, he arched his neck for a better look, not recognizing the BMW as anyone's he knew.

"Who is it, Dad?" Zach asked, probably hoping for company to break the monotony of his recent routine.

"Stay here, Zach," Clouse said, rising to answer the door.

He opened it to a totally unexpected visitor in the form of Dr. Martin Smith, the hotel's current owner, though Smith disliked the title at the moment.

He preferred to be labeled the hotel's caretaker or benefactor, though he paid the money to take it over, and much more in restoring it. Clouse knew the man was worth close to two billion dollars after his years of medical research paid off and his company made millions in pharmaceutical products used daily in hospitals nationwide.

"Dr. Smith," Clouse said with open surprise, forgetting momentarily to invite the older man inside. "What brings you out here?"

"I have some grave concerns about the hotel and what's been happening out there," the doctor replied.

In his sixties, Smith had more health than most men half his age, but the recent events had apparently taken a toll on him. A pale, ragged look took shape on his face instead of the usual easy smile and beaming green eyes. His gray hair appeared matted and unkept, as though a man of his stature held little value in his personal upkeep.

"Come in," Clouse said, finally waving the doctor inside the kitchen.

Smith looked suspiciously around, obviously aware that Clouse's wife had met her demise in the very room where he stood. It seemed he was aware of all of the recent events surrounding his hotel and its employees.

Zach came into the kitchen for a look, saw the doctor, stared a moment, then retreated to the family room for the empty comfort of television.

"So what can I do for you, Doc?" Clouse asked, walking into the vacant living room, turning on the overhead light before offering the doctor a seat.

"I talked to Rusty Cranor after the incident today, and I'm growing worried about the situation at the hotel," Smith confessed after occupying a cushy chair. "We need to stop work on the grounds immediately," he continued with distress in his voice.

Clouse could tell it deeply hurt the man to stop work on the property he personally invested so much time and money in.

"Are you sure that's the answer?" Clouse asked.

"It has to be. If there's no one there to kill, the murders will have to cease."

"I was considering leaving the project anyway," Clouse admitted. "This whole ordeal seems to hinge around me, but I don't know why," he added, shaking his head.

"Some sick bastard is getting his jollies, that's why," Smith said angrily. "And why someone would want to desecrate that beautiful landmark is beyond me."

Clouse settled uneasily in his own chair.

"What are you going to do now? You were so close to getting the renovation complete."

Smith looked up to the ceiling, and perhaps beyond, for the strength to say what he planned to carry out.

"I may sell the property, Paul."

"What?" Clouse said in shock. "You could be playing into the hands of whoever's doing this."

"How are you so sure this isn't a plot against *you*?" Smith retorted.

"If they really wanted me framed for this, they could have planted evidence several times over. I think the killer just wants everyone terrified of the hotel. That Father Ernest story has a *lot* of people spooked, especially so soon after Halloween."

"Regardless of whether I sell it or not, tomorrow is the last day for construction. No one else should die needlessly for the sake of a building. I would like you and Rusty to inform everyone tomorrow that they will be given a paid leave," Smith said, getting up to make his way toward the door.

"Who would you sell to?" Clouse asked a moment later as he walked the doctor to the door.

"There are a few potential buyers," Smith revealed. "I'm having my lawyer check out their reputations to see who would be a good match. If I don't find a buyer soon, everyone may get frightened off."

"Do you really think getting rid of the property will solve matters?"

"If it prevents more people from being murdered, I'll do it in a heartbeat," Smith answered, as though defeated in every other possibility. "Good night, Paul," he said, walking away as Clouse closed his front door.

"Good night indeed."

*   *   *

While most people readied themselves for bed, two teenagers snuck toward the West Baden Springs Hotel's back entrance, making their way to the cargo door.

Pressing their backs against the building, the two silently surveyed the sunken garden around the side of the building. They spied a flashlight beam bouncing further and further away from the hotel toward the storage buildings and the Jesuit cemetery.

"You sure you want to see this?" Dustin Thomas asked his girl-friend as she reached into her jeans pocket for a set of keys.

"Of course, silly," Melissa Cranor replied. "It isn't every day you get to see a murder scene firsthand."

Both stared at the yellow tape surrounding the ground where the body had fallen three stories. Getting a closer look would risk being spotted by the security guard. Besides, the real story began inside, where the murder took place.

"How'd you get your dad's keys?" Dustin asked in a hushed voice.

"My dad always leaves them lying around. I made myself a copy one night so I can get in here whenever I want to," Melissa replied, putting the key in the lock, pulling the door open before she turned the key. "That's funny," she commented, staring at the door.

Usually every door in the building was locked down with the guard stationed in a room between the two main entrances, able to see anything coming from the outside.

Unless, of course, he was on rounds.

Over the years, Melissa had grown to know the people her father worked with, and felt comfortable around them, and where they worked.

The hotel held a special interest to her because it was near her hometown, and such a historical landmark. Something about it drew her to the grounds more often than usual, often to visit her father. Even most of the security officers knew her on a first name basis.

Once inside, Melissa turned to look at the door once more. She had snuck onto the hotel grounds before, but the truck entrance was always locked. The guard had no need to unlock it, and it cre-ated more of a security risk if he did.

"What's the matter, babe?" Dustin whispered.

"That door is always locked," she replied.

"Maybe they forgot it in all the confusion. It's no big deal."

Melissa led her boyfriend through the darkened hotel, knowing her way around it well enough to navigate in almost complete darkness. Luckily the moon peered through several clouds, down through the atrium's glass dome enough that she could see the outlines of statues and doorways along the first floor.

"Stay close," she warned Dustin, knowing the guard was the only danger to their presence.

With everything the local papers had to say about the murders and the speculation around them, it was all the pair could do to wait so late before entering the grounds to snoop. Her father had arrived home, anxious to tell the tale of the day's murder, but unhappy about the hotel's grim outlook, knowing Smith never took pressure well.

Between the articles and community speculation, people were losing interest in the great monument, and respect in Smith. Her father feared Smith might sell the hotel hastily, rather than sacrifice his pride.

Smith had little to worry about since he was not responsible for the murders, but he would feel the public somehow blamed him, and rid himself of the troublesome source as quickly as possible.

"You think that fireman killed his wife and the people here?" Dustin inquired as they walked the first floor hallway to a set of stairs where Melissa could verify the whereabouts of the guard.

"My father swears he's innocent now," she replied, "but he wasn't so sure before today."

"I think he did it," Dustin commented as they rounded a corner. "Bam, sickle through the heart. Bam, slice and dice her insides. Gotta admit the guy's creative."

Melissa shushed him as they drew near the stairs, seeing something out of the ordinary ahead. Drawing to a stop, she peered ahead to a supervisor's office, seeing a flashlight beam dance across the frosted glass from inside. Her body grew tense, positive the guard had heard them talking.

Creeping closer to the door, Melissa saw another beam of light outside, meaning the person inside the room was *not* the guard.

Meaning he or she did not belong there either.

It explained why the door was unlocked, but not who the person was. Melissa suddenly felt defensive about her father's work at the hotel, and wondered if the murderer had come back to cover his tracks in some form.

She had to know.

"Dustin, we have to get help," she whispered quickly. "Whoever's in there isn't the guard, and it might be the killer."

"If we get the guard we get busted," her boyfriend warned adamantly.

"Fine. I'll go see who it is myself."

"Melissa, wait!" he demanded in as hushed a voice as he could muster, but it was too late. His girlfriend was heading for the room, unconcerned about the ramifications of trespassing and getting caught, much less possessing illegal copies of her father's keys.

Dustin could not stand by and watch Melissa confront an adult, any adult, alone. It was partly his idea to break into the hotel. He followed, watching his girlfriend cautiously approach the room, monitoring the flashlight beam intently.

Drawing near the door, both watched the beam go out as quickly as it had moved through the air a moment before. Stopping dead in their tracks beside the door, both knew there was nothing to do but wait.

If the person was done snooping, he or she would venture out any second and see them. There was nowhere to run and remain undetected, and the only chance of hiding was the room across the hall, if it was unlocked.

Deciding not to chance it, Melissa pointed to a nearby stairwell where the two could hide until the snoop left. Darting across the hall, Dustin was painfully aware of his tennis shoes squeaking, but made his way safely into the stairwell as a man with no identifying traits made his way out of the room and walked down the hallway toward the back entrance.

Darkness made it impossible for Melissa to see anything distinct about the man walking by, but she heard footsteps all the way down the hall, then a door open and close before she gave Dustin a nudge, urging him toward the room.

Strangely, the man had left the room unlocked, and Melissa recalled it being Dave Landamere's office, which made it stranger yet. She looked for the guard's flashlight, seeing it out toward the further reaches of the sunken garden.

Breathing a sigh of relief, she stepped into the room, throwing the light switch, anxious to see if there were any traces of what the man might have been looking for.

"What was he looking for?" Dustin inquired.

"I don't know, but take a look around and see if you find anything strange before that guard gets back. He'll see this light if we take too long."

Spending the next few minutes searching through the desk and shelves, the two were surprised when a person suddenly stepped into the room, staring at them.

"Oh my God, you scared me!" Melissa said, recognizing the man as one she'd seen around the hotel. "We saw someone snooping in here and thought we'd see if he stole anything," she tried to explain.

Saying nothing, the person simply stood, staring.

"But we'll be on our way now," Dustin quickly chimed in, clasping Melissa's elbow as he headed toward the door.

Shaking his head in a foreboding manner, the man blocking the door closed it halfway, revealing a handheld scythe behind the hinged object. As both teenagers looked in horror, he reached behind him to take up the weapon, never removing his cold eyes from the two intruders.

"Oh, come on," Dustin pleaded, moving in front of Melissa to protect her as the killer stepped slowly forward. "We didn't mean anything by-"

Before the young man could react, the scythe moved with lightning-quick speed, the point launching upward, lodging itself crookedly in his right eye socket, penetrating several inches into his brain.

For a moment the lifeless body shivered and twitched, refusing to fall, leaving just a gurgle to emit from his throat before Dustin's corpse slumped downward.

His body struck the desk, freeing the weapon from his head as Melissa shrunk back, possessed entirely by terror.

Like a timid puppy, she cowered along the other side of the desk, then bumped into it, causing her to dart frantically around it, using it as a shield from the man whose eyes seemed to know only one purpose.

Putting an end to her existence.

"No, please," she begged, seeing no remorse or emotion in the man's eyes.

To him, she was merely an object in the way of his ambitions. An object that needed to be disposed of.

Melissa tried circling the desk but the killer blocked her path, forcing her back to a defensive position, where she had no hope. Tired of cat and mouse games, the killer knocked the large desk over, opening a clear path between himself and the last victim who might identify him.

"You can't do this," she pleaded, backing away from him and the weapon that dripped her boyfriend's blood. "Please," she urged one last time, stumbling into an unseen chair from behind.

As she regained her balance, the killer found time to raise the weapon, letting the sharpened blade take flight toward her exposed neck, cutting off her piercing scream suddenly. Melissa's head tumbled from the body, landing neck-first, squarely on the floor with a thud and a splat, like a dropped piece of moist liver. Her corpse slumped against the desk, then landed limply on the ground near Dustin's.

No time remained for the killer to clean up the mess, and he was almost certain the scream had fallen on a pair of ears outside the hotel. Taking hold of the scythe, the killer shut off the lights and left the room, closing the door behind him.

*   *   *

"What the hell?" trooper Jason Brinkman asked himself as the scream crossed the sunken garden, hitting his ears on the way.

Working security at the hotel was more than he had ever bargained for, and he was determined to get another part-time job when an opportunity arose. He understood the risk of patrolling

Indiana roads, but never expected a security job to be dangerous, or as irritating as this had proven to be.

He was sick of people sneaking into the grounds, wanting a look for themselves at the hotel. Access to the upper floors was forbidden on the guided tours, but it was hardly worth sneaking a peek he thought as he raced toward the front entrance.

His heartbeat and the creak of his leather gun belt were the only two sounds he heard in his run.

Whoever was trespassing was in deep trouble if he got his hands on them.

Drawing his nine-millimeter, Brinkman raced up the main stairs toward the entrance, seeing nothing but several bulbs beyond the door that added to the hotel's decor, but did little to light the inside hallway. They were always on, but served only a cosmetic purpose.

Brinkman would be running blindly into the building, unsure of where to check first. Two sets of double doors made of thick clear glass stood between him and some answers.

Violently swinging the first glass door open, Brinkman stepped inside the building, throwing open the next right-hand door leading to the lobby. Though the doors added elegance to the hotel, they were sometimes a weighty hindrance.

Brinkman stepped inside, instantly lurching forward as the sharp end of a scythe carved through his abdomen. His gun hit the floor with a clack as the state trooper breathed in heaves, never given a chance to defend himself.

The trooper's attacker had hidden to the side of the glass in the hotel lobby, where lighting was scarce, and he was invisible behind a thick partition until the time to strike arrived.

Hunched over, Brinkman looked like an old-fashioned well pump as blood dripped from his mouth, bubbling up from his throat. The warm droplets hit the floor, creating a red pool from his injury.

Leaving the weapon where it was, the killer shoved the dying Brinkman back through both sets of glass doors, leaving blood streaks on all of the panels, until the brisk night air added a chill to the already eerie scene.

Standing along the edge of the balcony, with two flights of concrete stairs leading down, directly behind the slumped officer, the killer began prying the weapon slowly from Brinkman's insides, listening to the agonizing, barely audible cries from the trooper.

Both the weapon and victim trickled blood on the decorative concrete, staining it permanently as it pooled over the permanent carvings done decades before.

Tossing the weapon to the ground, the killer stood Brinkman up to his own level, grasping his uniform collar, looking into the officer's fading eyes. Blood trickled from Brinkman's mouth as he coughed involuntarily, the red substance forming a foamy mist as it forcibly spewed from his mouth.

Brinkman's end drew near.

"You son-of-a-bitch," the trooper gasped between breaths. "You shouldn't be-"

Shoving forward with both arms, the killer launched Brinkman down the three dozen steps that led to the front entrance, watching as the body tumbled side over side until it reached the bottom, rolling near the officer's own patrol car. Standing a moment, the killer watched for any movement from the resilient trooper.

Once the killer turned to head inside, Brinkman, determined to use the last of his life, reached for the radio transmitter clipped to his collar. Holding the button with a trembling thumb, he called the incident into his post.

"Officer down...officer...down," he said between gasps. "My...twenty...is...West Baden...Springs...Hotel," he added painfully, feeling blood trickles on his lip and cheek. "Send backup...officer...down," Brinkman added with his last breath, falling limp after the last word.

What the trooper could not have known during his dying, heroic attempt to stop the killer was that his radio unit was shattered, much like several of his bones, during his tumble down the hotel's grand stairs.

Like its owner, it lay devoid of life on the concrete walkway, overshadowed by the domed structure and its new legacy.

16

Clouse found the hotel in ragged condition the next morning when he and Zach arrived. At such an early hour, Clouse could not find any family members to take his son, and there would be little need to supervise the workers because their workday would consist of placing tools and supplies in storage once he and Rusty broke the news.

He imagined most of the workers were frightened about coming into work anyhow, with one of their colleagues murdered, possibly by someone they all knew. While no one else was present, Clouse wanted to evaluate what needed to be accomplished before the hotel could be closed down.

It still seemed odd that tomorrow there would be no activity within the mammoth walls, and that he'd have nothing to do on his days off from the fire department. Both he and his brother-in-law were given an additional week off by their chief to settle any family affairs that might linger.

Clouse figured it was the chief's way of wiping his hands clean of any potential criminal investigations within his department, particularly aimed toward Clouse himself. It would certainly look bad to have Clouse working while the city police investigated him, but the front office, like any other, kept Summers from working as well, so it didn't look as though they were only targeting Clouse.

Clouse knew, and understood, but their reaction served only to further annoy him.

Thanks to the unrelenting press, most of the Bloomington area seemed to know Clouse was the prime suspect in Angie's murder. It worried him, not being able to prove otherwise, or speak out against the allegations.

Stopping beside the state police cruiser, Clouse stepped from his truck, surveying the car, wondering why Jason Brinkman would still be at the hotel.

Usually, whoever worked midnight security would be gone by morning, locking all of the entrances and gates around the hotel before heading out. He might have thought little about it, except for the pool of dried blood next to the patrol car.

"Oh, no," he told himself, fearing the worst if he went inside.

Along the last several steps he could see chips of black plastic and more blood spatters. Signs of a turbulent fall were evident.

"Stay in the truck, Zach," he ordered his son, "and lock it."

Clouse walked the seemingly endless stained path up the steps, finding the front doors unlocked as he stepped inside. Cautiously walking into the unlit lobby, Clouse stepped in a pool of blood, still wet on the designer tile, which would cost a small fortune to replace.

"Shit," he said to himself, looking at the bottom of his boot, knowing he had already contaminated evidence.

Still, he could not help but see what horrors awaited him further inside. The firefighter observed the floor, finding nothing but a heavy flashlight, still lit, sending shivers up his spine. Now he wondered where its owner might be.

Clouse checked the atrium, barely illuminated by the dawn's hazy light from the glass dome above. Nothing inside was disturbed, so he took to the hallway and the nearby offices. Immediately he found more blood drippings near Landamere's office, and the door kicked in, but no one inside. He spied several blood smudges, worked into the floor in a circular motion, as though someone had tried to wipe them off.

He walked to his own office, finding the door kicked in, but nothing disturbed. The pristine condition of his office left him wondering if it was a decoy, or perhaps some other clever device to place blame on his shoulders. Of course there was no official evidence of more murder.

Yet.

"What are you doing here?" a voice called from behind Clouse, startling him.

"Damn it, Rusty," Clouse reprimanded the foreman. "I'm surrounded by pools of blood and you find it necessary to sneak up on me?"

"What am I supposed to do? You've got your kid locked in the truck out there and there's no one else here yet. I thought maybe that sicko got you."

"You'd better phone the police," Clouse said.

"Already have. I came in early to look for Missy."

Clouse gave a puzzled look.

"She must have snuck out with that creep boyfriend of hers last night, and never made it home. Thought she might have come out here, so I came in early."

"What makes you think that?"

"Oh, they like to find places they can make out," Rusty said with a wave of his hand, obviously remembering his days as a teenager. "Movie theaters, parking lots, old hotels."

"Thankfully I haven't seen her," Clouse said, referring to the implications of being on the wrong end of the bloody mess around them. "I haven't found anything besides blood, and I hope it stays that way."

"Any sign of that trooper?"

"Not yet. And I'm not looking through the entire hotel by myself."

"Good point. Let's wait for the police."

Carefully walking outside, around the blood this time, Clouse looked across the grounds before walking down the stairs, watching the morning fog lift as the sun rose over the horizon. Even this close to winter, the sunken garden looked like one large, intricate work of art, and Clouse wondered how it could be marred with blood, and by whom.

"Well, our last day here is off to a fine start," Rusty commented as the two walked down the stairs.

"And it might get worse, Rusty," Clouse replied, seeing the first county police car pull into the hotel's drive. "It just might."

*   *   *

Taking a sip of coffee from an irreversibly stained mug, Mark Daniels skimmed the local newspaper, finding little of interest.

He enjoyed a few minutes at home every morning before he hurried to work, but they seemed to go fast. If his wife worked, he rushed their daughter to the appropriate sitter before heading to the office, and if Cindy stayed home, he spent what time he could with her before heading off to the police station, knowing she would be working the afternoon shift when he got home.

Life with children was tough, especially with their second on the way. He was opting for a son, and suspected Cindy was too. In another five months they would find out for certain. Though the ultrasound had already revealed the baby's sex to doctors, the two were somewhat old-fashioned, choosing to be surprised when the time came.

Cindy supported her husband the best she could, but there were many aspects of his job, and his new position in detectives, he simply could not, or would not tell her. She knew the chief wanted some new blood in his division to attain better results, but Daniels never told her about the pressure he felt working around veteran detectives.

Many resented him for having so little time on the force and making the grade. Some disliked him working day shift when it took most officers considerably longer to get out of the midnight or afternoon shifts. Things that seemed trivial to Daniels and other young officers were the best issues veterans could come up with to bitch about.

Of any detective on his shift, Daniels worked the hardest. This also bothered the veterans, being upstaged by a rookie in their division. Regardless of where he was placed, Daniels worked constantly, never satisfied until the job was done. The chief saw this in him, and his ability to solve problems and cases, so Daniels was transferred to detectives after only three years on the force.

Just as his wife treated him like gold, Daniels kept an eye on his family. He drove his old Honda, or a utility truck purchased at a city auction a few years back. He cut costs everywhere, sometimes at the sake of his own pride, to provide the best life possible for his family.

By no means did it make him happy to see his fellow officers driving new sports cars or Harley-Davidson motorcycles while he drove second or third-hand vehicles that frequently needed repair.

He let Cindy have the good car, trying to look at vehicles as little more than transportation. His focus was on the house, which gave him bragging rights over most officers. Just outside of Bloomington they owned one of the best suburban homes the city had to offer.

Most police officers he knew rented, or bought homes a distance from city limits. Daniels typically thought little of himself when it came to providing a good life for his family.

He provided a good house, with good local schools. His appetite for practicality was satisfied with a home so close to work and shopping centers.

"Good morning," Cindy said, walking into the kitchen, planting a kiss on his lips as he read the comics.

"No news is good news," he said, flashing the paper's front page to her.

"Any new leads?"

"Nothing," he said dejectedly. "It has to be someone connected to the hotel, but I don't know who or why."

Cindy went about pouring herself a cup of coffee, prepared for a day of errands with their daughter before she went into work for the phone company. Both were just getting accustomed to full nights of sleep, now that their daughter was getting old enough to sleep through the night without crying, or needing a change of diapers.

"I got your photos yesterday," she said, handing him a packet from the one-hour photo service at the drug store down the street.

He wondered if the camera he found at the hotel would be his much longer.

Daniels began to open the pack, but a glance at his watch informed him how soon he needed to be at city hall. Standing, he patted himself down, assured everything he needed was on his shoulder holster, or in his pockets.

He opted for a shoulder holster during the winter months when it was necessary to wear a heavier coat. Daniels hated weighting his belt down when he wore heavy clothing. With his strong upper-body, the higher belt often went ignored, whereas a conventional gun belt dug into his side after a long day, and wasn't as easy to conceal.

As he stood, Cindy adjusted his tie for him, using the opportunity to sneak in another kiss, knowing she would not see him until the next morning. He smiled, knowing how little time they had together.

"Want to do something this weekend?" he asked, picking up his winter jacket.

"That would be nice," she said as he put it on, stuffing the photo packet into one of the pockets.

"Give it some thought," he said, opening the door. "When you decide, call a sitter."

*   *   *

Daniels walked into the investigative offices to find his partner ready for a morning drive to West Baden. He objected to Kendle's blood-sniffing, since they lacked concrete proof either way.

During the drive south he said little, simply admiring the countryside view. Several ideas came to mind of where he might take his wife for the weekend, but none seemed good enough for her after everything she had done for him.

"I'm going to nail your boy," Kendle said as they pulled into the hotel drive. "Then we'll see how smart you are."

"Whatever," Daniels replied passively as he stepped from the unmarked car, realizing the rift between he and his partner was completely due to a generation gap, intensified by friction in the workplace.

He felt Kendle acted unprofessionally simply to get at him. Around other people the senior detective kept his professionalism intact, but when it came to Clouse or his only potential protector, the man lost his cool much more easily.

While Kendle spoke to Rusty Cranor, Daniels walked inside, finding several state police officers photographing the stains, and taking samples from the various blood pools. He stepped over the primary puddle at the entrance, noticing someone had not, from the footprint left at one edge.

"Has anything but the blood been found?" he asked one of the troopers.

"We've had the county boys looking inside and upstairs, but nothing yet," one answered.

Daniels stepped outside a moment, looking over several county and state police cars from the balcony. He saw several construction workers approaching with perplexed looks across their faces. The detective couldn't say he blamed them.

He fished a cigarette from his shirt pocket, lighting it as someone approached him from the side. Daniels turned to see Clouse with an unsettling look on his face.

"Why does it seem you're everywhere there's trouble?"

"Just lucky I guess," Clouse replied sarcastically.

"That man wants your ass on his living room mantle," the detective noted, nodding down toward Kendle, who still spoke with Rusty.

"He might not get the chance. The reconstruction is being closed down until further notice."

"On whose orders?" Daniels asked with a quizzical look.

"Dr. Smith informed both Rusty and I last night that no further construction would take place until the killing ceased, or he could find a buyer for the hotel."

Daniels paced the balcony a moment, pensively thinking about what Clouse had just said.

"Who would be in line to buy such a place?"

"Someone with more money than you and I will ever see," the fireman stated. "You're talking about millions to reconstruct this place."

Daniels pointed his forefinger upward as a revelation raced through his mind, then crossed his face, showing sudden awareness.

"Yes, but what would the *selling* price be?"

Stumped, Clouse drew the same expression the detective had a moment before.

"You know, I'm not sure," Clouse finally answered. "Dr. Smith would probably be more concerned about what the person did with the property than he would about the money."

Without another word, Daniels took a final drag on his cigarette and flicked it over the balcony railing. He stepped inside the hotel, over the initial pool of blood again. Clouse followed, extremely careful to avoid it.

"You know who stepped in that?" Daniels asked.

"I think so," Clouse said in a voice that gave the detective his answer, especially since the print in the puddle matched that of his boot. "It was too dark to see."

Walking to Landamere's office, the detective flipped the light switch, illuminating the room. He walked in, surveying the room and the desk flipped over on its side. All of the drawers were removed, while papers strewn across the floor almost served as a carpeting for nearly half the office.

"What would anyone want from in here?" Daniels inquired.

"Hard telling. Dave kept most of his paperwork from the project in this office, but it wasn't anything useful to the layman."

"You have a key to the room, correct?"

"I do, and so does Rusty."

"So neither of you would need to be kicking in doors to look through his belongings," Daniels surmised.

Daniels knelt beside the desk, looking at and around the papers, finding something unusual among the scattered documents.

"Hey, troopers!" he called. "I need some latex in here!"

One of the state troopers brought Daniels a disposable latex glove, allowing the detective to finger through the papers, finally reaching the object that had caught his attention.

Snapping the glove tightly over his right hand, Daniels picked up a ring, smeared partially with blood. One of the troopers held out a plastic bag, allowing him to place it safely within its DNA-protective covering.

Taking hold of the bag, he examined the ring, finding a small red stone within a tiny white band which appeared diamond in nature, all encased within a gold frame. He assessed it a rare-looking ring if nothing else.

"Recognize it?" he asked Clouse.

Readily nodding, the fireman seemed unhappy with the find.

"It belongs to Dave Landamere," he answered. "Dave always wore it opposite his wedding band."

Daniels wondered if the ring had been there an extended period of time, or if Dave Landamere had come back to visit the night before. It looked quite authentic, which meant it was probably valued in the thousands. The ring was not something Dave Landamere would easily forget or drop.

"What do you think?" Clouse inquired, uneasy about the skeptical look on Daniels' face.

"I think I'm going to pay Mrs. Landamere a visit."

A few minutes later the detective and Clouse walked outside, seeing more construction workers gather around the front entrance, unsure of what to do until either Clouse or Rusty told them.

Clouse walked down the steps, giving them a quick briefing on what was found, then gave them instructions to pack everything away in protected areas until the construction could begin again. Before sending them off, he insisted they stay with another worker at all times for safety.

He took two men aside, instructing them to clean up the pools of blood as soon as the police were done, in order to preserve the tile if that was still possible.

"I checked on your grounds keeper," Daniels said once they were somewhat isolated from everyone again.

"And?" Clouse asked curiously.

"His full name is Vernon Black. It seems he's a throwback to the hotel's university days. He's a drunk who's been jailed a few times for disorderly conduct and public intoxication, but nothing remotely close to homicide. I doubt he's our killer."

"It was worth a try," Clouse replied, the hope of clearing his name fading just a bit more.

Clouse looked over to Zach, who was awed by the equipment in a police car.

Luckily one of the county officers had time to monitor the boy while Clouse spoke with Daniels. Like most boys his age, Zach found police equipment fascinating, despite the fact his father used similar devices on the fire department. There was an intimidating power police officers possessed that kids loved.

"What's going on?" Jane Brooks asked Clouse, pushing her way past a few workers once the meeting was over.

"What are you doing here?" he replied in surprise.

"It's my tour day. What happened?"

"We're not sure. I found pools of blood inside, but the police didn't find much else."

"My God," Jane gasped. "You don't suppose-"

"I hope not," Clouse cut her off. "Let's hope it's just some sort of prank."

He looked over to Brinkman's patrol car, finding little optimism in the situation. The circumstances were unusual, and state troopers didn't just disappear for no reason.

Rusty approached the two with the same worried look he had met Clouse with earlier.

"Sorry to break this up," he said, "but can you take over, Paul? I'd like to see if Missy ever got home, or at least to school."

"Sure, Rusty. Let me know what you find out."

Both watched as the foreman left, shaking his head. For parents, it was easy to understand the concern he felt.

"No matter how old they get, you never stop worrying," Clouse commented.

"I know," Jane replied. "Care for some company until my tour starts?"

Clouse somehow doubted there would be a tour, but he wasn't going to scare off his best company of the morning.

"Sure," he replied. "Can you tell me any good news?"

"I'll try."

"Let me introduce you to my son," Clouse said, walking over to the county officer's car.

Glancing away from the two patrolmen he was speaking to, Larry Kendle took notice of Clouse thanking the county officer standing beside his son, and a lady he did not recognize, who seemed quite concerned about Clouse's well-being.

From his own experience, he knew wives were troublesome when their husbands found someone new, and he wondered how far Paul Clouse might have gone to keep his wife from getting everything, if they had divorced.

Kendle suspected Clouse had murdered for money, and perhaps the detective had just stumbled upon an additional motive. He wondered who this woman was, and if she was more than just a concerned friend of the prime suspect.

He intended to find out.

*   *   *

Susan Portman had second thoughts about working at the hotel when she arrived late in the morning to find patrol cars around the building.

Recently hired to turn the hotel's gift shop, two crates containing post cards and a few small historical books, into an emporium, she had a daunting task ahead of her. Creating merchant accounts and doing enough paperwork to kill several small trees kept her busy enough, but the mental anguish from the strange events surrounding the hotel was almost enough to make her quit before she even started.

Near the second main entrance, what was to become her shop looked like a makeshift warehouse with boxes appearing randomly scattered throughout the room.

She pulled an invoice from one box, studied it, and found herself distracted by voices outside her window. Police were still buzzing over the reported spilled blood. Rumors were already circulating about the missing state trooper. A few of the workers stuck around to put their tools away, but few stayed very long.

Susan heard another rumor that Paul Clouse was the first person to discover the pool of blood. She wasn't sure whether to feel sorry for the man, or suspect him of cold-blooded murder. He seemed to be in the wrong place too many times to be coincidence, but no one had placed him directly at a murder site either.

Like most people involved with the hotel, Susan knew who he was, because she conducted occasional tours. Still, he was a relative newcomer to the restoration project, so she never made presumptions about his character.

Being around such an environment made her nervous, but she had confidence in the security staff, and knew the building like her own house.

An Orange County native, she remembered the various phases the hotel went through, including the time it was abandoned for the better part of a decade. Overgrown with weeds, the building had faded, lost shingles on its roof, literally fallen down along part of one wall, and suffered extensive damage to its glass fixtures.

Many statues were missing or broken at that time, and the floor looked deplorable. Tiles were dislodged, stained, and completely gone in chunks, as though someone had removed them with heavy machinery.

She remembered being inside the atrium when it rained through the dome where the glass panels had fallen in from deterioration and vandalism. For a time, the hotel was surrounded by gates containing warnings of dangerous conditions for those who trespassed. Like hundreds of other people, Susan ignored the signs, wanting a look at the hotel for herself.

That was years ago.

Now, she felt lucky to have been a retail store's assistant manager, which helped land her the job as the emporium manager at the hotel. Her position allowed her, and her husband, to remain close to family, while giving her a sense of doing something worthwhile.

Proceeds from the new gift shop benefitted the hotel, because funds from the shop and tours kept the electricity paid, with a little extra money for the upkeep of the building and grounds.

Returning her mind to the task at hand, she picked up another invoice, checked inside the box, then checked off the items as she found them. Many of the current items were related to the hotel's era, while custom books, models, and clothing were being manufactured locally that related directly to the building.

Ignoring the chatter outside, she went about her business, glad a dozen or so people lingered behind. The room she stood within was going to be an office one day, where she might keep her paperwork, phone clients and vendors, and make her life easier through the internet.

Using a sharp disposable knife, she slit the tape along the top of another box as a tapping noise, like a dropped pen, came from the hallway.

Her doors were open, so the slightest noise from the atrium or hallway echoed through the first floor, and into her gift shop, like it came from right beside her.

Hearing no other noise, like footsteps, or chatter, she chose to investigate. Walking to the closest door apprehensively, she figured the noise came from across the atrium, some hundred yards or more away from her.

"Hello?" she called softly. "Anyone there?"

Reaching the door, she realized all five of the doors that would eventually make up the emporium were open to let fresh air inside. New carpeting laid the week before gave off a foul odor, due to the adhesive used to bond it with the concrete floor.

The old windows were hard to open, and they were securely fastened with screws through wooden one-inch cubes atop each frame. Martin Smith wanted to make certain no one snuck into the hotel from the outside, so every door and window was secured in one fashion or another.

With stacks of boxes everywhere around her, Susan felt a bit uneasy about someone sneaking into the emporium while she distracted herself with invoices.

Peering into the hallway, Susan found no one in either direction. Writing the noise off as falling particles, she turned to find someone standing beside one stack of boxes, startling her as she let a brief shriek escape her throat before placing her hand over her mouth.

"Brent, you scared me," she quickly apologized to the retired state trooper who sometimes worked morning shift security.

"Sorry," Brent Guthrie said, chuckling. "I just wanted a peek at some of your goods before you put them out."

Susan paused a moment, letting her wits return.

"Have they found anything out about Jason?" she asked of the missing trooper.

"Not yet," Guthrie said solemnly. "I worked with the boy. He's not going to disappear, and he sure as hell isn't going to ignore his duty."

He looked through a box, but Susan read his emotions. Guthrie was passing time, simply keeping himself occupied, and his mind away from the grave matters at hand.

"It just seems things have been bad around here lately," he muttered. "If I was those Bloomington detectives, I'd be taking a hard look at that Paul Clouse."

"I would think they already are," Susan noted.

"One of them seemed awful chummy with him earlier."

Returning to her work, Susan opened another box.

"I'm just glad you're here," she told the retired trooper. "I take it you arrived to find the big mess outside?"

Guthrie shook his head.

"I got here at seven, like usual, and there was already a slew of cops out there. Things aren't looking good for Jason, and I heard Cranor say his daughter never came home last night."

"That's terrible," Susan said, genuinely concerned for the likeable foreman.

She stared into the dimly lit hallway, wondering if things were going to improve around the hotel anytime soon.

If they didn't, all of her hard work to land her new position was destined to be a complete waste of time. Hoping not, she turned her attention to another box needing her attention.

Susan decided to work as long as people were at the hotel. If they all left, she planned to quickly follow their lead.

17

It took Daniels nearly three hours to break himself away from Kendle, who was dying to find out the identity of the woman Paul Clouse was with at the hotel.

Though he found it strange the prime suspect would be seen with *any* woman so soon, Daniels focused on Landamere's disappearance, still convinced Clouse did not swing the scythe, and hopefully had nothing to do with the murders.

When the detective arrived at the Landamere estate between Bedford and Bloomington, near the area his work was based, Daniels could not help but stare at the beautiful landscape as he pulled into the driveway. He felt it was just as astounding as the hotel he had just come from, as he stepped from his unmarked car.

He began a stroll around the house, taking in details of the yard's beauty, earned from hours of labor and careful planning.

Sparkling with intricate design, the grounds displayed the remains of rich summer flowers, now wilted to tangled vines or pedals. More impressive were the statues, artistic flower beds, and benches placed almost perfectly across the expansive back yard where Daniels could picture a happy couple strolling through, wasting part of a day in their own back yard.

But the Landameres were not such a couple from what he had heard.

Staring at the grounds, he failed to hear anyone walk up behind him in the grass devoid of leaves. Not until Joan Landamere was within a few feet did he actually hear her coming.

"Do you like it?" she asked.

"It's beautiful," Daniels replied, quickly looking her over.

For a lady her age, Joan Landamere looked quite young and firm, even wearing a jumper which indicated she kept herself that way by design. He could see no lines along her face, and her gray hair, cut stylishly short seemed en vogue if Daniels recalled some of his wife's recent beauty magazine covers correctly.

Though old enough to be his mother, Daniels could not help but find her attractive. He wondered how Landamere could be unhappy with such a woman. From the youthful sparkle in her eyes, which seemed to display her pride, and the way she conducted herself, he had already gauged her an intelligent woman.

"I spend my summers working in the garden, finding something new every season to add to its beauty."

Daniels nodded easily, but said nothing.

"I'm here to ask you about your husband," he revealed, returning to his businesslike nature.

He quickly introduced himself.

"I figured," she said, obviously disappointed about having to talk about her husband.

"Can I take it you and your husband don't get along?" he asked, realizing his breath was visible in the cold air.

"You've probably heard we have a marriage of convenience, detective, and I'll save you the trouble of researching. It's true."

Daniels could hardly fathom being in such a situation himself. Perhaps money allowed people luxuries he would never understand as both a police officer and a family man.

"But you have no idea where he might be?"

"He does this, Detective Daniels. He'll just disappear for a week at a time. It's even in his contract with Kieffer Construction that he can take unannounced personal days for creative integrity."

"So you're not concerned?"

"Are you?" she answered with a question.

Daniels grinned. He had hoped for more of a straightforward interview.

"Let's get in where it's warm, detective," she said, leading him around the front.

"I have some genuine concerns about your husband's safety," Daniels confessed as they stepped inside the lavish three-story house.

It was far more than two people would ever need, and he could picture them throwing meaningless grand parties on the weekends, cooking on the industrial grill in the back yard, and swimming in the in-ground pool. By his own definition it was a mansion.

Daniels couldn't help but look around the house, and he was certain Joan viewed him as a kid in a candy shop. Everywhere he looked sat oriental rugs, hardwood floors, imported art, and more furniture in any given room than he figured his entire house contained. He wondered just how much Dave Landamere earned as a project manager.

"How did you come to get your house if you don't mind me asking?"

"David built it," she said, as though it was as simple as any weekend project. "It took him well over a year with help from a few of his workers."

She noticed him looking up the stairs, then into the doorways of several rooms on the first floor.

"If it puts your mind at ease, you can look through his office," Joan offered, appearing to enjoy the notion of someone rummaging through her husband's things, as though it would agitate him.

"I'll take you up on that. Thanks."

A few minutes later Daniels walked into the office, finding it much more elegant than the offices at the hotel. Full bookshelves were mounted to the wall, reaching the ceiling in the octagonal room. A lamp sat atop a small stand near one window while the large wooden desk stood beside the other, its top glowing from the light that streamed through the open blinds.

Daniels looked over the texts, finding most of them pleasure reading or construction-related. He set into the desk, opening the drawers one by one, seeing little except business letters, personal belongings, and several awards Landamere had won, either for his designs, or his humanitarianism, in efforts to save historic build-ings. Apparently the hotel was not his first preserved landmark.

He glanced over the letters, but found nothing to indicate either danger, or a reason why he would disappear. Still, Daniels felt a nagging sensation he was missing something of interest. He closed the desk drawers, thinking of what he might do if he was fooling around behind Cindy's back.

Though he would never do such a thing, Daniels had to think as if was, and it seemed he would need a place to hide letters or knick-knacks if he was concealing a relationship, if indeed that was what Landamere had done.

Daniels opened each of the desk's side drawers, feeling beneath each of them sequentially. On the bottom right drawer his hand rubbed a piece of tape, then a cold piece of metal.

He peeled the tape back, carefully pulling a gold-colored key from the drawer. Daniels inspected the key momentarily, contem-plating how much it would be missed since it was obviously a secret.

He placed it in his pocket and stood to leave.

His day was far from over.

                    *   *   *

Clouse found himself playing on the internet, registered as a guest on Angie's computer. He was waiting for Tony Dierker to break the main code, but his fellow firefighter needed to take his wife home from work before coming over.

In the meantime, Clouse ran a search of the worldwide web, try-ing to attain information about several of the hotel's potential buy-ers Dr. Smith spoke of.

He had managed to weasel a verbal list of prospects from one of Smith's board members. He used the excuse of possibly meeting several company presidents, wanting to do some research on them ahead of time so he didn't look a fool when they toured the grounds.

Unwittingly, the board member gave Clouse more than he expected, even phone numbers and website addresses in most cases. It was the companies without much information he worried about, and targeted first in his online search.

Most were nonprofit organizations, set up to restore old buildings, or preserve them. Some specialized in creating museums out of famous houses, or returning buildings to their original state, sometimes making a working exhibit true to the time period. Clouse cringed at the thought of someone decimating his hotel.

"Tincher Incorporated," he read a name aloud from his list, unfamiliar with the name or reputation of the company. Ironically, the listing provided a website, but no phone number or address.

Clouse typed in the address, quickly bringing up several impressive before and after photos of restored buildings. There were links to more photos of their insides, but he passed up the interesting stuff for an information search.

He found an Illinois address, a voice mail phone message number, and an e-mail link for the company, putting several of his fears to rest. Clouse tagged the site for future reference, typing in his e-mail address and personal information under the company's mailing list as he had the rest of the sites, in the hopes of receiving more information through the mail or internet.

In all, Clouse had looked at more than twenty sites that morning, hoping his contracting credentials would get him a response from each company. Every shred of information he attained about each company would help him determine which, if any, was involved in foul play. He finished looking over his list as a knock came to his front door.

He leapt to answer it, knowing Zach was napping upstairs.

"Tony," he said with a smile after opening the kitchen door.

"Hi, Paul. Finally made it over."

Clouse briefly explained the situation to his fellow fireman, letting Dierker seat himself at the terminal. Clouse grabbed a seat nearby.

Though his colleagues considered him a bit strange, they respected Dierker for his intellect and ability to think through most any situation. In a way, they thought of him as a nerd with his often unkept hair, lack of practical common sense, and an ability to focus on a computer screen regardless of what occurred around him.

Clouse figured Dierker could be in the middle of an inferno with his laptop and not flinch. When it came to dragging hose lines into a blazing building, Dierker kept the same intensity as he did with the computer, which earned him respect among other firefighters, even if they did find him a bit standoffish by times.

"This shouldn't be hard," Dierker said, pulling a diskette from his shirt pocket. He popped it into the disk drive, concerning Clouse slightly.

"You're not going to blow it up or anything, are you?"

Dierker chuckled.

"Not unless it's wired to blow if given a wrong password. And even then it would only kill *me*."

Clouse smiled, finding Dierker's humor entertaining for a change.

"My program will run a series of words, pretty much like a dictionary, then names, then random sequences of letters and numbers until it gets the right one."

"How long will that take?"

"It generates about a million codes per minute, so unless she had a fairly complex sequence of letters and numbers, which is recommended mind you, we should be in within the next ten minutes."

Half an hour later the program continued to run as the two firemen exchanged stories about fire scenes and some of the people they worked with. Clouse seldom spoke with the computer expert, since they worked different shifts and stations.

"I guess Angie had a decent code," Clouse surmised, looking at the tally of codes tried across the screen.

It was over the twenty-million mark.

"You would have been an eternity trying this yourself, Paul," Dierker revealed. "But the good news is, the program will tell us the code before entering it so you'll know, and you'll be able to change it if you want."

A few minutes later the computer beeped and a line of code flashed on the screen. It was the password.

"Zach82Mac," Dierker read aloud. "Mean anything?"

"My son's name, and the name of his favorite teddy bear, but the number doesn't mean anything. It probably didn't to Angie either. I'd have never gotten that."

Clouse wrote it down for reference while Dierker excused himself, his job being done.

"Thanks a million," Clouse said, tossing the diskette to him.

"Don't mention it. You can build me a house to repay me sometime," Dierker kidded as he left.

For the next half hour, Clouse browsed through Angie's mail messages, her online address book, and messages sent. Everything seemed ordinary except for one message sent, and another received.

Clouse confirmed that he was correct about Michael Hathaway keeping the purchase of the hotel a secret until it was actually done. He told Angie not to say a word to Clouse until the final paperwork was signed, leaving the firefighter to think it was only a possibility of the hotel being bought.

He also realized something that meant the world to him. In a reply message, Angie told Hathaway about their marital trouble, and that she planned to reconcile with Clouse when the time was right. He was overjoyed about the idea of Angie still caring for him, and upset that Kelli mislead him about the facts.

Clouse noticed the late afternoon time on the clock and decided to wake Zach up from his nap. He ran upstairs, shook his son awake, then walked to the upstairs bathroom, letting the door close partway behind him.

Cupping water in his hands, Clouse splashed his face, feeling a soothing cool as he rubbed his hands and the liquid into his skin. Dripping from the face, Clouse glanced in the mirror, catching a good look of someone standing behind him.

It was Angie in spectral form, dressed in a summer dress, like those she wore when they were first married. Her face held a placid look, taking Clouse back to the times they were happy for the split second before he blinked, losing the image. He looked behind him, seeing nothing, sure he was going mad.

Taking a towel from beside him, Clouse wiped his face, then looked in the mirror again, horrified by what he saw this time. Now his wife stood there, hands by her sides in a position of pleading, wearing a white dress completely stained with blood, accompanied by gashes and cuts along her body.

Her face and hair were sticky with dried blood and pieces of flesh and internal organs glued by the blood. The dress was torn in numerous areas, and she looked to be anything but peaceful as she mouthed the words "Help me."

Clouse turned away from the mirror, afraid to actually glance behind him. The horror was bad enough in the mirror, but when he looked again, it was gone, replaced by his son. He turned to Zach, only partly awake, and dropped to hug him. The fireman felt sure he was going mad, and wondered what was wrong with his mind.

"You okay, Daddy?" Zach asked innocently, unsure of why he was the recipient of so many hugs lately.

"I don't know, Zach. I just don't know."

18

Early the next morning Clouse fed the animals after his parents left with Zach. He scooped grain into several troughs, contemplating how soon he wanted to put his house up for sale. The images of Angie disturbed him, leaving him to wonder if the house was now haunted, or if there was something he should do.

He was dressed in sweat pants, an old T-shirt, and tennis shoes without socks. The combination made for a cool trip outside, but inspired him to hurry with chores. His hair crossed several directions, feeling oily because he had not yet showered. At least the cold weather now helped him sleep a little better at night.

Taking a look into the field which surrounded his house in nearly every direction, he spied most of the animals in the field, enjoying what little time they had left to walk in the open pastures. Hearing the phone ring inside the house, Clouse tossed the feeding scoop inside the barn and jogged inside, answering it on the third ring.

"Paul," a distraught voice said. "I received a disturbing letter today."

"Dr. Smith, what's wrong?" Clouse asked, recognizing the voice.

"Someone left me a letter ordering me to reopen the hotel or the killing would never cease."

"It's a trick," Clouse stated. "Don't reopen it. Call the police."

"I did," Smith said. "Now they want me to reopen it so they can stake it out and catch him."

Clouse shook his head, unable to believe the killer would make demands the hotel remain open. He was skeptical of police involvement because they would only monitor him all the more, letting the real killer run free.

"I may just take the best bidder I can find and sell the thing," Smith said with obvious tension. "I don't like all of this around me."

Clouse knew the pressure was getting to the doctor. Smith never intended anything but good for the property, but his dreams were being crushed by the insane crusade of one person.

"Do what you have to, Doc, but you should give it time. They'll catch whoever's doing this."

"I'll call you when I know something more, Paul. But it looks like we'll be going back to work with a police guard."

Great, Clouse thought sarcastically. He expected at least one officer to monitor his whereabouts at all times.

"This is your dream, Doc," Clouse almost pleaded. "Don't let it go that easy."

"I'm trying, Paul. I'm really trying. Goodbye."

"It's my dream too," the fireman commented as the click reached his ear.

He turned the phone off, tossing it to the couch. He hated days that started this badly.

"Goddamn it," he said, heading toward the bathroom for a shower.

As he dried himself several minutes later, he heard a phone ring from the living room, but it was not his cordless phone.

"Cell phone," he said, scurrying out of the bathroom without benefit of towel cover. "Hello," he said, clutching it from its charger.

"Hello, Paul," an unfamiliar, but clear voice said from the other end. It could have easily been the voice of a disk jockey, but it seemed too crisp, too unrealistic to be anyone he knew. Clouse wondered if it was a voice altering device doing the talking.

"Who's this?"

"That's not as important as where I am," the male voice replied. "Seems you have some people missing from your hotel. Guests check in, but they don't check out, is that it, Paul?"

"Who the hell is this?" Clouse demanded, sick of phone games. "I'm in no mood for this shit."

"Neither was your wife."

Stunned silence for a few seconds.

"You sick fuck! Why don't you-"

"Seems there's a lot of death around you lately, Paul. Everyone you know is dying, and you're always there. Too bad you weren't quick enough to save Beaman."

"Asshole!" Clouse stammered. "What the hell do you want?"

"I want you to rot in prison, then in hell for the crimes I commit. You've got it coming."

"Listen-"

"No, you listen!" the voice said, breaking its cool, calm demeanor for the first time. "You've got an hour and fifteen minutes to reach your precious hotel or a certain tour guide we both know gets a plot beside Father Ernest on the hill."

Clouse heard the click and froze, unable to move for a few seconds afterward while he pondered the authenticity of the call. Deciding it was real, he dashed to his bedroom to grab some clothes before he raced to West Baden in an unreasonable amount of allotted time.

*   *   *

While the bustle of morning work surrounded Mark Daniels, the young detective looked through the file of evidence surrounding the West Baden murders and that of Angie Clouse. The morning seemed to be the only time in the Bloomington police offices any work really got done.

Later, officers split up, took long lunches, or simply did work in the field. To Daniels, the office could actually be distracting in the morning.

He found little evidence of use inside the file. It seemed the killer was hiding his tracks well, but at the same time manipulated evidence and circumstances. If Daniels' hunch was correct, and Paul Clouse was not committing the murders, someone had gone through great lengths to incriminate him, yet left a lack of physical evidence to trace him with.

Daniels knew how easily someone could have left traces of Father Ernest's corpse in the back of Clouse's truck, or picked a better time to frame him for Angie's murder. At the fire station, he had a fairly potent alibi. There had to be better times when Clouse was alone with no witnesses. Perhaps the killer was simply being ambiguous with the fireman's potential guilt.

"Time," Daniels thought aloud, focusing on one of his thoughts.

Suddenly timing seemed the one thing he hadn't given much thought to.

Halloween?

No, nothing else tied into that.

West Baden Springs nearing completion?

Perhaps, but that seemed irrelevant.

Clouse's marital problems?

It seemed a good trigger to start the series of murders with, but held little consequence in the scheme of things.

A potential purchase of the property?

Daniels knew there were interested parties, but how serious they were, and who they might threaten, eluded him. He sat back, pondering where his search would lead him next.

Kendle was busy checking out what Clouse stood to inherit from his wife's death while trying to link physical evidence from the corpses to Clouse. The coroner would be able to determine, more or less, what height the killer was from the depths of the impacts, and whether he was left or right-handed by the angle of the cuts.

Daniels let his hands fall to his sides, slapping against his coat on the chair's backside. He felt a solid lump on the coat's right side, which puzzled him momentarily.

"Oh, the photos," he said to himself, finally remembering them.

Subconsciously he was afraid to look because the photos would probably show several people huddled in a pose, revealing who the owner might be, or perhaps some baby photos from a grandmother who had toured the grounds, accidentally dropping the camera on the way out. Daniels would never keep the photos or the camera if he had the slightest idea how to find its owner.

Reluctantly, he opened the packet.

"Want to go for coffee, Mark?" one of Daniels' old patrol partners asked, passing by his desk. He had just gotten off the midnight shift.

"Sure, Marty," the detective replied, stuffing the packet back into his jacket.

Its contents could wait a little longer.

*   *   *

Clouse swerved around several cars on a single-lane road as his unexpected trip to West Baden neared its end. Several cars honked as the truck awkwardly passed at its high rate of speed, but its driver did not care. He could not believe the audacity of the killer, actually phoning him and threatening Jane.

According to the clock on his dashboard, Clouse neared the killer's deadline, leaving him little option but to phone Ken Kaiser, who would hopefully be patrolling the county. He speed-dialed the number, hearing two rings before his friend picked up.

"Hello?"

"Ken, it's Paul. Where are you right now?"

"Working security at the hotel. Why?"

"I need you to find any tours going on, round them up, and get them to a safe place."

"Paul, what's this about?"

Clouse could feel sweat between his palm and the cellular phone. He realized how unusually nervous he felt, and must have sounded, to his friend.

"Just do it, Ken. I'll be there in about five minutes to explain."

"What do I tell them?"

"Whatever it takes. Just keep them together, and safe."

When the truck pulled into the hotel's lot, tires squealing from such a sharp turn, Clouse drove immediately to the front door, seeing no one outside. It seemed empty without the workers busily reassembling areas of the building.

Clouse dashed up the stairs, threw open the double doors, and entered, seeing a group huddled inside the atrium with Kaiser standing nearby. The officer's face showed his displeasure, but a quick glance at him, then the group, showed no Jane. Panic set into Clouse, then he saw the tour guide badge on an older man among the group members.

"Is Jane working today?" he asked the man.

"No, she toured yesterday," he replied.

Kaiser intervened, taking Clouse aside from the group, which probably figured he was the potential danger the county officer had corralled them from.

"What's going on?" Kaiser demanded.

"I got a call from the killer, Ken. He said he was going to kill Jane unless I got here in less than an hour and fifteen minutes."

"Why didn't you call sooner?"

"I got spooked," Clouse said. "If the killer saw a cop looking for him, he would surely kill her that much quicker."

Kaiser motioned for the tour guide to let the group continue on their way, afraid they might overhear the conversation. There was enough local media blitz already.

"Did he call you at home?"

"On my cell phone. My God, how could he have known the number, or that I'd be home?"

"Your number is posted in your office, Paul. Someone broke into your room a couple nights ago, remember?"

"Yeah, you're right," Clouse stammered slowly.

Clouse wondered why someone would lead him to West Baden for nothing. He could think of no motive, unless the killer wanted to monitor him, or to keep him out of Bloomington.

"Home," Clouse said aloud, knowing how easily someone could lead him out of Bloomington, only to plant evidence on his property or break into his house. He turned, heading hurriedly toward the entrance.

"Where are you going, Paul?" Kaiser demanded, growing more irritated with Clouse's strange behavior.

"I've got to get home quick, Ken."

"Don't be rushing off, Paul! You just broke every speed limit there was getting here. Stay a minute and cool off."

"I can't, Ken," Clouse said from an atrium doorway. "Can you find out who called my number almost two hours ago?"

"No. I'm not authorized to just check that stuff for fun."

Clouse wondered just how much of a friend Kaiser was. Perhaps the tension made him overreact, but he darted out to the truck without another word, desperate to outwit whoever made his life a game to be played at will.

*   *   *

In a corner booth at a local café, Daniels took a sip of his coffee, then a drag from his cigarette, realizing how many bad substances went into his body every day. He figured it made little difference anyhow because almost every food he ate held potential hazards.

"Ever notice how everything we eat is bad for us?" he asked Marty Hazen, sitting with his back to a window.

"It's always been bad for us," the officer commented. "When we were kids no one cared. Now they research everything people ever thought about eating or drinking."

"We live and we die," Daniels put it simply. "Guess in the end we choose our poison."

"You going to eat that donut hole?"

"No," Daniels said, taking a look at the local section in the paper. A small column under current events commented how there was no progress in the investigation of Angela Clouse's murder, and those at the West Baden Spring Hotel. He felt lucky the press didn't dog him for comments.

"So how is the investigation going?" Hazen asked of Daniels, noticing the same article.

"Peachy," the investigator said with disdain. "I've got an obsessive partner, an accused murderer who can't give me a solid alibi, and a group of murders without a single witness."

"Got any vacation time coming?"

Daniels laughed. "Kendle's already ripping me a new asshole. I'd be giving him ammunition if I took off."

Hazen munched on some bacon, then forked some scrambled eggs into his mouth.

"You sure you don't want patrol again?" he asked between several chews.

Daniels shot him a strange look for talking while eating before he answered.

"I've waited my entire career and most of my life for this. I don't care what the brass think, I don't care what the good ol' boys in that division think. I'll be damned if I'm going to give up this opportunity and go back to seeing every drunk, drug addict, and wife-beater there is in this town. Not that detectives is an easy division, but it gets me out, and might make a name for me."

"The chief seems pretty high on you," Hazen commented. "A lot of the guys call you his boy."

"Bullshit. He needs more of us young guys in there."

"It is kind of a stale division," Hazen agreed. "The old guys are probably starting rumors so you'll quit."

Daniels wiped his mouth with a napkin, taking a gulp of coffee.

"They'll have to do better than that."

"Damn," Hazen said, looking at his watch. "I'd better get home before the wife does, or she'll throw a fit. Let me use the john and I'll walk out with you, Mark."

While his old partner walked away, Daniels pulled out the pictures for a quick look at what he had put off for too long.

Opening the pack, he saw various shots of the hotel and the grounds, quickly assuming they were simply tourist shots of the hotel. If that was the case, he might not be able to identify who owned the camera.

Flipping through the shots, he stopped when he came to an almost pure blue photo, which he realized would be the sky with just a few trees acting as border for the picture.

"Who would take an awful shot like that?" he wondered aloud, flipping to the next one.

His eyes widened as he took in the view of a cloaked figure looming above the camera at a side view, holding what appeared to be a staff, or perhaps a scythe. There was no visible face, and the photo was partially blurred, but Daniels scanned it for every minute detail. He wondered if there was a possibility the figure in the photo was the killer.

A dark cloak, a potential murder weapon, the hotel as a setting. It all seemed to fit.

There was no visible blade as the staff ran off the visible realm of the picture, but the pose of the figure seemed threatening and calculating. Daniels could hear his breath, unable to look away from the photo for what seemed an eternity. Finally, satisfied there was nothing more to see, he slowly flipped to the next photo.

"Dear God," Daniels said as a horrible spectacle filled his eyes.

A slightly different angle, this time with a scythe in view and a hand clutching it from the victim's perspective filled the color photo. The hand loosely wrapped around the weapon, and it was apparent the camera was falling at this point, catching the last shot or two possible before it hit the ground.

Daniels could see blood on the hand, though most of the photo had a slight blur. He could tell from the orange hue in the sky's horizon it was late afternoon, probably near sunset when this occurred. The killer's profile was vague again, giving no real clue to his identity.

Only parts of him were visible in this photo. His arm and part of the torso were the only pieces captured behind the startling image of the weapon and the dying hand taking hold of it.

"Who the hell is taking that picture?" the detective wondered aloud.

Bracing himself, Daniels flipped to the last photo, unsure of what to expect. The result shocked him, and at the same time, sent a chill through his body, knowing there was finally something to go on.

"Vacation shots?" Hazen asked, returning from the restroom.

"No," Daniels answered almost blankly. "I've gotta run, Marty," he said, bolting from the table, stuffing a ten-dollar bill into his old partner's hand, implying he didn't have time to pay for the tab.

"Something come up, Mark?"

"You could say that," Daniels said, rushing toward the door. "Something real big."

*   *   *

Dust flew as Clouse pulled into the gravel-covered drive, slamming on the brakes as he reached the end. He nearly impaled himself on the steering wheel, but didn't care, bolting from the truck once it stopped completely.

Throwing the door shut behind him with one hand, the fireman stormed toward the house, catching a cold crosswind that stopped him for a second as he looked to the barn. Cautiously looking around, he saw no foreign vehicles, nothing disturbed, and no reason to panic.

Yet he felt highly apprehensive.

Walking to the barn, he rolled the main door aside, letting natural light flood the boat storage area and the stalls in the back as he stepped inside. A few minutes later he emerged, finding nothing unusual inside. Still, an uneasy feeling controlled him. Someone was toying with him, and his usually cool demeanor was nowhere to be found.

A moment later Clouse stepped inside his house, stopping in the kitchen, listening for any noises before closing the door. His eyes wandered to the ceiling as though he could see upstairs, but Clouse knew he would need to make a full inspection of the house before he could be satisfied.

Taking his jacket off, Clouse tossed it over a chair before making his way into the downstairs bedroom, then the living room.

Finding nothing out of place in either, he ventured into the family room, finding several boxes he had sifted through a few nights prior disturbed, their contents strewn across the floor. He started toward the mess, but caught a glimpse of a light to his right, coming from Angie's old office. Clouse turned, finding one of his largest potential leads lying in a heap on the floor beside the desk.

"Her computer," he said aloud, assessing the damage.

From the family room he could see the computer was a complete loss. Its sides were battered and the monitor appeared smashed beyond recognition. Papers and folders were strewn across the desk and floor, much like the items from the boxes. Clouse was about to inspect the damage when a noise from upstairs distracted him.

Jerking his head toward the noise, he stood a moment, breathing nervously. Deciding the police would probably arrive too late, or screw up his chances of catching the intruder, Clouse scurried to the kitchen, taking a hammer from a utility drawer.

Quickly, but quietly, he took to the stairs, heading up to see who or what was invading his house and destroying everything left in his life.

Reaching the top, he looked down the hall, seeing nothing. He opened Zach's room, seeing no one inside. A quick inspection revealed nothing in either the closet or under the bed. He left the room, shutting the door behind him.

Next was the guest bedroom.

It too held nothing in plain sight, or in the other areas. Above this room loomed the attic. Clouse listened for a minute but no sound came, assuring him no one would be in this room or above it. He carefully shut the door behind him, walking to the bathroom.

Flipping on the light, Clouse looked to his right where a brown shower curtain obscured the entire tub, showing nothing behind it. He drew in a breath, slowly reached for the curtain, and threw it aside, seeing nothing but typical sundries along the tub's side. He breathed a sigh of relief, turning to run the water in the sink.

Perhaps his paranoia was getting the better of him.

As he bent over, throwing cold water into his face, the noise of the faucet overcame that of the squeaking door behind him as the bathroom's only entrance closed. He rubbed his face thoroughly, feeling a sense of relief, thinking he was alone in the house before he had mistakenly called authorities.

Clouse looked up to catch a glimpse of the killer and Zach's baseball bat just before it struck his skull, rendering him unconscious, at the killer's mercy.

19

Clouse slowly awoke to the sounds of breaking glass and shuffling papers near his living room.

He moaned from the knot growing on his head, though he could not touch it because his hands and feet were tied together behind his back. Being hogtied was about the only way to ensure he would not interfere while the killer finished his business.

Within his scope of vision, everything looked hazy, like a dream in a television soap opera.

He could see none of the activity because the noise came from the kitchen. And he never saw who the killer was, because the person was masked when Clouse spied him. Somehow it didn't surprise the fireman he was in another compromising position, or that he had the misfortune of figuring out the killer's game, then getting beaten at it anyhow.

He was unlucky lately.

Adding insult to injury, the attacker stayed even longer to complete whatever objective he had set out to accomplish. He had no idea whether the killer was looking for something to take, or there to destroy evidence Clouse might have already have discovered. If evidence was in his possession, the fireman had no idea what it might be.

In essence, the killer took no chance.

Detective Kendle would simply believe it was an elaborate hoax set up by Clouse to remove blame from himself, and there was no evidence to support any notion otherwise. The killer knew how to avoid detection, and never left physical or trace evidence unless by design.

Clouse barely had time to think about a way out of the ropes, or what he might do if he accomplished such an impossible feat, before a car pulled into the driveway, startling both he and the killer. While he desperately hoped no one he knew would be placed in jeopardy, the killer bolted for the back entrance, toward the open fields for safety.

Nearly half a minute later a knock came to the front door. Clouse glanced to the open back door before answering, wondering if the killer might lie in wait for whoever was visiting.

Whatever he was looking for had to be important, for him to risk an entanglement with Clouse, but the captive decided not to leave whoever was standing at his door in the same jeopardy he had put himself in.

"Come in!" Clouse shouted, hoping the front door was open, trying to squirm in that direction.

It opened, and someone stood in his kitchen, obviously waiting for the host to walk into the room.

"In here!" Clouse shouted. "Help!"

He was surprised and relieved when Mark Daniels rushed into the room, though the look on the detective's face displayed equal shock.

"Kendle's going to have a bitch of a time pinning this on you," he commented as he began undoing the ropes.

"He just bolted out the back door," Clouse announced quickly. "If you'd quit jabbering, you might be able to catch him."

"I know who it is," Daniels said, looking to the door, then heading for it. "He's not getting away again."

"Hey!" Clouse shouted, finding the ropes weren't completely undone. He fought against the straps to free himself. He wanted to know everything Daniels knew.

While the fireman tried to free himself, Daniels darted down the shortest field on the property with the killer still in his view. The detective leapt a short wire fence in his initial pursuit, while the darkly-clad intruder darted into a short bed of trees, crossing into a neighboring farm.

Daniels found the chase easier since the field consisted of short, dead hay which occasionally stabbed his ankles through his thin dress socks. He sprinted the best he could despite a mild lack of stamina. He hadn't chased any suspects since his days in the uniform division, and it was never after someone of such an athletic nature.

Still, Daniels dodged small trees and hurdled thick brush after the mysterious man with equivalent ease.

He reached the thicket of trees, cautiously slowing down. He could see a white farmhouse and decaying barn ahead, with several small fields to either side, but no sign of the man he pursued. Tree branches whipped him as he pressed past them, noisily crunching the blanket of dry leaves on the ground as he stepped through the tree bed.

Looking to the ground, Daniels realized the leaf piles were not thick enough to conceal a person, so he looked at the trees surrounding him, noticing how dark the area appeared compared to the sunlit farm ahead. He passed each looming tree and its thick trunk, which could allow anyone to hide, then sneak attack, without much effort in hiding.

Reaching into his coat, Daniels unlatched the holster, letting his nine-millimeter slide into the palm of his hand. At the end of the trees the detective looked across the entire farm, seeing nothing.

A truck parked near the house implied people might be home, so his attention fell to the barn where the killer would likely hide, since no one was in the fields. Had the killer continued toward the fields, Daniels would have spotted him. It seemed doubtful the killer would have hid among the trees and doubled back to Clouse's residence.

Daniels reached the barn, finding its main doorway completely open from morning chores. He sucked in a breath, held it, and stepped inside, carefully surveying the troughs on the ground and hay storage tiers above him for any sign of the killer.

Most of the barn was clear of hay bales and tools, so the search was quick and easy as the detective walked from one end of the barn to the other.

At the end, he found an open door leading to a small field, partly obscured by trees. In the center of the field he could see a man-made wall of rocks, probably used to divide property, or keep a herd from straying. Daniels started walking toward the rocks, unsure of where the killer might have gone at this point.

Avoiding fresh manure piles, the detective spied the remains of a summer garden beside the rocky wall once he was closer, his fire-arm held cautiously to one side, clasped with both hands. The garden was partly obscured by the wall, with a scarecrow centered along the rocky mass to keep the birds from preying on summer vegetables.

Daniels kept a firm grip on his gun as he neared the wall, climbing it when he finally reached it, for a better view. He found it was more than a fence-high wall when he scaled it. The foundation also created a small walkway, or area to sit and rest, when the farmer's help grew tired of stacking hay bales in the summer.

As he reached the top, a voice called from behind him, distracting him from the garden, the view, and the scarecrow.

"What are you doing out there?" demanded an older man, most likely the property's owner.

Daniels turned, stuffing his pistol into his pants, ready to pull out his police shield when the scarecrow came to life, taking up a scythe found in the barn, then ambling toward the distracted detective.

Frantically pointing behind Daniels, the farmer realized his real scarecrow was nowhere to be seen, and whoever crept behind the detective meant bodily harm.

"Look out!" the farmer cried too late.

Daniels whirled around in time to grasp the scythe's handle enough to prevent the blade from cutting through him, but it still reached his innards. The detective's pistol popped loose, landing amongst the leafy blanket atop the rock wall.

Though not life-threatening, the injury was serious. Daniels slowly backed away, clutching his wound as he hunched over, trying to contain the bleeding.

He saw what looked like a small chunk of lined cotton candy bulging from his side, stained with blood, knowing it was part of a vital organ he would not attempt to put back. Instinct told him to keep pressure on it, preventing it from rolling out further.

Without his gun, Daniels seemed to pose no threat to the killer, who slowly stalked him, noticing the farmer had run back to his house to call for help.

Daniels fell to one knee, luring the killer close enough to strike him in the groin. The blow was potent, but Daniels felt the wound tear further, making his breathing more labored as blood trickled through the gash.

While the killer doubled over, the detective clutched the mask, ripping it from the killer's face. It was just as he had suspected, but it was also too late.

He felt blood reach his mouth from within, and a sudden cold chill shot through his body. Without help he could not last much longer, and any more attempts to slow the killer would drain his body of what life it still had.

Daniels backed away on one knee as the killer stood, picking up the scythe from the leaf pile. He hoisted the weapon high above his head, ready to swing it like an axe when another disturbance came from near the barn.

"Don't!" Clouse's voice echoed from the old building.

Not looking in that direction for fear he would be identified by the fireman, the killer finished the job, swinging the scythe with enough force to decapitate the detective and destroy Clouse's only hope to end his ordeal.

"No!" Clouse screamed, holding the word out several seconds before charging the rock mound as the killer darted off the other end, running to freedom.

Before Clouse could reach the rock mound, the entire scene faded to white and the world around him began spinning. A pain to the back of his head overtook him as he felt his consciousness wain, or perhaps return.

20

Larry Kendle flipped through several files at his desk concerning the recent string of murders at the hotel.

He began to understand his partner's theory about how Clouse would have trouble committing all the murders, but still could not fully buy into it. He suspected Paul Clouse was guilty as sin because he was the only one who had an obvious motive.

It also seemed odd the man would be associating with a hotel tour guide, whom he easily could have known for some time before murdering his wife. It seemed quite plausible the man could murder Angela Clouse, inherit all that they shared, and start a new life with someone whose company he preferred.

Though he gave Daniels a hard time, Kendle respected the younger detective's intuition and knack for overlooking the obvious to dig deeper into a case.

Kendle once had the ambition and tenacity to search harder, but after so many cases ending with the obvious suspect in guilt, and the jury going against Kendle's better judgment in those that didn't, the detective simply gave up and went with the flow, letting justice take care of itself.

Kendle spent most of his time gathering what evidence he could against Clouse while Daniels, in his opinion, wasted his trying to clear the man. Unfortunately for the detective, he found little but circumstantial evidence to go on. He could never place Clouse directly at any scene, and there were no witnesses who could truly prove or disprove his presence.

Kendle did not consider Rusty Cranor credible because he could easily be covering for Clouse in the murder of Scott Beaman.

He wondered why Clouse would involve himself in more murders than Angela's, except to throw authorities off track. He stood to gain nothing in regards to the hotel by killing off construction workers.

The detective had managed to obtain DNA samples for David Landamere through the hospital, and took both the samples, and the bloodstained swab, to a friend at Indiana University for comparison. Earlier that morning his friend had called back with the results.

He and his students had made a positive comparison from the two samples, verifying it was indeed David Landamere's blood found within his own car. Everything seemed to point toward foul play against Landamere, but Kendle wondered if he could possibly be helping or covering up for Clouse.

His loyalty to Clouse remained in question, and needed to be investigated further.

Kendle laid the files down as his phone rang.

"Kendle," he answered.

"Hello, detective," the voice said. "This is Andy Lewis with the coroner's office."

"Oh, hello," Kendle replied, recognizing the name, knowing the man as a forensic pathologist. "Have you got something for me?"

"I was combing the belongings of your latest victim in the West Baden case and found some interesting fibers in the clothing, as well as the body cavity. We've already bagged and tagged everything, but Gary said I should call you first so you could take a look before we ship everything off to the lab, in case you wanted comparisons done."

"Great," Kendle said, happy the coroner would keep him in mind on such an important case. "I'll be down in a little bit."

*   *   *

Half an hour later the detective descended the stairs to the basement of Bloomington Hospital where the morgue was tucked safely away in a corner.

Nodding to a passing orderly, Kendle took a familiar corner where he found partial darkness in the hallway ahead as the fluorescent light above flickered, nearing its end. The detective knew its starter was bad because janitors constantly replaced them in the detective division office.

A vibration stopped Kendle in his tracks as his pager buzzed at his side. He plucked it from its case, noting the number from his own office. It was probably Daniels wanting to swap information on their case, but there was no distress code after the entered phone number, so Kendle decided it could wait.

He looked ahead, noticing how dark the corner where the autopsy room's entrance appeared. Usually it was dim, but this was to the point that he could barely find his way to the door. He found it, however, and its numerous hazardous warning signs in bold red print atop a white background, proclaiming the room was indeed for autopsies and unauthorized people were not allowed.

Knowing he was authorized, Kendle gave two quick knocks to the door, then opened it slowly, finding the lights inside were also off. It seemed odd because the door was never unlocked without someone there. Yet it was, and no one seemed to be around.

"What the hell?" he couldn't help but ask aloud as he stepped inside the room, finding an orange glow from inside the main autopsy room further ahead.

Leaving the lights alone for the moment, Kendle slowly stepped ahead, wondering what in the world was going on. He heard the door shut behind him as he walked toward the next room, hearing only his footsteps in the darkness.

He suddenly felt vulnerable standing in the center of a darkened morgue.

Reaching the next room, Kendle's eyes widened as he took in the view of a plastic skeleton, its head covered by a lit jack-o-lantern. Instantly he placed the scenario closely with what he and Daniels envisioned Angela Clouse's murder scene to look like. His body stiffened as a chill of realization ran through him.

He flipped on the lights for a better look at the room as a cold piece of steel slid between his legs without touching a bit of his pants.

As the lights flickered to life, the steel blade of the scythe launched into Kendle's crotch before the detective even knew anyone was behind him. In one swift motion, the killer used both hands to hoist the weapon upward, then ripped it back, letting its sharpened blade act like a sword on its unwitting victim.

Kendle did not know the extent of his injuries as he grabbed what little remained of his groin area. After an initial cry of pain, he groaned intensely, hunched over, then dropped to his knees.

He fell to the ground in a fetal position, laying amongst a pool intertwined of his own urine and blood, created by his wounds.

He could not have known that his penis was severed beyond repair, or that the remains of his manhood lay beside him in a puddle of organic juice and layers of soft muscle tissue with two lumps of internal flesh that defined, in part, who he was.

Kendle only knew pain, and lots of it.

Groaning intensely, Kendle attempted to reach the gun at his side without looking up to his adversary, who was measuring him with calculating eyes.

Dressed in his black garb, the killer allowed the detective to reach the gun, already knowing what move each of them would make next. As Kendle pulled the gun slowly from its holster, still moaning, the killer waited until it was partly raised before letting the scythe fly again.

It had to look deliberate, the killer thought. It had to look intense and hateful, as though an emotionally invoked crime. There were no rules in crimes of passion.

Only bloodshed, and no conscious means to the act.

This time the weapon lodged itself partway in Kendle's hand, severing every vein in the wrist side as it struck, causing a yelp from the detective, then a scream as the killer pried the weapon loose. Kendle could not decide whether to clutch his useless hand or groin, but either way, he was at the killer's mercy.

Kendle rolled to his knees in an attempt to stand, and face his adversary if nothing else. Supporting himself with one hand, the detective drew himself to a crawling position, using his good hand to support himself.

Tired of waiting, and afraid someone might have heard Kendle's outbursts, the killer eyed his victim, drew the weapon back in a wood-chopping position, and let the bladed end launch forward.

It made a swoosh sound as it pierced the back of its victim, spliced his heart, and landed on the floor beneath him, cracking the linoleum tile below. Blood dripped like a leaky faucet to fill in the crevices.

Acting as the fourth appendage of support, the scythe kept Kendle's body in its knelt position while the killer searched for appropriate means of disposal, opening various cabinets throughout both rooms.

After looking at jar after jar of organs and samples, cutting tools, and paperwork, the killer found exactly what he needed, swiping it from a top shelf.

Walking over to the body, the killer tilted his head for a better examination of his work, stared a few seconds, then blew out the jack-o-lantern's candle, prepared to clean up his mess.

21

A brisk wind slapped Clouse in the face as he awoke among overgrown grass, feeling no pain from the brushy straw rubbing against him, because the rest of his body felt like a ball two off-road trucks had played catch with.

His ribs and face in particular had bruises and swelling. His kidneys felt inflamed as though someone had used them to practice kneading dough. He fought an incredible urge to wet himself, and barely had the will or the physical ability to prevent carrying out such an act.

Clouse knew he had been in and out of consciousness several times, but could not remember details. What exactly was real or conjured up by his mind during his unconscious spells eluded him. Struggling to look around him, the fireman rolled to his stomach, forcing his aching neck to stretch upward, seeing familiar grounds around him.

He was nearly to the top of one of his hills on his own property, and seemed to recall crawling and dragging his way up it during one of his numerous conscious spells. He looked around, taking note of the late afternoon sun, realizing how much of the day had passed.

To his left he saw an open field where several cows grazed, his house was to his right, and in the center stood the barn. In front of the barn he saw something strung from a rope, swinging slightly in the breeze.

It reminded him of his childhood days, seeing butchered cows hanging from a hoist at the barn doors with nothing but an empty, reddish inside and the open rib cage serving as an entrance point to the hollowed guts.

But this was no cow.

"Benny?"

Dangling in the wind like a porch chime, his favorite dog, a three-year-old Doberman, was gutted just like the cows Clouse remembered as a child, only with his intestines hanging like a knotted rope to the ground. Anger coursed through his body as he reached a hand upward, clawing the cold earth to pull himself to level ground.

Just as he rolled himself onto his yard, still wracked with pain, Clouse heard a car pull up his gravel driveway. At first he wondered if the killer had returned to finish the job, or if he was supposed to already be dead. Panic froze him as his eyes scanned the driveway to find a county police car drawing to a stop.

Clouse wondered whether Kaiser was friend or foe, once he realized who was driving the car. Propped on one elbow, Clouse maintained his position, cautiously watching the officer's movements as he stepped from the car.

With nothing except a T-shirt and jeans on, Clouse's body was frozen. The socks on his feet were not enough to keep him warm, but he didn't have time to wonder where his boots were. Like a partly domesticated animal, he remained perfectly still, observing what one of his best friends did, once outside the car.

Kaiser had parked near the barn, and appeared to instantly notice the gutted dog hanging at the front door. The officer, still in uniform, made a strange face at the sight, as though wondering what sort of strange thoughts might be going through Clouse's mind.

Clouse wondered if it could be an act, if Kaiser was the one who had attacked him, and returned to finish the job under the guise of concern. It would be an easy excuse to use, after the strange actions numerous people had witnessed the fireman carrying out around the hotel recently.

Hearing the smack of metal against an obstruction, Clouse and Kaiser respectively turned to look toward the house's front door. The storm door was swinging in the breeze, and Clouse had to wonder if the front door might be open, or worse, the killer might still be inside.

"Ken!" Clouse called too weakly for his friend to hear him.

His body was half-frozen from hours among the elements without proper clothing, and his voice was hoarse from being outside so long.

Shivering, Clouse pulled himself further across the yard toward the house and Kaiser, who was crossing the yard to reach the front door. Kaiser reached for his service weapon, obviously alarmed by the open front door.

"Ken!" Clouse shouted again as the front door closed behind the officer, forbidding the words to enter behind him.

Forcing his aching body to stand, Clouse lumbered toward the house, fighting the pain of his kidneys and stomach. He looked toward the barn, sure he saw something behind his mutilated dog. Clouse had only a glimpse of the object, but it looked tall, and pure black. He wondered if his fear was provoking his imagination, because the object did not appear in his second glance when Clouse reached the front door.

Taking no chances, Clouse pounded on his own front door, turning the knob with little result from his stiff hand. His fingers lacked flexibility enough to perform such a simple task as grasping a knob, but they could still help him make enough noise to bring Kaiser to him.

Clouse's full weight pressed against the door when it opened, sending him barreling into his friend, knocking them both to the ground.

"Goddamn it, Paul!" Kaiser shouted more from surprise than anger.

He immediately noticed the lack of movement from the firefighter and touched Clouse's cold skin, apparently building a mental image of what had transpired. He quickly called for paramedics on his radio, then returned his attention to Clouse.

"Hang in there, Paul. Help is on the way."

"Thanks, Ken," Clouse muttered.

"Did he do this to you? Was it the killer?"

Clouse simply nodded the affirmative.

"Damn," Kaiser said before springing to the living room for a blanket, noticing the mess in both it, and the computer room. He quickly collected his thoughts and returned to throw the blanket around his shivering friend.

Pulling a business card from his wallet, Kaiser used his friend's cordless phone to call Larry Kendle's number in detectives, but found neither Kendle, nor Mark Daniels available. He spoke to a Detective Peterson, their supervisor, and requested one of them, if possible, be sent to Clouse's address immediately to investigate an assault and burglary.

"Hang in there, Paul," he told Clouse after hanging up. "We'll find out who did this to you."

*   *   *

When Clouse woke up again, he was surrounded by several familiar people in a soft hospital bed. The blinds were drawn, but Clouse could tell it was probably late night. His body still felt horrible, but at least it was warm.

He could feel all of his fingers and toes again, but it would be some time before his body recovered from whatever physical abuse it had sustained.

"You're lucky to still have all your body parts," a doctor said, standing closest to him.

Clouse's parents and Zach stood at the foot of the bed while Ken Kaiser stood behind them, still in uniform, holding his hat. Everyone wore an expression of concern, yet they seemed relieved to see him awake.

"We managed to warm your body slowly enough that we saved all of your limbs," the doctor explained. "Too much longer in that weather and we would have been lucky to save you at all."

"Thanks," Clouse said.

"Would you like some time to rest?" the doctor asked.

"Kelli and Roger are waiting outside," his mother jutted in.

Clouse drew a smile, though it pained him.

"I'd like to talk to Ken a minute if I could, Mom," he replied. "Then I want to see everyone."

Ushering everyone else out the door before him, the doctor left Kaiser alone with Clouse, as his patient wished. Clouse barely mustered enough energy to speak, but he needed to know something before he could rest easily again.

"Did you see who it was?" Kaiser asked.

"No. He got me from behind."

"I called for Bloomington P.D. to comb your house for evidence, but they aren't sure what to look for until they speak with you. I told them it could wait until morning."

Clouse coughed involuntarily a moment.

"Ken, I was in and out of consciousness several times this afternoon and I'm not exactly sure what was real, and what might have been a dream."

"That's okay, Paul. What are you getting at?"

"I saw Mark Daniels get beheaded by the killer at my neighbor's farm."

Kaiser chuckled a second.

"Well, lucky for you he was the one who showed up at your house to seal it off until tomorrow."

Clouse rolled his eyes back in relief.

"So you saw him? He's definitely alive?"

"Yes and yes, but we can't seem to find his partner. Daniels said Kendle is probably pissed off, thinking you came up with another way to clear your name, so he won't return pages or anything."

"The consummate professional," Clouse said with a weak chuckle.

"I'll go ahead and get your folks," Kaiser said, ready to get home to his own family. "You're lucky I got worried about you after this morning. At least you haven't lost it like I thought you might have."

Clouse grinned.

"You been wearing that uniform all day, Ken?"

"Yeah," the county officer said, pulling lightly on the brown uniform blouse as he looked down at it.

"Smells like it."

Kaiser smirked, giving Clouse the middle finger before turning to the door.

"Ken?" Clouse called before the officer could leave.

"Yeah?"

"Thanks."

"Anytime, pal," Kaiser said before heading into the hallway.

22

"You must be fatter than you look," Clouse commented from the passenger seat of Roger Summers' pickup truck as his brother-in-law drove him home the next morning.

He tugged at the sweatshirt Summers had let him borrow until he could get into his own house.

"I buy the shit large in case it shrinks, brother."

"Uh-huh," Clouse said, unconvinced.

Summers was not permitted past the police guard at Clouse's residence until Mark Daniels had a forensic team comb the grounds with the fireman's help, so he had let Clouse borrow some of his own clothing for the ride home from the hospital.

"You sure you're up to this?" Summers asked, turning on the road that led directly to Clouse's house.

"I want it over with, Rodge," Clouse said, taking short breaths. His rib cage hurt whenever he took a deep breath, but luckily no bones were broken.

"You don't know where all those injuries came from?"

"I have a good idea," Clouse answered. "I just wasn't awake to see it coming."

Summers grunted skeptically to himself, carefully watching for oncoming traffic around a bend in the deteriorating county road.

"Looks like I go back to work next week," he said.

"Chief call you?" Clouse asked.

"I went in yesterday to talk to him."

"Funny I haven't been invited back yet," Clouse commented, unable to hide the bitter bite of his words.

"Well, the chief thinks-"

"I know what he thinks, Rodge, and he doesn't want to touch me with a ten-foot pole until this whole thing gets cleared up."

"You've got to admit this is some weird-ass stuff happening to you, brother. Time off ain't gonna hurt you," Summers suggested as he pulled into the drive, straight from the road.

"I just want a normal life again. God, what I wouldn't do to set things right."

Several unmarked cars stood along the drive as the truck pulled in. Clouse recognized one of the vehicles as the one Daniels drove. He felt a rush of relief when he spied the detective near the barn, but a sense of dread as the dangling body of his favorite dog retained its place, hooked through the jaw, and probably stiff as a steak pulled from the freezer.

As much as he loved the land, Clouse fully realized he would have to sell the house, because everything reminded him of death. There was nowhere left to go where he couldn't think about Angie, his dog, or the bizarre dreams and visions he'd been having around the farm. It was all one big nightmare now.

"You okay from here?" Summers asked, stopping near the police cars.

"I'm fine, Rodge. I'll call if I need anything."

Summers nodded as Clouse stepped from the truck. Daniels noticed the fireman's arrival and briskly walked to greet him.

"Heard you had a time of it yesterday," he commented.

"Well, I thought you were dead, so I guess we're both pretty fortunate."

Daniels gave him a puzzled look so Clouse explained the disturbing dream in detail.

"I don't suppose you really know who the killer is?" Clouse asked once he finished.

"No, but I have made some progress. I've got something to show you in a little bit, but first, let's get started on your place and figure out what the killer might have been searching for."

Clouse needed to see the inside of the house again, because he could not recall any memories after his initial blow to the head.

"How do I know this isn't all a dream?" Clouse pondered aloud.

Assured no one was looking, Daniels rapped the fireman on the bicep with the back of his hand.

"Ouch!" Clouse said, not expecting the detective to stray from his usual straight-laced behavior.

"Convinced?" Daniels asked, not breaking stride as they reached the front door. The detective opened it, motioning for Clouse to go first.

"I guess the banged up ribs and kidneys should have been convincing enough," Clouse commented as he reached the inside ruins of his house.

It looked much as he had expected with drawers overturned, papers scattered everywhere, and a tone of thoroughness that fit the theme of hatred the killer seemed to hold for Clouse.

"Where's your partner?" Clouse asked, beginning to look around the disaster.

"I'm kind of worried," Daniels admitted. "No one's seen him since yesterday, and he left no word about where he was going."

"Oh?"

"Left around lunch time and never came back. It's not like him."

Clouse pictured both as by-the-book investigators, and Kendle seemed even more regimented than his partner, so it was strange that he simply dropped from sight. Then again, Dave Landamere pulled it off, the firefighter thought.

"Were you doing anything out of the ordinary the last few days that might have worried the killer?" Daniels asked, kneeling to shuffle through some loose papers on the floor.

"Not that I recall," Clouse said, though thinking about his internet search and all the websites he left information at.

Perhaps he was closer than he thought, but telling Daniels meant giving away information he was not supposed to have to begin with. They would question where he found companies querying the hotel's sale and how he gained access to his wife's account.

"You sure?" Daniels asked, still shuffling through papers and scattered items on the floor.

Clouse only stared at him without realizing it.

"What?" the detective inquired, taking notice.

"I was so sure you were dead," Clouse said slowly, only half of his mind located where he stood. "I saw it so clearly."

Daniels stood, slightly agitated and uneasy about Clouse mentioning his death.

"Look, whatever you saw didn't happen," Daniels said sternly. "I'm still here. I don't know what that bastard did to you, but I need your head clear if you're going to help me catch him. I can't go slapping you into reality every time you have these weird lapses."

"Understood," Clouse said, drawing a grin until the pain of his ribs returned.

"He fucked you up, didn't he?" Daniels asked, leading the way into the family room.

"Yeah," Clouse agreed, following. "So what were you going to show me?"

"I've got some new photos you should look at. They're at the office, but they might shed some light on who our killer is if the right person sees them."

"And I'm that person?"

Daniels shrugged. "I'm not sure. Guess it depends on if you know the killer or not."

Both looked around the room a moment, seeing nothing but the mess left by the killer. Through a window Clouse could see the police crews outside, looking for evidence on the hardened, cold ground. He appreciated Daniels putting so much effort forth in collecting evidence, but doubt clouded his mind about ever finding the killer.

"Do you remember anything?" Daniels asked. "Something I should have the boys check for in here?"

Now that his dream was proven false, Clouse actually could not remember a thing after being knocked unconscious. If he did remember something, he would probably doubt its validity until he checked.

"I can't remember anything concrete," Clouse said. "The guy was wearing a black cloak, like I saw at the hotel. There wasn't a face or anything."

"Nothing after he struck you?"

"No," Clouse answered, closing his eyes as though trying to focus on the event. "I know I was in and out of consciousness a few times, but nothing stuck with me."

"What was the point of entry?"

Clouse gave a confused look.

"You know, where he came in?"

"I know," the fireman replied, his intelligence insulted. "I'm just not sure he broke in is all."

"Why is that?"

Clouse walked to the back door, turning the knob.

It opened.

"That's why. And I don't remember if I locked it or not."

"And if you didn't, who has keys?"

"Pretty much anyone in my family, and in Angie's for that matter. A lot of them came over to visit, babysit Zach, or keep an eye on the house when we were on vacation."

"So everyone's a suspect."

"You don't really think-"

"Don't close your mind to it, Mr. Clouse," Daniels said evenly. "I think it's someone pretty close to you."

"Then maybe I don't want to know," the firefighter answered. "But who around me would have any interest in the hotel?"

*   *   *

Hours later, the cleanup crews finished with his house, giving Clouse time to travel across town to a stretch of road he was familiar with, but not accustomed to visiting. Now he would be a regular, until the pain inside his heart and mind went away.

He pulled up to a large archway beside a small church, looking across the rows of granite and concrete with reverence, only now understanding how important the upkeep of cemeteries was to the living. They always seemed so vacant and lonely, and a million questions about death and the afterlife always flooded his mind when he visited them.

His truck pulled beside a familiar sports car and he saw Kelli placing flowers on her sister's grave, oblivious to the fact he was there. A fleeting thought told Clouse to leave before she saw him, but he stayed. It would be a wasted trip if he turned back, and Kelli would be crushed if she saw him leave without speaking to her, but he was quite uncomfortable around her at the moment.

"Oh, you scared me!" Kelli stammered when she turned to see Clouse after hearing his approach.

"Sorry," he said, placing a freshly-bought set of roses beside Angie's tombstone.

"Are you feeling better?" Kelli asked as she stood.

"A little," he said. "I feel weak and cold, but I'm going to settle in by a big fire tonight."

"Need any company?"

"No, but thanks. I'll probably start cleaning up the house tomorrow."

Kelli looked down at the grave site and the recently placed sod.

"If you need anything, just call."

"I will."

"Rumor is you have a new love interest, Paul," she said out of nowhere.

"Whoa," he said immediately. "Jane is not a love interest. We've only talked a few times at the hotel. Where did this come from?"

"Around," Kelli answered aloofly.

Clouse was growing frustrated with Kelli and her great interest in his life lately.

"So what exactly is your stand with me lately?"

"What do you mean?" she asked.

"All of this attention since Angie's death. You spend the night, and you keep finding excuses to come over. What gives?"

Kelli's expression changed to one of grave concern, as though Clouse misread her intentions completely.

"I've been taking care of you like a brother, Paul," she answered. "As for spending the night and allegedly getting close to you, I'm going to have to let you in on something."

Clouse stared, waiting for the answer.

"I don't bat that way, Paul."

His look grew slightly confused.

"Ever wonder why I didn't marry, Paul?" she said, raising her voice intensely. "I'm gay. And I'm not after your body and your life like you think, and I'm not trying to replace my sister. My interest in you is strictly family concern, and as of right now, I don't have much interest in you at all," she said before storming to her car, squealing the tires as she left.

"Ah, shit," Clouse said before looking to the grave, then to Kelli's car in the distance. Dust flew behind it as the dusk in the foreground nearly blinded him.

Another long night was ahead of him.

23

Everyone wondered where Larry Kendle was, his partner included.

Daniels flipped through the set of pictures, now smudged with his fingerprints, looking for any further clues he might have overlooked.

He wished his partner would show up to compare clues with him, but Kendle was missing from work another morning. Nothing of consequence had turned up at Paul Clouse's residence the day before, and Daniels would forever wonder if his partner's presence and expertise might have made a difference.

Dressed in one of his many white shirts with blue stripes, the detective tossed the photos atop his desk, opting for the file he put together concerning every murder since Angela Clouse's that seemed tied to her husband.

Often Daniels' wife teased that he was obsessive compulsive about shirts with blue. If he wasn't wearing a blue dress shirt, it had blue trim. It seemed to go with everything, and being the practical person he was, Daniels liked simplicity.

And he liked blue.

Kendle's wife had phoned him several times already, and it wasn't even lunchtime.

Daniels spoke to her half a dozen times, then had other detectives take messages, none of which he planned to return. It was difficult enough to plan his next move without distractions. He felt certain his partner was fine, probably intently investigating some part of Paul Clouse's deep, dark past. Daniels shook his head at the notions his partner came up with concerning Clouse.

"Kendle's wife called again," another detective said in passing.

"Tell her I was dead?" Daniels asked sarcastically, sick of being considered Kendle's keeper all the sudden.

"No, but it can be arranged," the detective answered with a slight roll of the eyes, indicating he was sick of playing secretary.

Daniels felt no desire to be mean, but he was at work. Being the consummate professional, he wanted to focus on what he was paid to do, and that meant investigating several murders when he wasn't busy preparing for court, or dealing with some leftover white-collar crimes.

He wanted to begin more intense interviews with Clouse's immediate family, especially those on Angela's side. More than ever, he believed Clouse was innocent, but could not piece together a connection between the hotel murders and that of Angie Clouse. He could see that someone was probably framing Clouse, but to what extent, and what purpose?

Daniels picked up the last photo of the bunch, staring at what details he could make out from the blur. Already he had reprinted it, and sent a copy, and the negative, to the state police lab in Indianapolis in the hope they could lose the blurriness or sharpen the image with their computers.

Feeling Clouse was hiding something from him, Daniels did not share the photo with the firefighter. He wanted to see what the lab could pull from the image anyhow, before he shared it with anyone.

He knew the fireman was intelligent, and probably carrying out his own investigation with knowledge beyond what Daniels could legally attain, so he understood why Clouse would not divulge his sources, but it aggravated him that they could be closer to solving the murder if they didn't keep secrets.

He and Kendle already had that working relationship.

Holding the picture firmly, Daniels examined the contents again.

Most of the picture's upper half was a black blur which Daniels knew was the cloak worn by the killer. From what he made out, after studying the picture for hours since first seeing it at the diner, he could tell the victim's leg had kicked up part of the cloak, revealing the killer's leg from the lower calve muscle up to the knee.

Though Daniels could not see the ankle or foot to determine what footwear the killer wore, he knew it could not be a cowboy boot, which Clouse nearly always wore to the hotel. This furthered his evidence Clouse could not be the killer, assuming the photo was authentic and not a hoax, or distraction created by the killer himself.

Daniels did not believe it was either.

From what little he saw of the victim's body, he guessed it was Robert Bennett. A few calls confirmed the man was an amateur photographer and indeed owned a fairly nice camera, though no one could inform the detective of its make or model. Bennett and his van hadn't been seen or heard from in a week, so there was no true way to verify the rumors.

What really set the photo apart from the others for Daniels, however, was a visible mark on the killer's right leg. The picture appeared too blurry for him to determine whether it was a blood spot, a scar, or possibly part of a tattoo. He hoped the lab could clarify the image, making it easier to determine exactly what color and shape the smudge was.

Any identifying mark would put him that much closer to finding the killer.

It would be several days before the lab technicians had anything concrete, since they were backed up with evidence from several other rape and homicide cases. Several recent departures had left the state police lab with a shortage of technicians, increasing the turnaround time on evidence analysis.

In the meantime, Daniels wanted to begin interviewing people around the hotel, now that construction was reopening. The more time he spent at the hotel, the less bad things were apt to happen. He knew Smith had little choice in the matter, and he knew county and state police would be keeping a close watch on the place, but he felt a personal touch would also help.

And without Kendle to override his decisions, Daniels could do most anything he wanted, as long as the chief and his sergeant saw results on a regular basis.

*   *   *

Clouse had most of his house looking normal by noon. His body ached too much to sleep in, but felt even worse when he moved. He tolerated the pain, ignoring it as best he could.

He had already phoned the fire chief, asking to return to work the next day his shift worked. The chief agreed, but only if he took an assignment with Summers at the same station. Clouse assumed this was at his brother-in-law's request, but the chief would not say.

Now he had two days to return his house to normal, make arrangements for Zach's babysitting, get a tentative schedule for the hotel, and mentally prepare for everyone to treat him like an outcast at work, despite several people now proclaiming his innocence.

Maybe working with his brother-in-law would be a bonus after all.

After digging through pictures and paperwork, Clouse found several items missing, which he assumed were taken, or destroyed, by the intruder. Most importantly, one page from his list of potential hotel buyers was missing. He was unsure if it was buried beneath some other piles, or stolen, but he assumed the latter.

Now Clouse had to question what the page's contents were. Without the computer he might never find out.

He picked up the remains of the computer from the floor, clearing the desk off with one swipe of his arm before placing it there. Taking a screwdriver from the kitchen, Clouse set to work, undoing the battered shell of the computer, using tin snips where the metal was too badly damaged and dented.

From the looks of the dents, and what Daniels guessed, they were made by a baseball bat or some other blunt object.

Whoever had broken into his house did not want the computer recovered.

Clouse worked up a sweat prying apart the metallic walls of the computer, hoping they did their job enough to protect the memory cards inside. He knew they were the heart of the unit, and could easily be placed in another body and reused. He wanted to phone Tony Dierker, but feared telling anyone about whatever moves he made in solving Angie's murder.

He trusted no one at this point.

Once the cover was off, though beyond repair, the fireman found most of the chips intact. One was broken completely in half, but the rest appeared fine, though that was only from an exterior view. Clouse knew the circuits inside could be severed or ruptured, rendering them useless.

When he went into town later, he would take them to a computer store for some advice, but wished he could confide in Daniels, having them sent to a secure lab for analysis without fear of the killer stalking him, or trying to destroy what evidence he had gathered.

Clouse left the computer casing on the desk to answer his cordless phone in the other room.

"Hello?" he answered.

"Paul, it's Rusty," the foreman said from the other end.

"How is everything?"

"Terrible," Rusty answered with a sigh.

It sounded as though something was bothering him.

"Any word from Missy yet?"

"No. That's what has me worried."

"Sorry to hear that."

Clouse decided not to probe any deeper. He knew if Zach was missing he would be beside himself with worry. Rusty was probably sensitive about everyone asking him questions every few minutes.

"You at the hotel?"

"Yeah. I was wondering if you were working this week."

"I'm probably going back to work at the fire department," Clouse replied. "I'll let you know my schedule once it's settled. Everything the same there?"

"I suppose. The workers are scared to death, my daughter and Landamere are still missing, and Dr. Smith has been here all day warning us to stay in groups and leave no one alone, even for a second."

"He's spooked," Clouse said, knowing the feeling all too well.

"He's not the only one, you know. This whole thing is making everyone's lives miserable. I can't take much more of this."

"Hang in there, old man. I'll let you know when I get my schedule."

"Take care," Rusty said, hanging up the phone from Landamere's office, which he now used as his own.

Rusty looked outside the window at several construction workers as they surveyed the hotel grounds. He knew they would do almost anything to avoid entering the building if they could help it. They were scared, but they were also protected by police, strategically surrounding the grounds. From several key areas, the county and state police performed surveillance details, but Rusty and his workers felt none the safer.

Taking up his hard hat and clipboard, the foreman left the office, shutting the newly-replaced door behind him. It was time to get back to work and appease his police watchdogs.

As he confirmed the lock was set, he heard a noise down the hall, like a stone ricocheting off the trim. No one else should have been inside the hotel at that moment, since it was a day to ready the grounds for winter.

"Hello?" he called down the hall. "Anyone there?"

No answer.

Licking his lips nervously as he thought about investigating, the foreman thought better of it and decided simply to join his workers outside.

Again, the noise came from down the hall, getting Rusty's attention. He involuntarily stepped toward the echoing noise before his senses caught up with his reflexes. Still, it was too late because the foreman had rounded the first bend.

He knelt beside two pebbles, almost in the same spot, picking them up as he looked down the hall. Seeing nothing, he wondered if they might have fallen from part of the wall, or been the closest physical evidence to a figment of his imagination.

Either way, Rusty had no intention of staying to figure it out.

A minute later he stepped out the front entrance, surprised it was such a sunny day in November, yet it was. Strangely, no warmth seemed to strike him as he zipped up his thick work jacket, looking across the landscape as he did, his nerves still tingling from the noises inside.

Rusty panned from one side to another, seeing nothing except usual activity. He saw none of the police officers, implying they were doing their job correctly, and better yet, he saw no sign of danger. He also saw nothing of Vern, the old grounds keeper. The man had been missing for several days, but that in itself was not unusual.

Drawing a deep breath, the foreman thought perhaps things would look up, and the day would pass without incident, and perhaps the police might call to tell him they had found Melissa safe and unharmed.

He could always hope.

*   *   *

Feeling somewhat dejected, Clouse continued to clean the rest of his house into the afternoon. With only papers and small debris left to pick up from the floor, he felt a sense of relief that he was nearly done.

Zach was with his parents, which left guilt weighing on his mind. As though it wasn't bad enough he was being accused of murder, Clouse worried about being a negligent father.

Looking around to his doors and windows, he still felt unsafe, as though someone might barge into his house any second. Worse yet, he felt virtually defenseless in his battered state.

He wanted to rest and recuperate, but didn't feel tired enough to try sleeping. Seldom did he nap at the fire station, and if he did, it was typically when he felt sick or extremely worn out from a lack of sleep.

As he picked up the last of the computer pieces, he heard a thunderous roar in the distance. Considering his driveway spanned at least the length of a football field, he wondered what the noise at the foot of his property was.

Drawing close to his kitchen window, Clouse looked outside, spying a motorcycle cautiously navigating his driveway. He knew instantly who the rider was, but wondered why Tim Niemeyer was paying him a visit.

Though they were buddies in high school, the two were lucky to see one another twice a year at best.

Ordinarily, Clouse might think his friend was paying him a visit to check on him, but he had good reason to be suspicious of everyone around him at the moment.

Stepping onto his porch, Clouse watched Niemeyer put the cycle's kick stand down, then dismount. Wearing a bandana, half-gloves, and a black leather jacket, Niemeyer looked the part of a renegade biker. He had begun growing a goatee to accompany his mustache since Clouse saw him at Angie's calling hours.

"Hi, Tim," Clouse said neutrally, offering his hand.

Niemeyer shook it, but only to pull his friend into a long hug.

A big teddy bear. Gentle, caring, and blatantly honest was how Clouse always described Niemeyer to others. Even in high school he was a stocky individual, but he carried his weight, a solid mix of muscle and girth, very well.

"I was worried about you," the construction owner said, his Southern drawl coming through.

Part of his upbringing meant staying with his grandfather from Tennessee. Since middle school, Niemeyer always had the lingering drawl.

"Ken told me about what happened," Niemeyer revealed. "I thought you might like to see a friendly face."

Clouse stood awkwardly a moment, contemplating what he truly wanted at the moment. Niemeyer shifted his stance uneasily, licking his bottom lip in obvious anticipation of a reply.

Realizing he looked like a terrible host, Clouse finally decided some company might take his mind off his problems awhile.

"I'm sorry, Tim," he finally apologized. "Come on in."

Leading the way, Clouse closed the door behind them. He walked to the refrigerator, taking out a beer for each of them, opening his own before downing half the can with one upward tip.

"You sure you're okay?" Niemeyer questioned aloud.

"I've been better. I'm just not sure who I can trust these days."

Niemeyer opened his beer, taking a sip before setting it beside him.

"I hate drinking before I ride the bike," he admitted.

"Sorry. It's just instinctive to have a beer around you and Kenny."

Niemeyer smirked.

"I can remember some times when you two were pretty tanked."

"I don't remember all of them," Clouse noted, forcing a grin.

He looked out the window at the new Harley-Davidson sitting in his driveway.

"I take it the construction business is paying pretty well?"

"I do okay," Niemeyer said with an indifferent shrug. "I think I've got Kenny wanting a bike now."

Clouse shook his head slowly. He never had any desire to own a motorcycle. His boat was adventurous enough for him.

"He's always had a stiff one for motorcycles. It's just a matter of time before the wife lets him buy one."

Looking to the beer can beside him, then to Clouse, Niemeyer had a perplexed look.

"Where's your boy?"

"With my folks," Clouse answered. "He's a lot better off with them for the night."

He paused a moment, realizing once again it was strange for his friend to visit him at home.

"Tim, what really brings you out here?" he asked.

"Well, I'm worried about you and Ken."

"Ken?" Clouse asked, leaning against his kitchen counter, folding his arms. "I didn't realize my recent turmoil was causing him grief."

Niemeyer shrugged.

"He's afraid he might lose his second job, and he's more afraid you might be, well, you know."

"Guilty?" Clouse questioned, raising an eyebrow.

"It just looks bad for you," Niemeyer admitted. "I know you'd never do anything crazy. And again, I'm sorry for your loss."

Clouse decided to lighten up toward Niemeyer.

"I appreciate it, Tim. As much as I hate to see the hotel close its doors, it might be safer for Ken, and everyone there, if it did."

"Any ideas who might be killing those people?"

"If I was a betting man, I'd say it's the same person who killed Angie. I can't trust anyone around me anymore, Tim. Whoever it is knows my habits and where I'm going to be. It has to be someone who knows me well, like a family member, or a good friend."

Niemeyer swallowed hard, getting the point. He picked up the beer, taking a long drink, before setting it on the counter.

"What's the matter?" Clouse asked, taking notice of his friend's sudden change of heart toward drinking.

"Nothing," Niemeyer said too quickly for his friend's taste.

"It's about Ken, isn't it?"

Stalling for time, Niemeyer took another drink from the beer can.

"He says he's doing it to protect you. To make sure nothing else bad happens there."

"What are you talking about?" Clouse asked sternly.

Looking almost helpless, Niemeyer's face had an expression of grief, as though he was about to open the gates of hell to shove Kaiser through them.

"He's been working a lot of overtime at the hotel."

"Ken works there regularly," Clouse noted aloud. "What's the big deal?"

"I'm not talking about his regular shifts. He's been picking up extra shifts, sometimes working two a day when he's off-duty from the county."

Clouse was puzzled. He felt certain he would know if his best friend was working so many shifts.

"A lot of the shifts are in the overnight hours," Niemeyer stated. "He thinks that's when people are sneaking around the grounds, disrupting things."

"Like graves," Clouse muttered quietly.

"Ken's just not been himself lately. Maybe you can talk to him."

"Yeah," Clouse said almost absently. "Sure."

Niemeyer seemed to look uncomfortable, almost as though his sole purpose for visiting was to bear bad news.

"I didn't mean to come out here and dump all this on you," he admitted. "God knows you have enough on your mind without me bugging you."

"It's okay," Clouse assured him. "I didn't mean to be harsh, earlier. Like I said, I'm just wary of everyone right now, but now isn't the time I need to be pushing my friends away. You guys have helped me through a lot of tough times."

Niemeyer nodded in understanding, probably realizing the times Clouse and Kaiser helped him through some ordeals.

"I was worried about you staying alone," Niemeyer confessed. "In this house."

Niemeyer looked to the floor, as though expecting to see blood stains where Angie was brutally murdered and hacked to pieces. His blue eyes quickly returned to Clouse.

Deciding that company wasn't such a bad thing, Clouse wanted to make his friend feel a bit more welcome. Alienating Niemeyer wasn't something he planned on doing, but he was apparently doing just that.

"Let's go have a look at that bike," he said, putting an arm on the burly man's left shoulder as they walked toward the door.

24

Ian Briscoe hated calls in the middle of the night.

When he took a deputy coroner position, he knew murders were more common during night hours, but how so many came to be found at all hours of the morning baffled him.

Lately, things were slow within Bloomington city limits, but the Angela Clouse murder was still fresh on a number of minds.

Briscoe was now on a call for a rape and murder retrieved in the south end of the city. He had already examined the scene, finding little useful information, and now walked with the paramedics who wheeled the body into the morgue, where he would do a fresh examination.

He already knew she was killed by a bladed object, but he needed to determine what drugs, if any, were in her system. She was a known prostitute who occasionally used drugs, and homicide detectives would throw a fit if the coroner's office failed to dig up any details.

Though dead tired, Briscoe didn't mind doing his job. He was thorough, and enjoyed helping the police however he could. It beat his usual nine to five job at the hospital in the x-ray lab where he often specialized in boredom. He hated the area, but worked diligently at moving up in the medical profession, which was why the coroner picked him as an assistant soon after they shared lunch with a common friend one day.

Barry Andrews, one of the hospital's resident doctors, who also ran his own clinic, took a liking to Briscoe's work ethic, promising the young intern a spot under his wing, and his practice once he was ready. He felt it would be great experience, and a test of sorts, to place him in the morgue examining corpses, while learning about human anatomy up close. The lunch went well and the rest was history.

"Just pop the bag up on the table," he told the paramedics once he had unlocked the morgue.

If he needed it moved to the freezer in the near future, Briscoe planned to recruit the assistance of a security guard, or a male nurse.

Dressed in an unpressed pair of slacks with a polo shirt, Briscoe intended to be seen at this time of morning only by people in the same condition as himself. His long hair was uncombed, looking like a perm gone wrong. It felt unkept and oily because he had found no time to shower, and probably wouldn't before going to work.

The combination of his hair and the old pair of glasses he found to put on at such an early hour created the look of a terrorist from any number of early '80s flicks.

Briscoe didn't care, as long as he found ten minutes to sharpen up his look and put his contact lenses in, before his shift began.

He watched as the paramedics placed the black body bag on the exam table, leaving it zipped to ensure no contents spilled out. As they left, Briscoe examined the room, finding a new odor to his dislike. He saw the room on a weekly basis, but it seemed to change a bit every time he walked in.

Briscoe took notice of the skeleton sitting in the corner atop a stool, apparently set there around Halloween by one of his colleagues. He also saw the remains of a jack-o-lantern in the trash, which explained the smell. Traces of the pumpkin's innards remained atop the skeleton's head, causing him to wonder exactly what went on around the past holiday, since he was out of town.

Other than the smell and the disarray of the plastic skeleton, Briscoe saw no difference in the two rooms forming the morgue. He looked to the two examination tables, side by side, and wondered where to begin. By now he had conducted several such examinations, and observed over two dozen others. This would be open and shut, though it would take several hours to complete, depending on what he found.

Starting with the body bag, Briscoe unzipped it, carefully sliding the body, half at a time, to the adjacent clean table. Assured everything was out of the bag, he took it to the sink where he thoroughly washed it. When he gave items back to police or EMS he preferred they be perfectly clean, so his rapport remained equally so.

Once it was clean, he turned it upside down, shook it out, and began looking for a place to store it once it dried.

He looked through several cabinets before recalling where the coroner usually stored objects needing to be returned. There was often a small collection when the coroner waited for the organizations to retrieve their equipment. His relationship with them was not as strong as Briscoe's.

Opening the cabinet, he noticed a space in the right-hand corner. It took a moment before he remembered what was usually there, and ironically, it was the permanent body bag the coroner's office owned.

"Where in the hell is it?" Briscoe wondered aloud, beginning to search drawers, knowing he would be blamed if it came up missing.

Frantically, he searched drawer after drawer, finding nothing except chemicals, preserved body parts, household cleaners, and other things he didn't care to see. His search, however, allowed him to find more evidence of horseplay inside the lab.

He found candle wax atop the steel counter and strange smudges along the floor as though whoever last used the lab did not properly clean it. He knew the lab came clean easily enough, with just a few minutes of work and the correct cleaners.

"Damn it, guys," Briscoe berated his absent colleagues, certain they knew better.

He knew the bag was around somewhere, or someone had broken the golden rule about removing equipment from the lab when it wasn't needed.

No one dared do that, or the coroner would be on them like flies on shit.

To Briscoe's knowledge, there were no bodies currently in the freezer, but he decided to check all eight doors anyhow.

Inside, each compartment held a sliding steel tray, though none were actually divided by any sort of wall. Briscoe opened the first compartment, peering inside, but only seeing to part of the third compartment due to lack of light. He moved down, opening the last top and bottom doors, finding his body bag inside, apparently filled with something.

"Oh, you guys," he said with a shake of his head, figuring someone had thrown a secret Halloween party in the lab he'd missed, then hidden their mess for cleanup later.

Tugging the black bag from the bottom compartment, Briscoe found it heavy until it landed on the floor with a thud.

"Heavy," Briscoe muttered, taking hold of the zipper, prepared to find blackmail material to use against his colleagues for a later date.

He unzipped the bag fully with one swipe, caught a whiff of one horrific smell, and gasped audibly.

"Holy shit," he said, stumbling back until he hit the exam table, falling to a seated position on the floor, stunned from what he had viewed. It would take several minutes to recover before he could phone for investigators.

At least there was no need to call the coroner's office.

*   *   *

No one inside the room could truly keep their cool when the bag was fully unzipped and the body of Larry Kendle was curled up inside, assuming a fetal position. Kendle's suit was wrinkled and soiled with various internal liquids.

Inside one sport coat pocket, and sealed in a plastic bag with an unmarked label were the remains of his testicles, their surrounding tissue, and part of his penis picked up from the floor. They appeared to be marinating in a mix of juices, also cleaned from the tile surface. Every police officer in the room cringed with discomfort when the evidence was viewed.

On more than one level.

"I can't believe this," Mark Daniels said, slumped in a corner stool, staring at the group around his partner. It was all he could do to sit up as nervous shivers ran through his body.

He never envisioned this happening to his partner, or even himself, but now his mortality was laid out before him in a black bag. One simple look at his dead partner broke down Daniels' usually calm, cool demeanor in front of several people he worked closely with.

A blank stare crossed his face, showing the stages of shock, and an inability to cope, that came with someone close to him dying. He didn't care how he appeared, and neither did anyone else in the room, considering they were experiencing the same feeling.

Dressed only in blue jeans, an Indiana University sweatshirt, and tennis shoes, Daniels almost didn't get past the police guard because a new officer failed to recognize the detective. His hair looked somewhat like a bird's nest with strands sticking up in little patches, as he sat, hands nervously in his lap, looking as other detectives performed his usual job, examining his partner with the scrutinizing detail he often used at murder scenes.

"You don't have to be here, Mark," one of the other detectives said. "We've got it under control."

Seeing that Daniels would not budge from the corner, his eyes simply staring intently at the body bag, the detective walked away. Daniels folded his arms, not moving his eyes from Larry Kendle's corpse or the helplessness it seemed to exhibit.

He desperately wanted to step outside for a smoke, but he knew once he left the room they would not let him return, and he was determined not to leave his partner, even in death.

Even if they weren't as close as partners should be.

Maybe it's my fault, Daniels caught himself thinking. If we hadn't been so determined to work on this separately, I would have been there for him. But then the killer would have no reason to target him, he deduced. An array of thoughts and emotions ran through his head, but nothing seemed worth dwelling on at the moment.

Within the examination room, Daniels recognized the coroner, two detectives from his division, a forensic photographer, one detective from the state police, and Ian Briscoe. He could tell Briscoe desperately wanted out of the room, but the state police detective was asking him several initial questions.

Daniels expected some to be asked of him later.

Without him realizing it, his right hand assumed several positions every minute. It would scratch his chin, rub his cheek, set in his lap, and take any number of other positions without him realizing how much nervous fidgeting it did.

Daniels was not thinking like a police officer at the moment. For now, he could only be a supportive partner in the most final sense. His thoughts would only wander to police thoughts occasionally, but they quickly bounced back to Kendle's wife and three children, and how his murder might have been prevented.

For him, the most unfortunate thing was the lack of clues left at this crime scene, and how much that would prolong him in finding the killer when the time came. The one thing Daniels did realize was the nature of the crime and how hateful it appeared.

Insulting Kendle's character by placing the body, and its loose organs the way he had, the killer had set out to write the detective's demise with as much of a humiliating conclusion as possible. Such an end was meant to anger the police, and especially the man's partner.

And it did.

After another fifteen minutes the state police detective approached Daniels, who was simply waiting for an excuse to leave by then. He was too proud to just walk out on his own accord, subconsciously fearing others would say he left his partner when he didn't have to. Daniels had to see it through with Kendle until they laid him to rest.

"Can you go to the post and answer a few questions?" the state detective asked Daniels, looming above the seated man.

"Sure."

*   *   *

After close to an hour of explaining the case to the detective, Daniels finished, lighting a cigarette as the two walked outside the state police barracks. It was time to talk more informally.

"Could this Clouse have killed your partner?" Detective Ben Edwards asked of his fellow police officer.

"Highly unlikely," Daniels said before taking a drag. "If he is involved, he's not the one swinging that scythe."

"Then you think he might be behind it?"

"The more I'm around him, the less likely it seems," Daniels explained. "It would be real hard for anyone to take a beating like he did yesterday, even if he was trying to cover up, and the way his dog was gutted and left hanging, I don't know," the detective said, shaking his head to free it from the gory image it harbored.

"He wouldn't really have any motive in the hotel killings, then, other than trying to remove the suspicion of murdering his wife away from himself."

"Even at that, it would be awful risky to orchestrate so many murders," Daniels explained. "And I doubt anyone would do so many hits for what little he could pay them."

"Are we talking two separate sets of murders then?"

"I don't think so," Daniels noted. "Everything we've gotten back from the lab indicates the same person swung that scythe in every murder, that it's a right-handed male around six feet in height, and that he has at least a fairly strong build. That describes Clouse, but at least a tenth of our city fits that profile."

"Our office will likely take this investigation over," Edwards noted cordially. "Or we might work out a joint effort with your chief."

"I know. I've got a few things coming back from the lab I want to look at, then you guys can have everything. I'll help you however I can."

"Thanks."

Edwards never expected the detective to relinquish control of the investigation so easily, but they both knew Daniels would keep searching for the killer on his own. He felt a sense of responsibility to Kendle, as though he had missed something in the case that might have saved his partner's life.

Daniels said a goodbye to Edwards then walked toward his car, thinking about where to start. He knew the department brass would want him to take time off, which would leave him free enough to investigate the case as he saw fit, with the ability to check on the lab's progress through their photo analysis, and any other evidence in their possession. They would not know he was on leave, and Daniels saw no need to tell them.

Tomorrow he would begin investigating his way.

25

Clouse reached the edge of town in his pickup, anxious to see if any of the computer could be salvaged. The morning paper informed him of Kendle's murder, which failed to impact him deeply, but concerned him for several reasons.

Somehow Clouse knew the killer wanted to implicate him in the murder, because Kendle certainly did not endanger the killer's spree by exclusively investigating the firefighter. Though he did not know the details, Clouse suspected the murder was gruesome and meant to look vengeful, as though he performed it.

Also, it potentially turned Daniels, his only ally of significance, against him, or at least away from finding the truth. This was a last-ditch effort by the killer to keep the public believing Clouse was guilty of murder.

"Where are we going, Daddy?" Zach asked from the passenger seat.

"To see if our computer is fixed," Clouse answered.

After reading the bad news that morning, Clouse took the remains of the computer hard drive to a local dealer, then picked Zach up from his parents' house. He had taken time to clean the house and properly bury his dog, though it disturbed him to see Benny treated like a deer cleaned in hunting season.

That was his favorite dog.

"How did it get broken?"

"It fell on the floor, Zach."

"Grandma said someone bad hurt you. Why would they do that?"

Clouse had to think on a four-year-old level for a moment. There were some things his son just could not be told yet.

"Some people have something wrong with them, Zach," he explained. "They don't like anyone, and they don't know anything but how to hit people and hurt them. I think I made one of those people mad, and he decided to hurt me."

Zach sat for a moment, accepting what he understood of his father's explanation as gospel before asking another question.

"What does gildy mean?"

"Guilty?"

"Yeah."

"It means someone did something wrong, Zach."

Silence.

"Why?" Clouse asked his son.

"Grandma and Grandpa took me out to eat and someone with a newspaper said you were gildy. Did you do something wrong?"

Shit, Clouse thought. It was times like this he missed having Zach in preschool. When he returned to work for the city in a few days, Zach would return to his school, mostly for his own good. Consistent, familiar surroundings would do the boy good, he thought.

"I haven't done anything wrong, Zach, but some people think I'm the one who made Mommy go away. See, the newspaper doesn't always print what's right."

"So they're wrong then?"

"They are," Clouse confirmed, pulling into the parking lot of the computer dealer.

A moment later the fireman and his son walked into a maze of computer tables and glass cases. Toward the back, the owner saw the cause of his most troublesome repair job in recent memory return, and waved Clouse to the back repair area.

"Welcome back," the man said with a smile that indicated he'd managed to do something right for the firefighter.

Clouse saw a complete computer setup along a long table with printer, scanner, monitor, and several other pieces of hardware he was unable to identify. On the screen were several programs and files Clouse recognized from Angie's computer. Perhaps his luck was getting better.

"Good news and bad news," the dealer said. Clouse still didn't know his name. "The chips were so fragile a few of them actually broke when I put them into slots. I managed to salvage most of them, however, and get everything downloaded into my system here."

"Do I need to buy your system?" Clouse joked.

"Not quite," the man replied with an understanding smile. "Using an external drive, I downloaded everything inside my computer onto this disk," the man said, handing Clouse a rather large and sturdy diskette. "Is there anyplace you can use that?"

"I know someone with one of these drives," Clouse replied, thinking of Landamere's computer at the hotel. No one else would be using it.

Clouse walked with the dealer to the counter and paid him.

"Let me know if you need any more help with that," the man said as the firefighter left.

"Will do," Clouse said with a nod, happy he could set to work on finding his attacker.

*   *   *

On the other end of town, Mark Daniels stood across the counter from an old friend in the locksmith business. If anyone knew where the key he took from Dave Landamere's house came from, it would be Lee Colton.

With a stack of locksmith magazines and technical manuals on the shelves behind him, Colton examined the key with a keen eye. Daniels could tell he found it vaguely familiar, but seemed unable to place its origin.

"Safeblock," the locksmith read the name on the key aloud.

As he had expected, Daniels was called in by the police chief, and given a week off from work with pay. Departments bent over backwards to give employees time off with pay because they knew placing stressed employees into work after a traumatic situation sometimes led to potential problems. Sometimes those problems led to lawsuits much greater than one week's pay for any given employee.

Daniels figured he had time to investigate several things on his own that he otherwise might not have, which led him to an old friend.

Colton was one of the few people the detective had known since high school who actually knew what he wanted for a career, stuck with it, and made a good living. With four kids, he apparently had sufficient free time, and the money to support them.

Daniels had never met anyone with such a calm demeanor. The man seldom displayed emotion, and did everything with a deliberate, cautious manner.

His patience was incredible, and in his line of work it needed to be. He never hurried a project. By the same token, he never seemed to err. His product knowledge of locks and keys was the best Daniels had ever seen, even topping forensics experts he'd worked with from much larger departments than his own. The detective had faith his friend would provide an answer much quicker than the heavily burdened state labs.

"What do you think?" he asked Colton, who continued to scrutinize the key.

"Goddamn, it's familiar," the locksmith noted aloud. "Don't know that I've ever seen one of these in person, but it caught my eye in a catalog once," he continued, putting the key down to search for a particular booklet.

Built like a grizzly bear, Colton often intimidated people when he came to fix their lock problems, but Daniels knew the man was far more docile than he appeared.

He could even recall a time when several friends of theirs in high school found fun in taunting a hapless snapping turtle. Despite urging from his friends, Colton would have no part in toying with nature, or a creature that stood no chance against a swarm of teens. He simply objected by standing back and crossing his arms. Eventually the others followed his lead, rather than causing the animal any permanent damage.

Daniels knew Colton as a silent leader. Strong, intelligent, and occasionally witty, the quiet locksmith impressed the detective more as the years passed.

"I don't suppose you ever lose books or files, being the organized police type?" Colton asked, feverishly digging through his magazines for the correct issue.

"No, never," Daniels replied with a sarcastic tone.

At work, everything went through the commanding officer in his division, so organization was easy. At home with a child, however, proved a different story altogether.

"Aha!" the locksmith said after a few minutes, yanking an issue from the bulk stack.

"What have you got?" Daniels asked as his friend flipped through the pages.

"This," Colton said as he folded the magazine over, fronting an advertisement that stumped the detective for a moment. "There's an article about this thing in another magazine, but it'll take me a while to find it."

"Not necessary," Daniels said, staring intently at a large, metal lockbox in the ad.

Shaped much like a footlocker, the box contained several drawers and looked immensely heavy. The box seemed the height of a night stand, but held three drawers controlled by one lock above a bottom drawer, apparently with its own lock. The detective read the features listed on the side, and it seemed to be an impressive invention. Made of a lightweight version of the metal used in safes, the box was dent resistant and portable, with the special cart it came with.

Daniels looked at the cover of the magazine, finding it dated two years prior. He was lucky Colton knew how to keep relevant information handy.

"Did it help?" the locksmith asked.

"I think it did," Daniels replied, certain he saw no such box at Landamere's residence when he visited.

He thought about it, realizing the box was too industrial to be used in the home. It seemed more appropriate in a garage, or perhaps a hotel renovation.

*   *   *

Clouse pulled into the hotel, unsure of what to expect anymore.

He recalled when the job was fun, when he could expect to see Dave Landamere's face within the first few minutes of his arrival, put in several hours of work, and return home to his loving family.

Now he might discover pools of blood, rotted corpses, or his office door kicked in. He no longer enjoyed driving to West Baden. Still, he was drawn to it after spending so many hours laboring there.

Today he needed to be there.

"I thought you weren't coming in," Rusty said as Clouse stepped from his truck, greeted by several unfriendly stares from the construction workers.

Though Rusty now swore his innocence, the workers either refused to buy into it, or just considered Clouse the source of their troubles.

Zach walked around the side of the truck, taking his father's hand.

"I've got to use Dave's computer to read this disk," Clouse replied, holding the diskette firmly. "Any news on Missy yet?"

"Nothing," Rusty said dejectedly. "It's like they both just disappeared. No one's seen her car either."

"I'm sorry to hear that," Clouse said, thinking perhaps no news was good news with two teenagers in love. He wondered if they might have simply run off.

"I've got to check on some of the workers," Rusty noted. "I'll see you inside in a bit."

Clouse nodded, taking Zach toward the hotel entrance. He had little time to waste, considering the impending events building around him. The next evening was the reading of Angie's will, which would bring no surprises to him, considering they had written it out together less than a year before.

State police wanted an interview with him about Larry Kendle's murder. He hoped to be exhumed from guilt, since the murder apparently took place while he was in the hospital. Still, he was the one Kendle had investigated closely for the better part of two weeks, so Clouse again found himself a prime suspect.

Unlocking the new door to Dave Landamere's office, Clouse let himself and Zach inside, closing the door behind them.

With a clean, new look, the office appeared better than before with the exception of Landamere's papers and books stacked randomly in a corner beside the bookshelf. Toward the back of the office stood an antique hutch as high as the ceiling. To the best of his knowledge, the hutch, and the computer hidden inside it, were never touched or damaged during the break-in, or any other time.

While Zach occupied himself with the globe on Landamere's bookshelf, Clouse walked to the hutch, finding it locked.

"Damn," he said under his breath, knowing it was never actually locked before.

He could hear the computer running inside, which was unusual, since it seldom remained on, when not in use. Clouse recalled it being off the last time he left the room and actually checked, which was after Landamere disappeared.

Unfortunately, Clouse did not own a key, which explained his unhappiness with the situation, but more importantly, someone did have a key who should not have, or Landamere had come to check on his computer.

Either way, Clouse needed at the computer.

Luckily the hutch had no back to it, and after a few minutes of mustering all of his strength to move it, Clouse had it far enough out that he could reach inside with a small screwdriver and remove the clip from the lock, letting it fall freely out the front.

Assured nothing was permanently damaged, Clouse opened up the front of the hutch, pulling a chair up to the computer as he turned on the monitor. He could hear the hard drive running heavily. Once the monitor's screen warmed up, Clouse saw the computer downloading information from the internet, but a gray message box blocked his view of whatever crucial information might help him identify who had been using the computer.

Clouse knew Landamere could easily be avoiding people, perhaps vacationing or spending some time at a resort. Maybe he was just checking on the hotel from time to time, assuring himself things were running smoothly.

Just maybe, but that did not sound like the Dave Landamere Clouse knew.

If the project manager was abducted, his captor would have access to his keys and everything Landamere knew. With everything he'd seen so far, Clouse felt obligated to fear the worst, because he trusted Landamere too much to expect anything less than the man's greatest effort on the hotel.

To Clouse, the hotel was probably the greatest feat in his life. He understood Landamere had done all sorts of restoration projects, and even a few major saves like the West Baden Springs Hotel, but he could not picture the man as the type to suffer burnout just as a project neared its end, regardless of what the man's wife, or Rusty, thought.

Carefully working around the message box, Clouse looked for indications of what the computer was being used for. He copied down the information from the website address box and whatever other tidbits he could find in various internet boxes that might prove useful.

He debated momentarily whether or not to break the link to the download, and ultimately decided to, knowing he could print the information from his disk and investigate any downloaded information in the appropriate download file.

"Daddy, this is neat," Zach commented.

He had been talking to himself the entire time, but not directly to his father.

"What have you got, kid?" Clouse asked without removing his eyes from the screen.

Momentarily, Zach presented him with a framed plaque of shiny silver paper containing black type across it. It was presented to Landamere almost a decade prior in Chicago for his contributions on the restoration of an old school, which became a senior citizen activity building.

Did Dave live in Chicago? Clouse wondered. He recalled Landamere mentioning several areas in which he lived prior to Southern Indiana, including one project overseas that lasted almost a year. In such a profession, one could not expect to remain local, due to funding drawbacks and an eventual lack of work.

Landamere was a journeyman manager by design, so it ultimately made sense he had spent time one state over.

"It's cool," Zach said, staring at the shiny paper, probably wanting to color on it.

"Yeah, it is," Clouse replied, holding a different opinion as to why.

He had always assumed Landamere grew up locally, and figured he always returned home when his projects were done. As he thought about it, there seemed little Clouse truly knew about his boss's past. He knew about Landamere's training and his work, but little about his personal life or past.

Within a few minutes Clouse printed the useful information from his disk and began searching the computer hard drive for anything downloaded, but little was legible. He began looking under recently visited websites when the room's door opened.

"Jane," he said as both he and Zach were startled by her presence.

"I was just getting ready to leave for the day when I saw your truck outside," she said. "I hope I'm not interrupting you."

"Just about done," Clouse said, turning to write down the last few sites on the screen.

"Are you getting any closer to the truth?"

"Slowly," he said, taking up the remainder of the papers he would have to sort through later. It would take some time to compare what he had to the new information.

They talked a few minutes about the impending reading of the will, the hotel's progress, and what might happen if Smith decided to sell. Both knew the results would not be good. Smith would be hasty to sell, and probably to the wrong party.

"My brother is an excellent attorney if you need one," Jane suggested.

"I'll keep him in mind," Clouse replied, "but I should be okay."

"Let me know when you're up for breakfast sometime, okay?" Jane said as she headed for the door, knowing he wanted to finish with the computer.

"I will," he said with a sincere grin. "I go back to the fire station in a few days. It's not far from your clinic, you know."

"Good," she said. "Maybe we'll get a chance to talk."

As she left, Clouse turned to click into several more windows, searching for more crucial information about whatever was being downloaded. If Landamere wasn't accessing his computer, someone else was. Clouse realized he was ruining the chance to catch whoever it was. He also knew the police would never monitor the room upon his request, and talking to Daniels was too risky, considering the information he had already kept from the detective.

Clouse's options were limited.

If the police perimeter was as tight as they claimed, and someone gained access to the computer, it meant they were someone who actually belonged at the hotel, or had knowledge of how to evade surveillance. Of course, that person would have to know there was a police presence in the first place, and very few were informed of such.

Clouse finished writing down every shred of information he felt might possibly help him discover the user of the computer, and filed the paper in a manilla folder. Pocketing the external disk, he grabbed his jacket from the chair and stood, turning around too quickly to avoid bumping chests with Ken Kaiser.

"Hey, Paul," the county officer said. "Doing some computing?"

"Mine's broken," Clouse explained, noticing Zach had been too preoccupied with a jigsaw puzzle on Landamere's shelves to see the door open.

"Did it crash?"

"You could say that," the firefighter said, uneasy with the fact Kaiser stood so close to him, using an almost accusatory tone of voice.

Kaiser finally backed up a few steps, allowing Clouse to gather his things and call over to Zach that it was time to go.

"Feeling any better?" Kaiser asked, following him to the door.

"Somewhat. I've been too busy trying to find the killer to really care."

"Getting anywhere?" the county officer asked as both stood at the doorway.

"I guess I'm realizing you can't trust anyone."

"No, you really can't," Kaiser said as though it was a golden rule.

"This job, this hotel was everything I ever dreamed of working on, but now it's just a place where, I don't know, it's-"

"A place where people check in, but they don't check out," Kaiser said in a tone that seemed half joking. "Kind of like that Eagles song, eh?"

Feeling a chill run through his spine, Clouse realized it was past time to leave.

"I've gotta go, Ken," he said to his friend, who suddenly seemed more ominous after uttering the words Clouse had heard over the phone just days prior.

"Take care of yourself, Paul," Kaiser called as Clouse led Zach toward the closest exit. He simply gave a quick glance back.

He only wanted to get home where it was safe to peruse the new information. He was too close to simply give up.

26

Settled beside a warm fire, Clouse reviewed the files lying beside him slowly, looking for any details that might disclose who was using the computer in Landamere's office.

He planned to visit a local copy shop in the morning that rented out computers by the hour, for printing or online access to the net. Several key sites continued to plague him as he read through the dozens of laser printouts.

Zach was tucked in for the evening, leaving Clouse feeling less guilty after finally spending a day with his son. He felt safer keeping Zach close to him, especially now that the killer had made the ordeal personal by attacking him. Kids made easy targets for people with hostile intent, and Clouse had no idea how far the game might escalate.

Most of the information would have to be accessed through the internet when Clouse found a computer to use the next day. Once he plugged in some of the websites, he figured everything would be revealed to him, and he would be that much closer to knowing who was using Landamere's computer.

Hearing a knock at the door, Clouse shoved the papers into a folder, setting them beneath his couch cushion.

"Rodge," he said, finding his brother-in-law at the other side of the door.

"Hey, Paul. Is this a good time to talk?"

"Sure. Come on in."

After the two sat in the family room, Summers talked a few minutes about how he looked forward to working with Clouse again. It was only two days away, but Clouse didn't feel as optimistic about working around his brother-in-law.

"I came to make sure you were ready to get back to work," Summers confessed from the recliner he chose to sit in. "I didn't want them rushing you back or anything."

"I'll be fine, but I'm not so sure it's a great idea to stick us together, Rodge."

"Sure it is. We haven't been stationed together in almost two years."

"It's not that. It'll just look strange is all."

"Come on, brother. I'm not going to let anyone say one bad word about you. Anyone gets out of line, I'll take care of 'em."

Clouse groaned to himself. He wanted to return to work on his own terms, not saddled with an overly protective brother-in-law who would lay his fellow firemen out if they spoke out against either one of them.

"It seems you managed to piss Kelli off," Summers said almost offhandedly.

"That I did."

"You didn't know?"

Clouse's face flushed red.

"No one ever told me. She's been acting kind of strange lately so I confronted her about it."

"She'll be okay. She just couldn't believe you thought that of her."

"Oops," Clouse said apologetically.

"It's okay. When I got out of the service and started looking for a job, I noticed Kelli didn't act the same as she had when we were kids. It took her almost another five years to fess up to me."

Clouse stood to throw another log on the fire.

"Is Kelli going to forgive me?" he asked, returning to his seat.

"Oh, she'll be fine. I think she was just a little shocked at what you thought." Summers shrugged. "We're all pretty tough in our family. I met people in the service who weren't as tough as that girl."

"What branch were you in again?" Clouse inquired, barely recalling it ever mentioned.

"Navy. I was an engineer. I was lucky enough to stay close to home. They always had some projects going in the Midwest."

"You never got shipped overseas?" Clouse asked.

"A couple of times, but never for more than a few months. I had it pretty easy working for the government."

"But you came back home."

"I had some pretty good offers," Summers admitted. "But I'd already tested for the fire department during my leave time, and decided to wait it out until my name reached the top of the list."

For the next few minutes the two talked about how good it would be to get back to work and move on from Angie's death.

"I'd better get home," Summers said, standing up.

"I'll see you at work in a few days, if not tomorrow," Clouse said, walking him to the door.

"Don't sweat it, brother," Summers said reassuringly. "You'll be fine."

I hope, Clouse thought as he watched his brother-in-law climb into his truck to depart.

After closing out the chilly weather, Clouse locked the door and returned to the paperwork at the couch. With a hi-lighter he went through, marking repeated e-mail addresses and websites. Several addresses continued to appear as places where e-mail was forwarded.

"Orangeco," he read one of the e-mail addresses aloud. From the looks of it, the address belonged to someone who worked within Orange County, where Kaiser patrolled.

Of course, Orange County was also where the hotel stood.

He planned on checking the e-mails for a user profile or origin in the morning. Though well before midnight, Clouse decided to turn in early for an early start to the next day.

27

Before heading to the copy store the next morning, Clouse decided to take Zach to Deacon Park, at an old church outside of town.

To entice enrollment in their church, the Church of Christ built an extensive playground and nursery facility to draw families to their location. If nothing else, it seemed to provide more funding for the congregation. Others, like Clouse, simply took advantage of the open playground without joining the church.

Recently remodeled, the church was growing. Clouse remembered Angie wanting to join, because it was relatively close, without the hassle and detachment of a city church. Clouse never took action on the situation, preferring to keep his Sunday mornings to himself around the house with his family.

As Clouse and his son walked to the park from his truck, he spied someone familiar with a swinging girl behind her.

"Jane?" he asked, drawing closer.

"Paul. What brings you here?"

"I've got Zach all day, so I thought we'd hit the park before I do my busywork."

"Katie and I had the same idea," Jane said, looking to her daughter, happily swinging behind her.

While the children began playing together, Jane walked with Clouse over to a nearby picnic table where parents often monitored their children. They took a seat at the table, each waiting for the other to begin a conversation.

Clouse zipped his jacket halfway, stuffing his hands into its pockets as a gusty wind passed through the park. Leaves shook in the trees as their fallen counterparts danced across the barren, hard ground.

"Are you any closer to what you need?" Jane asked.

"Getting there. Sorry if I seemed distracted yesterday."

Jane looked over to the children, who seemed to be enjoying the merry-go-round as they pushed it to a high rate of speed and jumped on, pretending to cling for dear life. Smiling and laughing, they didn't have a care in the world, unlike their parents.

"They're a handful, aren't they?" Clouse wondered aloud.

"Katie certainly is. She's always wanting to do something, or be somewhere."

"Do you have custody?" Clouse asked, breathing on his hands for warmth.

Jane gave a look of disdain in no particular direction as she thought out her answer.

"Her father sees her once every three or four weeks, and that's his choice."

"I see."

"It doesn't help that she asks about Daddy all the time and wonders why he isn't there for her soccer games and karate lessons," Jane said with a disgusted tone. "He's too busy with his projects in other states."

Clouse began to ask what her ex-husband did for a living, but thought better of it. He felt his face begin to flush from the cold wind's assault, and decided to limit how long Zach stayed outside.

"This weather is horrible," he commented.

"It's supposed to be a rough winter. I'll bet that makes for some long days at the fire station."

"It can," Clouse replied. "It's bad enough to begin with, then the water and cold mix for some dangerous conditions. It doesn't take long for the cold to eat through our gear when it gets wet."

Both sat silently a moment, watching the children play on the slides, then the swings.

"Is that detective getting any closer to finding out who killed your wife?" Jane finally asked.

"Haven't really spoken to him lately. Unless he finds forensic evidence, he won't have any more than I do."

"Maybe something will turn up."

"Maybe," Clouse said doubtfully. "So, it looks like you won't be doing any tours for a while."

"I heard they're shutting the renovation down again so that foreman can search for his daughter. I got the call last night."

"And with me returning to the fire department, they really don't have anyone to manage the construction until Dave Landamere comes back."

Jane gave a quizzical stare.

"Don't you mean *if* he comes back?"

"I think he will," Clouse said. "He's done this sort of thing before."

"But never at such a bad time, has he?"

Clouse shrugged. "I suppose we'll find out soon enough where he's been."

He felt terrible leaving the construction by the wayside, but he had a career to return to, and the hotel was not a safe place for anyone to be, even the police who performed the surveillance. Now, to his understanding, there would be no one working security at the hotel, leaving it entirely unprotected.

Though Clouse hated the idea of an abandoned hotel, he considered human life more important than steel beams and concrete.

After the kids had played a little longer, Clouse decided to begin his errands. He called to Zach, said a goodbye to Jane, and headed for his truck. A full day of activities awaited him.

*   *   *

Despite his week of leave from the police department, Daniels felt obligated to check for mail and messages in his office.

Wearing everyday attire, he walked into the investigations office, seeing few of his colleagues sitting at their desks. The few who weren't at lunch shifted their eyes in other directions when they saw the young detective walk into the office.

Daniels felt uncertain of exactly what they were thinking. Blame could be placed on him for not being closer to Kendle, or they might have simply felt bad because it could just as easily have been their partner killed on an assignment gone wrong.

Ignoring the cold shoulders, Daniels walked to his desk, which appeared just as orderly as he had left it, except for several sheets of paper and a large envelope in the center. The first two messages were inconsequential, but the third, from Dave Landamere's wife, appeared more important. He read, then reread it, thinking he was mistaken.

"David called and spoke to me briefly yesterday," he read it aloud. "Thought you would like to know."

Surrounded by quotation marks, the officer had obviously taken the message verbatim over the phone. Daniels decided to speak with Joan Landamere immediately, but not over the phone. He wanted another opportunity to scope out the grounds and house as much as possible.

As he walked out of the office, Daniels again tried making eye contact with the other detectives, but there was none returned. He slipped his index finger beneath the envelope's flap, prying it open as he reached the stairwell leading down.

He sauntered down the stairs amongst dim lighting, pulling an enlarged and computer-enhanced photo from the envelope, which had arrived from the state police lab that morning.

"That was fast," he commented to himself, pushing the door open to the main floor. Once in better light, he observed the photograph better.

He was amazed how well the lab technicians had removed the blurriness and regained clarity, simply by using a computer. He knew the state bought programs that were ahead of the common market, and Daniels felt this program was one of their better purchases.

Standing beneath a recessed light, the detective peered at the area in question on the killer's calve muscle. Though still rather dark in color, Daniels made it out to be a tattoo of some sort. Much of it seemed to be cut off, but the edge he saw appeared to be part of a shamrock, or perhaps the edge of a cross. The photo did little for him except verify that it was a tattoo, which enabled him to eliminate suspects rather easily if he could verify they had no artwork on the bottom of their right leg.

Feeling a bit more confident with new evidence, Daniels walked outside, strolling across the street to his Honda. Opening the door, he felt a strong wind hit him in passing, as though to indicate winter was closing in. He stepped in the car, starting it, fully unaware someone in a parked car across the street monitored his every move.

*   *   *

Clouse considered himself the most unlucky person on the planet. As he stared into a nearly blank screen, he felt completely dejected.

Neither e-mail address turned up a profile or any sort of true origin. The first three common websites Clouse had found seemed to lead to nothing, because they were mere subdirectories for a larger site. His search ended there in all three instances.

While Zach contented himself with building blocks in a children's area outside the computer bay, Clouse cursed himself for not being able to find anything concrete, with so much information already provided. Worse yet, he may have blown the only chance he had to discover who was using Landamere's computer, especially now that the hotel was closed off to everyone.

He searched through the printouts again, looking for any key words he might have missed the night before. Knowing how tired he had been, it might have been easy to overlook something as simple as one key word or an address.

"Tincher Incorporated," he said, finding it five sheets later amongst a pile of paragraphs and gibberish. It would have been easy to ignore the night before in a state of fatigue.

Clouse quickly typed in the website, finding the same images and text as before with an Illinois base-of-operations. He jotted down every shred of information the site provided him, opening every possible window, noting every project the company had claimed to work on, and the organizations it claimed to have worked with.

The more he wrote, the more Clouse convinced himself the company was a sham, explaining why he had never heard of it before one week ago.

He recalled giving his information to the company the day before he was severely beaten, and his house ransacked. Clouse touched his ribs for proof of the pummeling he had taken. They were nowhere near fully healed, but he could breathe normally again. He knew exactly who to call, and where to check on the legitimacy of Tincher Incorporated. It would take just a few phone calls to some people who owed him favors.

Armed with a new source of information, Clouse closed down the computer, took up his folder of papers, and walked to the front counter to pay for his computer time. As he called Zach over from the play area, his cellular phone rang.

"Hello," he answered.

"Paul, it's Mark Daniels."

"Hi, detective. I wasn't expecting to hear from you this soon."

"Just have a question for you."

"Shoot," Clouse said, handing his credit card to the unhappily employed teenager on the other side of the counter.

"What kind of tattoos do you have?" Daniels asked pointedly, leaving the question open-ended on purpose.

"I don't have any," Clouse answered quickly enough to assure the detective he wasn't lying. "Any reason?"

Daniels hesitated, knowing what he was about to do went against his training and standard police policy. Then again, Clouse was probably the most useful source of information he had, since he could reasonably be eliminated as a suspect.

"If I send you a copy of a photo I received back from the lab today, do you think you might be able to identify some body art for me?"

"I can try. You think I'm into some weird stuff, don't you?"

"No, it's not that," Daniels explained. "I have a feeling you may know the person responsible for the murders and just don't realize it. There's what I believe to be a tattoo in this photo. Where can I send it?"

Clouse took his credit card back from the counter person and signed the receipt, taking Zach's hand as he left the copy center.

"Well, my computer's broken," he said, exiting through the sliding glass doors. "You could fax it to the fire department and I could pick it up later."

Daniels considered that a bit too public, but no one would probably understand what significance a photo of a leg meant anyhow, especially if he didn't accompany it with any vital information.

"Okay," Daniels agreed. "Give me the number."

Clouse stopped to pull his fire department work calendar from his wallet, then gave the detective the fax number.

"I'll take a look and see if it's familiar," Clouse said. "You think the killer's in this photo?"

"Almost certain, so get back to me if you find something out. I don't want you holding out on me," Daniels warned, airing his suspicions.

"I won't," Clouse promised.

Daniels clicked on his phone's talk button and looked to the Landamere house before stepping out of his car. He surveyed the grounds his entire walk up the driveway, seeing little that might lead him to the whereabouts of the lockbox he sought. He could see no storage shed, and their garage was used to keep their vehicles, not as a workshop.

Before he even reached the front door, it opened, revealing Joan Landamere.

"Hello, detective. I didn't expect such personal attention."

"I wanted to see you in person because I have a few questions for you," Daniels replied, following her inside.

She led him to the living room where they both took a seat on opposite sofas.

"I suppose you want to know what David said when he called?"

"That would be a start."

"He said very little really except that he was out of town and expected to be back within the week. He said there was a project he'd worked on previously that needed some attending to."

"I find it difficult to believe it was too inconvenient for him to let any of his staff know about this," Daniels said somewhat scornfully. "Did he act artificial perhaps, as though someone was forcing him to say those things to you?"

"Not particularly, but David is a rather dry speaker to begin with. If you're implying that someone would abduct him, I seriously doubt it. There's no sensible reason to keep him hostage."

"Not to you and I perhaps, Mrs. Landamere, but one never knows these days."

Walking to the kitchen, Joan pulled a kettle from the stove, pouring a cup of coffee for herself, and another for her guest, almost as though she had expected him. Daniels thought back to several mystery movies he'd watched where guests were poisoned by their hosts, often through coffee or tea. He quickly shook off the notion.

"Did you have another question for me?" she asked, handing him a cup of coffee. "Sugar or cream?" she questioned before he could reply.

"Cream," he answered. "Does your husband have a storage box around here with a bottom drawer that locks separately? It would be a fairly large unit."

"Is it metallic, with about five drawers total?"

"It is."

"He keeps it at the hotel, full of things he doesn't want me to see, I suspect," she replied as though it might contain dirty magazines or things husbands knew their wives hated them having. Daniels could relate from his own marital experience.

Hesitantly, the detective took a mild sip of the coffee before setting it on the coffee table in front of him. He berated himself for being so suspicious, but decided it was time to go.

"I hate to rush off, but I've got a lot of ground to cover, Mrs. Landamere."

"You do what you have to," she said, much like he remembered his grandmother doing. Daniels remembered hating it when she put guilt trips on him as a teenager, as though he was always abandoning her. "You're welcome to drop by anytime."

"There's nothing else you can think of?" he asked as they strolled toward the front door.

"No. Nothing stands out."

"If you think of anything, even if it seems insignificant, please call me."

"I certainly will," she replied, opening the door for him.

"Thanks for your time, Ma'am."

Daniels felt compelled to check on the box at the hotel, despite the nagging feeling he was walking into a dangerous situation. Like Clouse, he felt there was no one left to trust. There were still too many suspects and not enough clues for him to narrow it down.

He hoped to reach the hotel before dark and discover some new evidence in the box, assuming he could find it.

28

Daniels was surprised to see the mammoth archway gate of the West Baden Springs Hotel lit by a great number of bulbs when he pulled up to the front entrance. He expected everything about the hotel to be shut down, and dead in appearance.

Including the lights.

From the road he spied no one on the grounds. Several antique lamp posts along the brick path leading to the hotel were lit, and the arch entrance held no physical impeding gate, so he would have easy access walking to the hotel. If what he heard was accurate, there would be no security posted anywhere at the hotel, but the doors would be locked.

After befriending locksmith Lee Colton for so long, Daniels knew several tricks about entering buildings without detection, and leaving no signs he was there. Colton let him borrow several lock picks for just such an occasion with the knowledge of how to use them efficiently.

Daniels felt terrible about breaking and entering, but he had no intent to steal. He simply wanted to observe, and search for the final pieces of the most difficult puzzle he'd ever been asked to solve. Without department backing, he was desperate to find his partner's killer and put an end to the senseless slaughter before more people wound up dead or missing.

No matter the cost.

At the end of the brick walkway, Daniels stared up at the looming building. Two of the four giant towers appeared to stare back.

Behind them the dome glistened with its curved glass fixtures and painted black frames.

An eerie orange glow emitted from the horizon, indicating within minutes it would be fully dark outside. Daniels wanted access to the hotel before nightfall so he could find the lights inside and make his way around the hotel with ease. He already knew how to reach the basement and storage areas, but turning on sources of light would prove more difficult if he could not see.

Daniels reached the first set of steps leading to the main entrance, catching a whiff of some foul odor in the wind. The smell, to him, was that of death. He had worked enough homicides, and grown up around enough hunters, to know what a dead carcass smelled like. He turned to look at the cemetery in the direction the smell emanated from, saw nothing out of the ordinary, and turned to the double glass entrance doors atop the steps.

A form of deadbolt lock blocked his way to the inside but he was prepared with some helpful advice from Colton.

Within two minutes he had successfully used lock picks to steadily get inside the lock and move the metal bar toward him, unlocking the door. He replaced the picks to their case, then stuffed them in his jacket pocket before letting himself in.

"God only knows how I'll lock that up," he muttered to himself.

Stepping inside the main lobby, Daniels looked up to the balcony, then past an arch, into the atrium where half the rooms overlooked the floor where so many social gatherings had occurred over the years. He was amazed at how many of the lights were turned on, able to lead him down any path he chose.

He chose to visit the basement and look for Landamere's chest.

Daniels began to understand why the construction workers referred to the basement as the dungeon. Beneath the hotel it was much colder and damp, suited only for the tools they stored there.

He made his way along the dusty concrete floor, looking cautiously around him, seeing nowhere a person might leap out and ambush him. Daniels felt very uneasy entering the hotel, and especially this target area alone, under such conditions.

Various cabinets and doors stood along the walls of the basement, making Daniels' search even more complicated. He suspected the trunk would be found by itself, not surrounded by power tools or building materials. He looked along the floor for the most traveled paths, noticing one particular door had little or no foot traffic leading to it, while the others appeared significantly used.

Daniels prepared to take the pick set from his jacket, but found the door unlocked. He opened it, patting the wall down for a light switch. He found it a few seconds later, illuminating a nearly empty storage room. The only object inside the room was a large metallic storage box, exactly like the one he was searching for.

"Too damn easy," he muttered to himself, his suspicions of foul play reaching a new height.

Digging for the key in his pants pocket, the detective walked toward the box, looking around the room to assure he was alone. Wasting no time, Daniels knelt down at the foot of the box, becoming oblivious to everything around him except the lock, and the key he was about to place inside it.

Before he truly conceived turning the key, the drawer popped open and Daniels realized his mind was not where it should be. He was so consumed with solving the case, his actions superceded his thought process.

Pulling the drawer open, Daniels let the faint light of the room reveal a blanket covering several unidentified objects. Slowly, he pulled the blanket toward him, revealing a soft pad taking up most of the bottom drawer's space with an indentation across it.

An indentation shaped much like that of a scythe blade.

"Shit," Daniels thought aloud. "If it's not here, where is it?"

For a moment, he remained knelt beside the box, looking to the door, listening intently. Nothing broke the silence, so he started toward the door to leave the room, almost convinced Dave Landamere was behind the killings to obtain the hotel for himself.

It made perfect sense for him to draw Clouse into his confidence, learn everything about the man, and use him as a pawn in a scheme to obtain the property potentially worth a small fortune.

Now he had some circumstantial evidence to back his theory.

Daniels carefully headed toward the door, anxious to exit the hotel grounds and return in the morning for some further explanation. He wanted to contact the state police, who were now handling the investigation, to inform them of a tip he had just received about a certain box in the basement of the hotel.

Leaving obscure clues with the new investigative team was about the only power he had left.

Locking the hotel doors and returning the box's key to Landamere's study were issues he could deal with easily enough. Creating the perfect story, complete with evidence to hand the state police investigators would prove more difficult. Daniels had obtained some of his evidence illegally in the eyes of the court, which would let the killers escape courtroom justice if the case came to that.

As he ascended the stairway toward the main floor, the detective heard several shrill screams and a plea for mercy from a distance. It was a woman's voice, and he thought it sounded much like Joan Landamere, after just visiting with her.

Hurried, but cautious, Daniels reached the top of the staircase, stopping to listen for more screams.

They came once again to his right.

He reached behind him, pulling his duty weapon from the back of his pants where it was tucked. Keeping close to the inside wall of the circular hallway, Daniels continued to listen for any noises, occasionally hearing a few to pull him forward. It seemed as though he was heading toward one of the small corridors leading into the main atrium.

He rounded another bend, finding the corridor, then spotting Joan Landamere lying at the threshold of the atrium entrance. Running to her, he felt for a pulse, discovering she was only unconscious, a few drops of blood under her nose.

Glancing to his right, he found a green staircase leading up to the second floor, and an elevator adjacent to it.

A ring from the elevator sent Daniels dashing to its side, waiting for the door to open. His back almost pressed against the staircase, the detective pointed the firearm at the elevator door, waiting for it to open. He hoped it would reveal the perpetrator of every crime he had dealt with the past two weeks, and the entire ordeal could end.

It didn't.

Just as the doors opened, Daniel raised his weapon, unable to see someone descend the stairs behind him, just far enough to have a solid swing at him with a wooden-handled weapon. Too focused on the contents of the elevator, Daniels would have needed to look completely behind him to see the figure standing there, ready to swing down at him.

"Damn it," the detective uttered before the small gardening shovel connected with the back of his head, creating a loud clank before he fell face down on the floor.

29

Clouse considered his first morning back to work fairly mundane, much as he expected.

After the usual truck check and cleaning, he was free to do as he pleased. It was an administrative holiday, so there would be no training, and most of the firefighters were sitting around, watching television upstairs in the living quarters, or working out downstairs, but Clouse found solitude in the game room beside the pool table with his list of things to check, and his cellular phone.

What he was discovering through several phone calls, was that Tincher Incorporated had existed less than a year under that name.

It seemed the construction company was indeed real, but there were no known current projects, and none of the listed contact people could be found. Clouse wondered how the company expected to prove legitimacy to buy the hotel, if no one could be contacted.

He smelled trouble.

Clouse had asked one of his contacts to cross-reference the jobs Tincher claimed to have done, to jobs done by other companies and individuals. The results would be one solid way of proving legitimacy, or the fraudulent nature of the company.

Due to the Chicago connection, and Landamere's previous experience, Clouse expected to find jobs done by Landamere under an old company name. He was beginning to piece together the likely scenario for the hotel's takeover.

Apparently Landamere wasn't happy with just managing the construction job. He wanted the property for himself, and intended to bring it down to his price range.

No one else made sense as the killer, at this point.

Clouse wondered why Landamere would want the property. There was millions of dollars worth of renovation yet to be done, and the upkeep alone would be more than the project manager could afford on his salary. There had to be something more to the plan that Clouse had yet to find.

Long ago, the hotel had harbored antiques and art worth a fair amount, but even selling those would never equate the funds necessary to fund a working hotel.

Royalty had visited the grounds at one time, and legends of the jewels and gems they left as gifts passed down through several generations, but the notion they could still be somewhere on the grounds seemed unfathomable to the firefighter.

"What are you working on?" Summers asked, walking into the game room.

"Checking on some construction companies," Clouse replied a half-truth.

"Looking for a new job?" Summers inquired, picking the pool table's balls from the corner pockets.

He gathered them on one side of the table before racking them, much to Clouse's dismay.

All morning long, Summers had kept his brother-in-law within eyeshot. Clouse didn't need protection from his fellow firefighters, nor did he feel alienated. He kept to himself for a specific reason, and as long as his associates made the necessary phone calls, it would pay off. Clouse was trusting no one, because people tended to talk, and he knew what could happen when people talked.

While Summers practiced his pool shots, Clouse buried his nose in the papers, searching for overlooked evidence. He was waiting for several important phone calls, with little else to do but bide his time. He thought of something he needed to do, stood, and stuffed the folded papers into his back pocket.

"Where are you going?" Summers asked almost defensively as Clouse walked out of the room.

"I'll be right back, Rodge."

A moment later he returned with shoe polish and an old T-shirt he used as a rag to shine his station shoes. Clouse preferred shiny shoes like military personnel wore, so they were easy to clean. Seldom was polish necessary but he occasionally took the time to spiff them up.

He took his shoes off, opened the cap of black shoe polish and scooped the rag into the polish when the dispatch tones went off.

Without a word, he and Summers looked at one another and started toward the door. Clouse quickly stuffed his papers under a chair cushion before rushing toward the pole where he followed Summers to the truck room below, feeling the brass pole between his arms and legs for the first time in several months. All the other stations Clouse had worked at recently were single story.

Clouse reached the ground wondering how he would react in a fire scene again, or if this was an actual fire. According to the dispatcher it was a reported working fire, but so many times the trucks were called back to the station after just a few minutes because of false alarms. As he stepped into his protective boots and took hold of his bunker coat, Clouse sensed this wasn't one of those cases.

He was right.

Five minutes later he found himself standing in the middle of a burning feed store on the south end of town. He, Summers, and two other firefighters stood in the middle of the room armed with an attack hose line and two pike poles. Clad in full gear and breathing apparatus, they were ready to face the challenge before them.

Clouse and Terry Jarvis, the other firefighter riding the pumper truck with him that day, used the charged hose line to down the growing flames before they consumed the entire store. Summers and his partner, Gary Pierce, were riding the ladder truck, which meant they were extra manpower in this instance.

Using the pike poles, they tore down accessible areas of the wall, allowing the water to penetrate and kill off any smoldering areas. The fire itself seemed to provide little threat to property, as most of it was contained within a minute, but parts of it had climbed into the ceiling, making their job a bit tougher.

Made entirely of wood, the feed store carried bags of grain, pellet feed, and lots of hay. Not quite half had been ablaze, making it possible to save the store if the firefighters contained the rogue flames. Summers worked diligently, breaking apart the thin wooden boards along the walls. As Clouse helped Jarvis man the hose, he heard an officer shouting orders behind them, before heading outside to check the progress of the other crew.

Clouse watched as several flames danced atop the baled hay in front of him, sneaking in from behind the bales where water had not reached. Water streamed in from a hose line above, cascading from the roof to help extinguish the various sets of fires below. Clouse turned the hose several times against different flames inside the building that seemed to cling to life. He knew fire would continue to survive, unless thoroughly soaked, or robbed of oxygen.

There were already too many cracks and crevices in the structure to deplete its air supply.

After making a round with the hose, Clouse and Jarvis paused a moment to remove their face masks, now that visibility was much better and the smoke had thinned out with help from the ejector fans. They traded places so Clouse had to take a break from the nozzle, which got somewhat heavy pumping hundreds of gallons per minute. Supporting the hose for the front man wasn't much easier, but he knew his forearms would feel better in the morning if he wasn't wrestling the nozzle the entire time.

Hearing no activity to his left, Clouse looked over, seeing his brother-in-law standing there, holding the pike pole at his side, simply staring at him. He waited a few seconds, wondering if Summers might be waiting for a cue from him to come help, but it never came.

Summers had stood there too long to be taking a break, and no one had come to relieve his crew yet, so he was technically abandoning his duty.

Clouse quickly analyzed the stare. It looked as though Summers stared right through him, as though Clouse had somehow severely wronged him. Clouse sensed his brother-in-law was pondering whether or not to do something. He wondered if he was the object in question, or if Summers simply happened to be eyeing his direction.

"What's the matter, Rodge?" another firefighter finally asked, catching Summers' attention.

As though shaking off a trance, Summers immediately set to work helping his fellow firefighters destroy the blaze with a second attack line that had been dragged in, sending water streams everywhere they were needed. Few could man a hose as well as Summers. He had both good size and natural instincts when it came to putting out fires.

Clouse set to work again, keeping Summers in the back of his mind. Perhaps his self-doubts were misguided, and Summers was the one who needed more time off. And perhaps putting them together wasn't such a good idea. Clouse knew his job required continuous focus and attentiveness to one's surroundings. Summers knew it too, yet something else was enough to distract him from a fire, sometimes a life-threatening situation.

Clouse wondered what it was.

*   *   *

An hour later the firefighters settled back into the station. It took more time to clean up than it did to actually put the fire out.

Clouse recognized the unique odor fire scenes left in his bunker gear, but he actually felt happy to have it back. He took off his gear, setting it beside the truck, which dripped water from several areas. The trucks usually left puddles beneath them from the overfill in their water tanks.

Down to his station gear, minus shoes, Clouse started toward the door leading up to the living quarters when Jerry Guinn, the deputy chief, stopped him for a moment, handing him two sheets of paper. He was dressed in gear suitable for fishing, particularly on an administrative holiday.

"These came for you yesterday," he informed Clouse.

"By the time I got here yesterday the office was closed," the fire-fighter replied. "Thanks, Chief," he added. Guinn simply gave a playful salute and headed out the back door, apparently finishing whatever business had brought him into the administrative office for the day.

He was one of the few officers who knew how to have fun, Clouse thought. He had missed the deputy chief the day before because the office closed early for a presentation on the Indiana University campus. It had already been closed when Daniels faxed over the sheets.

As he climbed the stairs Clouse looked at the cover sheet which said little more than nothing, then to the darkened black and white copy of the original photograph Daniels had possession of. Clouse studied it a moment, trying to make out what the photograph was supposed to be, before figuring out what Daniels was talking about.

"Damn," Clouse said, realizing what the photo was when he saw the handle of the scythe and the mostly-cloaked leg of the figure.

Like Daniels, he suspected this was Bennett's death.

Clouse reached the top step, almost hit by the door leading to the living quarters as one of the firefighters swung it open to head down.

"Sorry," the man said after Clouse barely caught the door in time to save his face from being rammed.

As he walked through the quarters toward the locker room, Clouse found better light by which to study the copy. He began to make out part of the tattoo, but it was difficult to confirm, due to the darkness of the paper.

Clouse walked into the locker room subconsciously wanting a shower, but still too intent on the photograph to undress. After a few minutes the edge of the body art began to take shape for him and he realized there were edges, and they appeared to be rounded, but Clouse felt almost certain it was a flaw in the original photo because he knew tattoos could distort from a side view with bodily curvatures.

"Could be a cloverleaf," he said doubtfully under his breath, stepping toward the bathroom, realizing there was only one person he knew with a tattoo on the backside of his leg.

"Or a Maltese Cross," he thought aloud, looking at the one tattooed on the right leg of his brother-in-law, who was standing in front of a sink, covered only by a towel as he combed his hair, now that his shower was over.

For a moment, Clouse simply stared, much like Summers had toward him at the fire scene. He asked himself what seemed like a thousand times why his brother-in-law would commit such heinous acts.

There were no ready answers, and Clouse felt compelled to ask Daniels for more proof before he questioned Summers. Somehow it all seemed to fit, yet Clouse couldn't bring himself to believe the man who was like a big brother to him would kill so many people he worked with and cared for.

He looked to the red and gold Maltese Cross permanently etched on Summers' right calve muscle. It seemed ironic someone who wore a symbol depicting protection, worn as a badge of honor, was capable of cold-blooded murder.

"Need something, Paul?" Summers asked, apparently over whatever had bothered him at the fire scene.

"Just seeing if a shower was free," Clouse replied. He stuffed the fax in his back pocket, unbuttoning his shirt. "What kind of engineering did you do in the Navy, Rodge?"

"Structural, brother," Summers replied, turning from the mirror. "We built stuff."

"Oh," Clouse said, satisfied with the answer.

"You sure you're okay?" Summers asked, apparently taking notice of how apathetic Clouse appeared, because mild shock still overwhelmed him.

"I'm fine," Clouse said, undoing the last button on his shirt. "I think I'm going to do a workout before I shower though."

Summers nodded before heading into the locker room to put his station attire back on.

A few minutes later Clouse stood downstairs, locked in a restroom with his cell phone, desperately wanting to talk to Daniels.

"What do you mean he didn't come to work this morning?" Clouse asked the detective who answered the phone at the police station. "Did he call in?"

"No, I don't believe he did," the detective said, sounding more than a bit concerned. "He just never showed up."

"And you didn't bother calling him at home?" Clouse asked, somewhat irritated at the lack of forthcoming information.

"I'm sure they tried."

"His number's not listed. Any chance I could get it to give him a ring?"

"Sorry," the detective said. "We can't give out that kind of information, but I'll give him a call, and leave him a message if you want."

"Okay, thanks," the fireman said, hanging up before he said something he might regret to the detective.

Whether the man was unwilling to give out anything remotely personal concerning Daniels, or just a moron, eluded Clouse, but it was already apparent something bad might have happened to his only true protector.

Clouse knew Daniels well enough to believe the man would never skip work without calling in first. He knew of only one place the detective might have gone that would have placed him in danger.

And Clouse had no way of getting there until morning.

He stepped out from the bathroom, literally running into his station's captain.

"Sorry, Captain," Clouse quickly apologized.

"Paul, are you sure you didn't come back too soon?" the older man asked, genuinely concerned. "Rodge says you acted kind of strangely at the feed store fire."

Clouse found it odd his brother-in-law would say that, when it was Summers acting out of character.

"Maybe I am still a bit distracted," Clouse told a half truth, hoping the captain would take the bait.

"I don't need you endangering yourself or the others if you're not mentally ready to do this job. I'm going to call someone in and give you the rest of the day off."

Clouse was overjoyed inside, but couldn't let it show.

"You sure, sir?"

"Yeah. Get your gear and I'll see you in two days."

Clouse nodded.

As the captain left, he took the fax from his back pocket, crumpled it up, and walked outside to the dumpster behind the station, tossing it in. As he walked back inside Clouse looked up to the second story, seeing his brother-in-law looking down upon him. Summers had seen him toss the sheet of paper, but probably had no idea what it was.

Anxious to leave the station, Clouse did not bother to retrieve the fax. He simply wanted to locate Daniels and get some concrete answers.

Without saying a word to the others, he gathered up his belongings upstairs and headed away from the station feeling empty inside. The world around him felt like it was caving in, and his guts hurt from anxiety. He hated not knowing the answers, feeling as though Daniels had left him hanging. Clouse had a fleeting thought the detective could simply be toying with him, hoping Clouse would reveal some break in the case to make it easy.

He now trusted Daniels, and knew better deep down.

As Clouse pulled into his driveway, the sun began to set, leaving a strange glow across the fields surrounding his house. After a change of clothes he would head to the hotel, and hopefully find some answers.

30

Dressed in more familiar attire, Clouse pulled his truck up the hotel drive, seeing a county police car parked near the hotel's main entrance, when his truck's headlights panned across the vehicle.

He still felt wary about who to trust and how accurate Daniels' information was. He remembered Kaiser echoing the very same words the killer used the day Clouse's house was ransacked and he was beaten half to death.

He had also spied Daniels' car parked at the front gate, glad his hunch was correct, but worried for the detective's safety. There were still a number of possibilities running through Clouse's mind as to who the killer might be. Daniels was the one person he trusted by default. The detective could not have been present during all of the murders, due to his job.

As his boots hit the ground, Clouse closed his truck door, zipped up his jacket and recognized a smell crossing the sunken garden with the breeze. Perhaps he now knew the smell of death too well, but the fireman felt sure it could be no other odor. Though he barely saw it through the few overhead lights on the grounds, the cemetery sat across the garden.

Climbing the stairs to the main entrance doors, Clouse noticed the wind pick up as though the sky might let loose with precipitation. It seemed deathly cold for rain, and too gusty for snow, but hail or sleet might be possible, he thought.

It also seemed fitting.

Clouse tugged lightly on the entrance doors when he reached the hotel's balcony, expecting them to be locked. He wasn't really surprised when they opened, leaving him extremely wary of what to expect inside.

He walked inside slowly, noticing the lights seemed to be turned on selectively. He could see his way to the atrium, but barely. It was like being in a haunted house, only without any sense of fun. Clouse walked carefully, unsure of what to expect or who he might find, dead or alive. He fought back an urge to turn back only because he wanted assurance Daniels was safe.

Zach was safe at preschool, Jane was at work, and no one else Clouse knew would be in danger except the detective. Ordinarily, Clouse would not be so concerned, but Daniels was the one person who believed in his innocence when no one else did. The fireman felt obligated to return the favor, putting his neck on the line the way the detective had for him.

As Clouse stepped further into the lobby, he spied a glimmer from the floor, created by a single row of bulbs along the second floor balcony, selectively turned on above him. After standing frozen a moment, Clouse shivered in realization, moving closer to the pool of blood in front of him.

Drawing nearer, the firefighter realized it was more than just blood as a body came into view. He could make out a torso, legs, and shined shoes at the very end.

But there was no head.

Gasping, Clouse took a step back with a deep breath to regain his composure, praying it wasn't his high school friend. Even rescue runs on the fire department never prepared him for something as horrific as finding a dead friend. Seeing a corpse usually did little to phase him.

Knowing such an act on any human being was intentional, chilled him to the bone.

"Damn," Clouse said, reluctantly kneeling near the body for a closer look, careful to avoid the pool of blood where the head had been.

He felt the brown vinyl jacket, looked at the uniform pants, and knew it was a county officer. Lying backside up, the body yielded no clues of who it might be. Warmth emitted from the torso, implying the death was quite recent. The pool of blood came mostly from the neck, but there was a large tear in the jacket with blood bubbling upward.

Clouse figured the officer never saw the blade coming. He also suspected the beheading was done posthumously to intimidate Clouse further upon his arrival.

It worked.

He wanted to know whether it was his friend or not, but figured knowing might scare him out of the hotel completely. Clouse refused to turn the body over to look at the name plate.

Stepping over the headless corpse, he found the service weapon missing from its holster.

"So much for sense of security," he thought aloud, hoping to have found some form of protection from the fallen officer.

Clouse continued down the hallway, unable to see much except dim light bulbs ahead. He heard the footsteps from his boots echo down the hallway, wondering who else heard them. As he passed an open door, something brushed against him.

Whirling to see what it was, the fireman gasped again as the stiff body of Robert Bennett hung from two ceiling hooks in front of the door. Clouse looked at the blood-covered body, stumbling backwards as he did so.

Two sharp hooks pierced the shoulders of Bennett, giving him the appearance of a beef slab, hung for storage. Bennett was fully clothed, but somewhat dirty, as though stored in a basement, or maybe a pile of dirt. The skin appeared ghostly pale, even in low light, and a creaking sound emitted from the hooks where they screwed into the ceiling.

He had only met the electrician once, but remembered Bennett, who spent more than an hour touring the entire facility with Landamere and himself. Soon after that Bennett had started his work, then disappeared.

Clouse stared, continuing to back up until he felt another bump from behind.

"Shit!" he exclaimed, turning to see Vern, the grounds keeper, hung by the neck from the ceiling, a small gardening shovel still stuck in his abdomen with dried, crusted blood along its edges and his clothing.

His eyes were still open as though asking what he deserved to die for, while a dried trickle of blood streamed from his mouth. He appeared as discontent in death as he had life. Clouse never liked the man, but knew he deserved better than the death he received.

Wanting to avoid any more bodies, Clouse hurried his walk down the hall toward the beam of light crossing the hallway from the atrium entrance. At least in the center of the atrium he would be able to see in every direction with ample light, and guard himself from all sides. The area was too big for anyone to surprise him.

He approached the light carefully, looked around the corner, and saw a grand spectacle awaiting him from a distance.

"Dear God," Clouse muttered, horrified, yet obligated to walk inside for a closer look.

Along two portable support posts, Dave and Joan Landamere were tied and gagged, looking to the floor until they heard Clouse's footsteps. They both turned to see him, and gave muffled cries through their gags as he approached. Apparently realizing they might endanger Clouse too, both quickly silenced themselves, certain they had his attention.

Nearby, the firefighter saw Daniels lying belly down, hands rope-tied behind his back with a gag as well. He appeared unconscious from what Clouse could tell, but he would not draw any closer until the rest of the horrifying scene in the large atrium was revealed, serving as a grand stage for the killer's sick, playful imagination.

Against one of the marble statues, Melissa Cranor's headless body leaned forward, arms stretched upward as though reaching to the heavens for help. Her boyfriend's body was stuffed inside a giant vase, only his shoulders and head visible above the rim.

Clouse could see where the throat was slit. The body was a bluish hue with the eyes only partly open as the head lie slumped against the side of the oversized decorative object. It was almost like visiting a wax museum, but realistic beyond Clouse's wildest dreams. He never expected to walk into anything so gruesome as the scene before him.

Beside the vase was a jack-o-lantern seated on the floor, flickering from the inside as a candle burned. It was becoming symbolic for death within this entire ordeal, which started on the most creepy holiday of the year. Clouse realized just how much trouble one person had gone through to set the stage for this final act. One way or another he would find out the answers to every question he had posed the past three weeks.

As he approached Daniels' unconscious form, Clouse spied a state trooper's uniform, previously hidden behind Joan Landamere. Haplessly laid to rest on his front side, arms sprawled out on the floor, Jason Brinkman's corpse appeared stiff, and somewhat dirty, much like Bennett's had been. The eyes were closed, and of the bodies, his appeared the most at peace if there was any such thing for the victims.

Avoiding the Landameres for the time being, Clouse knelt beside Daniels, finding a pulse along the detective's neck as he placed a small blade in Daniels' partly opened hands in case anything happened to Clouse and the detective woke up. At least one of them would hopefully make it out alive. Clouse knew the end was quickly drawing near in one form or another.

"I see you've made it to my little gathering," a voice called from some distance behind Clouse, echoing through the mammoth atrium.

Bolting to his feet, the firefighter whirled to see Roger Summers carrying a head in one hand as he crossed the atrium floor toward his brother-in-law.

"Heads up," he said, tossing Melissa Cranor's head to Clouse, who refused to catch it, letting it thump against the floor beside him, leaving bloody patches as it bounced off the ceramic tile.

"You're no fun anymore, Paul," Summers said, acting much more at ease than he had that morning.

Almost fully relaxed in fact.

As though this was all rehearsed.

"You managed to get here quickly," Clouse noted, refusing to let Summers near him. Summers circled around him, stopping as he drew near Daniels. Clouse also stopped in front of the helpless Landameres, keeping a watchful eye on Summers in case he tried to harm the detective.

"I have some good connections," Summers said. "After all, I'm not the one accused of murdering Angie by everyone in Bloomington, am I?"

"You're smooth all right," Clouse commented bitterly, realizing all of his fears were completely true.

"Somehow you don't seem totally shocked, Paul," Summers commented. "Seems your buddy over here is smarter than you are," he added, walking over to lightly kick Daniels' motionless form. "You should watch what you throw away at the station."

Clouse refused to take his eyes off Summers, not noticing that directly behind him, Landamere was loosening his bonds.

"I'll keep that in mind, brother," Clouse said with a sour tone, mocking how Summers always referred to him.

Dressed in a black cloak, but without the benefit of hood or mask, Summers still appeared creepy in the costume. He was an imposing form, and it was no wonder victims fell so easily.

"We've got a lot to talk about, Paul," Summers noted. "But it will have to wait."

Before Clouse could ask why it would have to wait, Dave Landamere dropped the ropes from their loose position around his hands, to the floor, taking up a small garden shovel from between his legs. With one swift motion he clocked the fireman in the back of the skull, sending Clouse unconscious to the floor with a thud.

31

"I didn't want Roger to have all the fun," Landamere said as Clouse regained consciousness, rubbing his head as he sat on the tiled floor.

Though he was not bound like Joan Landamere and Daniels, the gun in his brother-in-law's hand was enough to keep him where he was.

"Dave, I can understand your stand in this," Clouse said, still feeling his head, "but Roger, I don't get your angle. Why, Roger?"

"Why, Roger, why?" Summers mocked him, waving the gun airily. "Paul, that's the dumbest question you could possibly ask."

Summers paced the floor a moment, thinking about where he wished to begin his tale. He looked to Landamere, smiled, and knelt fairly close to Clouse, the gun dangling in one hand across his knee. He seemed to be having fun with this at Clouse's expense.

"Let's start from the beginning," Summers said. "You already know Dave worked in the Chicago area but what you didn't know was that we met on a common project while I was in the Navy, stationed there.

"To make a long story short, I moved back, Dave moved back, and we decided to collaborate on a different sort of project. See, we knew if we scared the shit out of the people around this hotel we could drop the price and eventually buy it for pennies on the dollar."

Landamere stepped forward to speak.

"But we knew Smith would never sell to just anyone, so we created Tincher, a company that cared about its work, and the investments it purchased and ran. You probably didn't have much time to research deeply into that, did you, Paul? See, the guest book was kind of our tracking system for snoops who might look at Tincher for the wrong reasons."

"The original idea was just to scare the people through the Father Ernest legend and some ghostly sightings," Summers added. "We thought about it though, and decided it would take a little more than just that to scare Dr. Smith and the workers away."

"So you went and hacked people up?" Clouse asked, shocked at the notion of murdering for financial gain.

"Well, Roger did most of it," Landamere said, giving credit. "But I got a little dirty with those two unruly teenagers and that trooper."

"You did pretty well," Summers said with a complementary nod. "I have to admit it was a hell of a lot of fun roughing you up, Paul, and destroying that computer before you could research us anymore. Now, cleaning up after the old detective's body parts proved rather gory, but I managed to itemize everything for the police."

Clouse shook his head in disappointment, amazed the one person he knew and trusted for so long committed such acts. A person completely instrumental in making his life as he knew it exactly what it was.

"And as for the rest of the money to finish up and run this place for an unholy profit, we simply need to have you finish up your rampage of murder right here and now, Paul," Landamere noted.

"You see, after you walk in here, dig up all these bodies, and kill both my wife and your detective friend using his own weapon, you'll take your own life because you'll finally realize you've destroyed everyone you love, and life is no longer worth living," he summed up the end of the plan.

"You still don't have a concrete alibi for any of the murders, and after you blow away Detective Daniels, there won't be anyone left to dispute your guilt. And no one will even care, Paul," Landamere added with a maniacal grin. "It'll all be swept neatly under a carpet, and no one will care that you, a psychotic, delusional murderer, took his own life."

"Oh," Summers butted in. "We invited your county police friend but he was unable to make it."

"So hospitable of you," Clouse said bitterly, finally realizing where the master plan was heading.

"From the insurance on Mrs. Landamere we should make enough to finish the hotel at cost, or at least enough to take out a large insurance policy," Summers noted. "We play it by ear, see if there's interest in the property, and if the money isn't there, the hotel has an unfortunate accident and we collect the insurance. Both Dave and I know how to work the system, Paul. We would have brought you into this, but you've always been too straight-laced."

"I still want to know exactly what turned you into a scythe-wielding maniac," Clouse insisted.

"Now that's the one part you should know," Summers said with a laugh. "You murdered my sister after everything I've done for the both of you, just so you could collect the insurance and have everything to yourself, so I decided to do the same exact thing and take everything from you."

Clouse's shocked look caught Summers off-guard.

"I had nothing to do with Angie's murder, Rodge," Clouse said steadily, looking Summers straight in the eye. "How the *hell* could you ever believe I did?"

"Finish this," Landamere whispered hurriedly to Summers as his fellow conspirator shot him a quizzical stare.

"No," Summers replied. "This needs a proper ending. There's a lot to be said for how things end."

Clouse looked over to Daniels for a moment while the two debated exactly what to do with him. Without looking up, the detective took the small blade Clouse had placed in his hands, and began to work away the rope binding his hands.

"Do you really think I could have gone home and killed Angie when I was working that night, Rodge?" Clouse insisted, purposely barging in on their conversation.

"You could have," Summers said, outwardly growing less certain by the second.

He seemed to still genuinely believe Clouse was to blame for all of his family's problems after Angie's death.

"Angie and I weren't on the outs as someone led you to believe," Clouse noted, shooting a glance toward Landamere. "Who pushed the idea of murdering the workers here, Rodge?" he asked insistently. "Who had the most to gain from this whole thing?"

Slowly, Summers looked to Landamere, who looked from his bound and gagged wife back to his fellow conspirator.

"Finish him, Roger," Landamere insisted with a hiss. "Don't let him lie to you like that."

Summers looked at his hands, and the gun clutched in one, possibly realizing Clouse was correct, or possibly ready to aim at his brother-in-law and pull the trigger.

"You've known me ten years, Roger," Landamere stated. "You don't know *him* that way," he added, pointing to Clouse as though he were a complete stranger to both of them. "Day after day he kept coming to work here, telling me his marriage was failing and he didn't know how he would ever pay the bills. I warned you months ahead of time what Paul was capable of, then it happened. He took that insurance policy out on your sister, then killed her for profit."

"Bullshit!" Clouse yelled at Landamere. "You are a piece of work, Dave. You've had this master plan worked out all along," he said, slowly standing up, keeping them both from looking to Daniels, who had cut most of the ropes. "The thing I want to know is when your conscience abandoned you, because it was obviously long before you met me."

"You can't trust him, Roger," Landamere almost pleaded. "Blow him away and let's get on with making millions."

Shaking his head, Summers turned away from them, holding his hands up in frustration. He shook the gun enough to make both Clouse and Landamere nervous. For the first time, he realized he had murdered on the premise of mere words from a man he deeply trusted.

Trusted too much, perhaps.

Joan Landamere shrilled from within her gag, uncertain of what to expect as well.

Taking advantage of Summers' distraction, Landamere decided to protect his own interests, pulling the fallen county officer's gun from within his jacket, ready to fire at Summers if necessary.

Clouse shot a quick glance to Daniels, who looked up for the first time, barely lifting his hands behind him to indicate he was free. He returned his attention to Landamere, just as the project manager drew a gun from his jacket. Clouse rushed toward him, knocking it free, back toward the detective.

Turning around to a complete scene of confusion, Summers looked past Clouse, who hit Landamere with a hard right hand, toward Daniels. The detective stood, scrambling for the gun, which provided the only threat to Landamere and Summers pulling off their scheme if they could still coexist.

Taking quick aim, Summers fired the service pistol, missing completely on the first shot, but firing a second directly into Daniels' backside, flooring the detective. As Landamere fell to the floor from a second punch, Clouse looked to Daniels, who lay motionless halfway across the atrium. A blood pool formed atop his back, through his jacket.

"Damn it, Roger," Clouse said quietly, giving a mixed look of shock and disdain to his brother-in-law. "This has to end."

Clouse didn't care anymore. He would say whatever he chose and face the consequences. Almost everything he knew and cared about was destroyed during the past two weeks by the man he looked up to and respected like a big brother. Only now did Summers realize the extent of his mistake and his misplaced trust in Landamere.

Now that it was too late.

Frustrated that his emotions were toyed with by Landamere, and that his once good nature was tarnished with utter evil, Summers felt his eyes water, knowing he could not return to a normal life, nor could he finish this lie, this evil ploy with Landamere, learning it was based completely on greed and deception.

He pointed the gun at Landamere, who held up a foreboding hand with wide eyes, silently begging for mercy.

"You killed my sister," Summers finally spoke what he had come to realize.

"All for this," he added, looking up to the glass dome, loosely holding the firearm. A serious look etched itself across his face as he composed himself again.

For what seemed several minutes the betrayed firefighter took careful aim at Landamere, then turned toward one of the atrium entrances, tossing the gun like a frisbee. It hit the wall, echoing as its metal frame collided with solid concrete.

"I'm sorry," Summers said to Clouse, stumbling away with the realization his life as he knew it was over.

He headed toward one of the atrium exits, possibly wanting it completely over as he stripped away the black cloak from his body, tossing it aside.

Clouse also saw him undo the bulletproof vest beneath it, then toss it against a wall before he exited the atrium. Several stopped slugs were visible from where Timmons, the missing teenager, had shot the reaper several times before his untimely death.

Clouse turned his attention to Landamere for a moment, full of rage he would not be able to contain, were he not preoccupied with Summers' new revelation.

"You son-of-a-bitch," the fireman scorned the project manager.

"You had this set up from day one," he said, realizing just how long they had worked together. "You bided your time, waiting for the right opportunity. When Angie and I separated, you found out from Roger, and put your scheme into action."

"Just admit it, Paul. It was brilliant, was it not?" Landamere said, cracking a slight smile, not bothering to rise from the floor.

Clouse soured even more.

"But now it's over. I'll see this hotel imploded before you ever own it," he said, looking to Daniels, who still lay motionless across the atrium. "You asshole."

Quickly darting over to the detective, Clouse saw the pool of blood emanating from the center of his back, near the spine. Summers was a better shot than Clouse ever imagined. Putting that fact out of his mind, he knelt beside Daniels.

"Talk to me, Mark," Clouse said, avoiding the usual formality in names.

"Can't feel my legs," the detective answered quietly so Landamere would not hear. He was still belly-down on the ground, and stuck that way because Clouse would not risk moving him. Snatching Landamere's gun from its nearby spot on the ground, Clouse placed it in the detective's left hand, assured the man could still grip a weapon.

"I'll be right back, Mark. I'm calling the police and getting Roger before he does something else stupid."

"I'm not going anywhere," the detective answered quietly again, knowing he could do little to protect himself once Clouse left the room. He pulled the gun closer, tucking it beneath his jacket, hoping to avoid using it.

Clouse wanted to stay with the detective, but felt a deeper urgency to save Summers from his own destruction, despite everything his brother-in-law had wrongfully done.

He walked out of the atrium to find Summers under Landamere's watchful eye. The project manager knew he could not confront Clouse without a weapon, and the only useful gun he knew of, lay across the atrium against a wall.

Besides, he knew Clouse would be back once he and Summers were finished. He hoped they might kill one another and give him an easy conclusion to an otherwise complex situation.

32

Clouse entered the circular hallway, listening for his brother-in-law's footsteps, hoping they weren't in the direction of the dead bodies. He no longer felt any sense of danger confronting Summers, and sensed what frame of mind the man was in.

Unfortunately, he probably knew the hotel's layout just as well as Clouse did.

Down the hall he heard the elevator door close. Taking off his jacket, Clouse tossed it behind him before running down the hall to discover he was too late for the elevator, which was heading to the top floor.

"Shit," Clouse muttered, knowing two exit points led to the roof above.

This elevator was one.

Another was a long flight of stairs leading to a door on the roof. Clouse had no time to climb six stories before the elevator delivered Summers to his destination. The second elevator, across the atrium, only went to the sixth floor, and not the roof access, so Clouse still had a run ahead of him if he tried to use it.

No, he decided. He was waiting for this car to return.

He pushed the up button several times, anxious to discover exactly what Summers was up to.

Down the hall in the atrium, Landamere looked up to his wife from a sitting position where he recovered from Clouse's attack, smiled sadistically as she stared down at him wide-eyed, and stood, slowly crossing the atrium to retrieve the gun Summers had tossed away, assuming Clouse had taken the other weapon with him.

As he picked up the weapon, the project manager strolled toward Daniels first, seeing no movement from the detective. He stopped short of the motionless man, viewing the bodies and the bizarre horror around him. Smells of death and dirt intertwined for an unusually foul odor inside the freshly-cleaned atrium.

"Too bad you figured it out too late, detective," Landamere said, kicking Daniels over to his backside, surprised to see him still alive.

"You're still finished," Daniels said between labored breaths, the bullet in his backside plaguing him several different ways.

Being overturned put his back in agony.

"You won't be able to wrap everything up neatly before Clouse calls the police."

"You'd be amazed what I can do," Landamere said confidently. "I have several contributors to this project who will do anything to see it succeed. People you and your pathetic department would have no chance of discovering."

Landamere checked the gun over, released the safety, and pointed at the detective's waist, slowing tracing his torso up to his head.

"Don't worry," he said. "I'll put you out of your misery, just like the wounded animal you are, detective."

Daniels' hand had slowly crept toward his jacket during the course of the conversation, but he would never draw before Landamere put a hole in his head. Still, he had to try. He only needed the murderer to shift his attention for a second.

"Freeze!" he heard from across the atrium, barely able to see the county officer drawing a bead on Landamere with his service pistol.

From what he could see in such a prone, limited position, Daniels thought it was Kaiser, though they had only met once. From the way Summers had spoken, he figured the county officer for dead. Then again, they had been so determined to make Clouse as miserable as possible before they killed him, they probably twisted the truth.

Daniels knew there was no way Landamere would surrender to the county officer, but he felt compelled to keep quiet since a nine-millimeter duty weapon was still pointed directly at his head. For a moment the three men exchanged glances, almost like the multiple person showdowns in old westerns.

"Drop your weapon, Ken, or the detective gets a lobotomy the hard way," Landamere instructed the familiar officer.

After a few seconds of thought, Kaiser set his weapon to the ground, rising to a standing position, unaware of what Landamere had in mind.

Kaiser failed to react to Landamere's surprise turn of the gun on him. One shot fired from the weapon tore through the officer's chest, flooring him with a thud, as the impact took his feet out from under him. Left groaning in pain, the officer rolled to one side, blood oozing from his chest and shoulder area.

Landamere smiled with the utmost confidence, unaware that shooting Kaiser had left an opening for Daniels to draw the concealed gun from his jacket and aim it upward at him, with as steady an aim as the detective could muster.

Once he saw the pistol pointed at his forehead, Landamere's smile quickly faded at the same moment Daniels pulled the trigger, jerking the project manager's head back as a red spot appeared instantaneously in the center of his forehead.

A shocked look crossed the man's face the second before he died, as his fading eyes looked into those of the detective. Landamere was genuinely surprised anything spoiled his plan after so much effort to keep it all together.

His body wavered a second or two before collapsing to the floor in a heap.

Daniels breathed a sigh of relief while Joan Landamere sighed through her gag, looking off in a different direction, apparently glad her ordeal was over.

Strangely, no one in the room was in a position to get help because Kaiser's radio was in his patrol car, since he was officially off-duty for the day. Daniels simply laid still, getting some satisfaction knowing justice was served, even if he might never walk again.

He hoped Clouse returned soon, because no one else was going anywhere.

*   *   *

When the elevator finally reached the roof access, Clouse stepped from the car, into a small room containing a door that led onto the roof.

He stepped into the brisk air, finding the black, rubbery surface wet in several spots from the recent rain showers. Treaded mats created a safe walkway along the roof. Parts of the roof felt spongy when walked on, so a path of durable tread circled around the dome part of the roof.

A few small buildings atop the black roof contained heating and cooling units, while a few small shacks held ducts for the units. Standing beside the dome, Clouse noticed the windows allowing a peek into the atrium from high above, but ignored them.

A rusty ladder, that looked somewhat like a staircase along its bottom portion, led to the top of the dome. A rounded room known as the crow's nest provided an access point where lights were changed above the chandelier. Paintings far older than Clouse lined the metallic walls of the old room, and graffiti marred their beauty, identifying people from the hotel's various eras, bold enough to sign their names.

Clouse figured Summers had no intention of getting inside the rounded room to dive into the atrium. It was a tricky climb, and getting through the small hatch along the floor of the tiny room was no easy feat.

Instead, Clouse rounded the first bend along the roof, finding a shell of the man he once trusted and loved beside one of the four towers.

"Talk to me, Rodge," Clouse said, not getting a response from his somberly pensive brother-in-law.

Summers stared over the edge to the brick walkway below, and several trees that looked to obstruct any jump from such a height.

As the two stood a safe distance from one another, the sky let loose with sleet and rain to accompany the heavy winds sweeping through the hotel grounds. Ordinarily, Clouse liked being on the roof, seeing everything for miles around.

All of the hotel's other buildings, including the storage rooms and the old sports utility building, seemed so small below.

For Clouse, nothing compared to the bird's eye view into the glass dome of the atrium, seeing the giant steel rails below, holding up a literal ton of glass. It gave him an entirely different perspective of the hotel and what craftsmanship went into building it so many decades before. He also marveled at old fire stations the same way.

The same way he once admired his brother-in-law.

"I was so self-involved," Summers said after a minute. "Dave lied to me for so long in setting this up that his word became gospel," he added, a tear coming to his eye, realizing everything he had thrown away.

"He screwed us all, Rodge," Clouse said, desperately thinking of a way to dissuade his brother-in-law from thinking of suicide. "You've got a wife and kids. Let's get out of here and go see them."

"No. They're better off with me dead," Summers said, looking back to the edge from the black roof surface below him. "I never realized everything I might throw away. I was so damn bent on revenge and making things right that it never occurred to me it might all be one big lie."

"I'm not letting you do this, Rodge," Clouse said with the greatest of confidence he could muster.

"Why? So you can enjoy watching me rot in prison? Or die in the gas chamber?" Summers asked angrily, finally looking toward Clouse. "I'll be a disgrace to everyone on our department, and my family will know I was partly the cause of Angie's death. I can't live with that, Paul. Let me do this," he said, nodding toward the unforgiving concrete below.

"No," Clouse answered with a foreboding tone.

At that moment, Summers realized he had lost his big brother role and Clouse was now the responsible one. The one in control.

He smiled awkwardly, determined to end his own life, rather than face the ones he loved in shame.

There was no explaining what he had done, and there was no going back. He realized what he had to do, and climbed the short wall of the roof to jump.

"No!" Clouse yelled, grabbing his brother-in-law by the seat of the pants to pull him back.

Summers turned suddenly, hitting Clouse with a strong right hook. The younger fireman staggered, trying to shake off the punch.

"Don't make me do this," Summers insisted. "I've already hurt everyone too much. Just let me go."

Without a word, Clouse charged forward, taking Summers down with a football tackle before crossing left and right fists across his face. Though nearly equal in size and strength, Clouse always had more of a tendency to excel when under pressure, frightened, or both. Summers wanted no part of him like this.

Clasping the younger man by the shirt, Summers tossed him off, now ready to fight if necessary. He wiped the blood from his lips as the rain soaked him. The combination of rain and sleet made the surface of the hotel roof slick. He consciously kept track of his footing as the two contemplated their next moves.

Moving toward one another, the two locked stares, each determined to foil the other's intentions. Summers threw a jab first, hitting Clouse in the jaw. The roof surface tripped the younger man, landing him on his posterior as Summers staggered toward the edge of the roof once again.

"Damn it!" Clouse said to himself, regaining his footing enough to run and baseball slide against the wall, catching Summers by the foot before he could lift it over the wall.

"Give it up, Paul. I'm going," Summers stated.

Doing as he said, Summers broke his foot free from Clouse's grasp, pulling himself up to the wall. Once again Clouse tugged him back, throwing a right hook that landed squarely against Summers' jaw, teetering him back several steps.

Before Clouse could follow up on the punch Summers bolted toward one of the four towers alongside the hotel. The slick surface slowed him down enough that Clouse could follow closely, but both lost their footing several times in the trek toward the huge tower as the roof iced over.

Reaching the tower first, Summers let himself in, slamming the door against Clouse's head. Falling back several steps as he held a hand to his head, Clouse wondered if it was worth such pain to save a man who wished to die.

Nonetheless, he pushed on, bursting through the door in time to see his brother-in-law climbing a ladder to the higher portion of the tower where it would be a cinch to jump without intrusion or inter-ruption. Clouse quickly followed, trying to avoid snagging his cow-boy boots against the ladder rungs.

He reached the top level just as Summers leapt over the railing, but managed to dive forward enough to catch one of the man's hands. It was a situation he had experienced only twice as a fire-fighter where someone's well-being hung literally in his hands. This was the first time he recalled the situation definitely being life-threatening.

Bracing himself against the tower railing, Clouse grabbed for Summers' other hand as they both stared down, now even further than before. Still, Summers showed no fear of dying. Clouse real-ized it was all but over, refusing to let go of his tight grip.

Catching a foot alongside the tower wall, Summers braced him-self, beginning to climb back toward the tower railing as though he had changed his mind. He took a few steps upward, Clouse assist-ing him by pulling with every bit of strength he had.

Suddenly, Summers paused.

"Let me go, Paul," he insisted, looking up to his brother-in-law, not the ground below.

"You know I can't, Rodge."

Summers closed his eyes a few seconds and nodded in under-standing. He would do the same thing if their roles were reversed.

But they weren't.

Placing his feet against the wall, Summers pulled himself up a few more steps and looked at Clouse with a strange grin. Taking hold of Clouse's hands, he crossed them over, making his brother-in-law's grip more difficult.

Summers then let his weight fall entirely downward, smashing Clouse's forearms against the railing. Wracked with pain, immediately thinking one of his wrists might be broken, Clouse felt his grip break loose. This sent Summers into a downward spiral, tumbling against the building several times before the deadly impact with the ground arrived.

Clouse slumped against the tower wall, ignoring the pain in his forearm as the emotional pain intensified. Perhaps selfish motivation, remembering the good times gone by, made him want to save Roger Summers, but he felt doubly hurt by the man now.

Summers had always been a man of strong convictions in life, and perhaps those rules he lived by made choosing death easy for a man with so much pride.

Only now did Clouse realize how easily manipulated even the best of men could be. He planned to teach his own son the value of true friendship and family. In the end, little else mattered.

He stared down at Summers' distorted body, wondering what else was left.

Was it finally over?

Subconsciously he straddled part of the railing, looking down at the spot Summers had hung from, wondering if he could have done anything more to save the man.

"Don't do anything stupid," a voice said from behind him as someone clasped his arm, tugging him back softly.

"I'm not," Clouse answered, turning to see Kaiser standing behind him, using his left arm and a thick towel to put pressure on the wound to his right shoulder. "What happened to you?"

"Got shot by your buddy Landamere."

"And you climbed up here like that just to check on me? I'm flattered," Clouse replied, stepping back into the tower, ready to follow Kaiser down the ladder.

Kaiser gingerly stepped into the hatch first, descending the ladder. Clouse followed, careful to give his friend an ample lead.

"And he's not my buddy anymore," the fireman added as he stepped down, glad the ordeal finally had closure.

33

Less than a week later Daniels was able to have visitors other than his family. Though still unable to walk, the prognosis was good. The swelling in his spine had recessed enough that doctors could evaluate him.

Just a few days prior, Daniels had given his statement to state police, corroborating both Clouse and Joan Landamere. According to Joan, her husband had abducted her after Daniels visited the house, and made haste to the hotel, luring the detective into his specially designed trap.

It appeared Landamere had everything planned far in advance, but didn't want to carry out the plan any sooner than he had to.

"They say I should be up and walking within a few months," Daniels told Clouse from his hospital bed where he sat propped on a few pillows, with a tray of less than desirable food in front of him. "I should regain feeling in my legs within a couple weeks."

Clouse lifted the cast on his wrist, displaying his own battle wound. It was evaluated as a hairline fracture.

"Looks like an excuse to get off work," the detective scoffed.

"God knows I haven't had enough of that," Clouse joked. "I'm just glad to have something I can call a life again."

Both looked past the pleated curtains to the outside, at the season's first real snowfall. The holidays were quickly approaching, and neither planned on having their best time ever among family. Things would never quite be the same for either man.

Without carpet, the hospital room felt chilly. It was another sign that winter had officially arrived. Zach was asking his father to go find a Christmas tree, perhaps in a subtle attempt to put the past further behind them.

"What's this I hear about you being nominated for police officer of the year?" Clouse asked, suddenly recalling an article from the morning paper.

Daniels chuckled.

"My chief jumped right on that one," he said. "It'll be awful hard to sum up my nomination in just one paragraph after all this."

"You'll get it," Clouse said confidently. "After all you've been through, there's no one more deserving."

"Thanks."

"It's me who should be thanking you," the firefighter said. "You were the only one who gave me a chance through this whole thing, and you almost got killed trying to prove my innocence. I can't repay that."

"Then don't try," Daniels said. "But *do* fill me in on some of the details I haven't heard about yet."

"Like what?" Clouse asked with a quizzical look.

"Like where all those bodies were stored, and why the state police never found them."

"Easy enough. Landamere used Father Ernest's grave site to store them since it was freshly dug, and police usually refrain from disturbing graves. He just piled them inside and discarded the extra dirt in the woods."

Daniels knew the police probably couldn't disturb the grave site, even if they had suspected it, because a warrant would have been necessary on private property and they were still technically looking for missing people at the time.

"And the vehicles?"

"Landamere had a storage facility in town where utility vehicles were stored for Kieffer Construction. Thing is, they were all summer work vehicles so no one would have had any reason to visit the building. Both Melissa Cranor's car and Bennett's work van were found there the next day."

"So Landamere knew Roger for a decade and once they found one another in Indiana they devised this plan to scare people off from the hotel?"

"True," Clouse answered, still amazed he never knew a thing about their relationship beforehand. "But things changed when I came to work for Dave. He saw the opportunity to push the scare even further and used Roger. From almost the time I started the West Baden project, Dave was feeding Roger lies about me and my marriage, establishing a revenge motive early on. When Angie and I split up, he used that fully to his advantage and made me sound desperate for money and a way out of my marriage. Neither was true of course."

Daniels nodded.

"So what's going to happen to the hotel?"

"Dr. Smith is pleased things are back to normal," Clouse answered. "Kieffer Construction is interviewing for a new project manager. If he's up to it, I suspect Rusty will be the man for the job."

"That's horrible what they did to his daughter."

"It's been horrible for all of us," Clouse added. "I wish I could say things will return to normal, but there *isn't* a normal anymore. Roger's family and our department agreed to bury him without ceremony just to keep things quiet. I doubt I'll be on speaking terms with any of his family again."

For a moment both of them sat silently, each wondering different things.

Daniels seriously questioned the extent of his stay at the hospital, while Clouse thought about the future, and whether or not Angie would want him to move on. He was in no hurry to rebuild his life, but the horrific visions of his wife haunted him. Clouse never wanted to remember her as a bloody mess the way Dave Landamere had left her.

"How did Landamere get into your house that night to murder Angie?" Daniels questioned, as though reading Clouse's mind. "I mean, she did lock the doors, didn't she?"

"He probably lifted Roger's key to my house then returned it, or just copied it. Once you got to know Rodge, he got too trustworthy, even with his possessions."

"Sounds like he had Roger under his thumb."

"A little too much," Clouse admitted. "You were right when you said it was someone close to me."

"But I didn't expect a pair," Daniels noted.

"Me neither. Care if I use the commode before I take off?" Clouse asked, thumbing toward the tiny bathroom.

"Go ahead."

Clouse closed the door behind him, did his business, then washed his face in the sink. When he looked up, a ghostly figure stood behind him dressed in the purest white dress, with the most peaceful smile Clouse had ever seen on her face.

"Ang?" he asked aloud, wondering why on earth his wife's spirit chose a hospital restroom to visit him again.

Perhaps timing was her motive.

Without a sound, the specter looked at him in the mirror's view, blew him a kiss, then disappeared.

There had been no blood, no discontent.

Perhaps Angie was now at peace. Clouse sensed he could move on with his life, even with the possibility his imagination was playing tricks on him.

"Everything okay?" Daniels asked when he emerged from tiny room, staring at his hands.

"Everything's just fine," Clouse replied, a grin crossing his face. "Take care of yourself, detective," he said as he opened the door to leave.

"You too," Daniels with a voice that echoed the uneasy feeling in his own heart. He watched as the firefighter left, wishing he could have emerged from the incident so unscathed.

His destiny would be determined by willpower and months of rehabilitation, but he intended to live a normal life once more.

Epilogue

By August the next year, things had changed for the better.

The hotel was almost fully renovated, rooms and everything. Clouse was content with both of his jobs, since Rusty had eventually taken the project manager position with Kieffer Construction, and his relationship with Jane was blossoming quite nicely.

In fact, he had set his mind on proposing before the holiday season came. Things could not get much better for the couple and the two children. Clouse had eventually sold his house and moved in with Jane. She lived in town, but the two actively searched for a country home more suited to the lifestyle they preferred.

"I can't believe Dr. Smith actually gave you a personal suite here," Jane commented, seated on a blanket inside the atrium.

Clouse had brought a picnic basket and white wine for a picnic in front of the hotel's grand fireplace, settled on one side of the atrium. It was large enough for several people to stand inside.

He had obtained permission from Smith to light a fire for such a special occasion. He was more proud than ever of his achievement at the hotel, now that it neared an end, and wanted this to be the place he asked Jane the most important question he could ever ask.

"It's only two small rooms," Clouse said, carefully opening the wine bottle before pouring himself and Jane a glass. "Still, it was a nice gesture."

"I can't believe we have a day without the kids," she commented, looking up at the clear blue sky through the atrium's glass dome six levels above the blanket they sat on.

"God, I feel like I own the place," Clouse said, happy Smith had been so generous toward him.

Not only had Smith decided to maintain ownership of the hotel, he had ordered it finished by Kieffer Construction, to be dedicated in late October, and opened soon thereafter.

"You've got the keys," Jane said. "That's the next best thing."

Clouse smiled. He did that quite a bit more lately.

He looked up through the dome for a moment, lost in the sky as Jane had been a moment earlier.

"What are you thinking about?" she questioned.

"How everything seems so right," he said pensively, still looking up.

"You seem so much happier than when I met you," she said, caressing his face with her soft hand, drawing a long kiss from him.

He finally felt comfortable being intimate again, which was part of the reason he could ask Jane the question that had plagued his mind the past few weeks.

Clouse looked at the fire brewing in front of him, wondering why Jane hadn't questioned his lighting a fire in the middle of summer. The recent cold front was temporary, and by no means chilly. It was nothing more than a few days in which people would avoid their swimming pools and eat inside.

"Did you want a sandwich?" Jane asked, searching through the basket.

Now was the moment to ask.

"Jane," he said seriously, gaining her attention. "I want you to stand over here with me."

Clouse led her to the edge of the fireplace, looking into her eyes as the fire reflected within them. Reaching into his jeans pocket, he pulled out a small box before dropping to one knee. He watched the curious nature of her eyes turn to delight as he opened the box to reveal a sparkling diamond ring, enhanced by the glowing orange light from the fireplace.

"Will you take my hand in marriage?" he asked, not so much as blinking when he did so.

He wanted to remember every split second of this occasion.

Her hands cupped her face as she smiled, and mist came to her eyes. She was genuinely speechless, and to his amazement, she seemed surprised.

"Yes," she said after a moment of recovery. "Yes, I will."

For a moment several tears trickled down her face as she tried to collect herself. For months she had wondered if the day was coming and it finally had. She never pushed, knowing how tormented Clouse was after his first wife died.

She had wondered if he would ever recover enough to spend his life with another partner. Now Jane was assured Clouse had been thinking about the same topics recently, and finally proved himself able to commit.

She led him back to the blanket with something besides food on her mind. For almost a year since Angie died, Clouse had felt shell shocked about developing a relationship and sharing his life, and his bed, with someone else. Part of it was Zach's understanding, and how others might look at him.

Once Zach seemed content with the idea of having a stepsister and a new mom, Clouse decided to live his own life and ignore what others thought or said. It was none of their concern.

"Are you okay with this?" she asked, tugging his polo shirt lightly.

"I'm fine," he said, kissing her again.

Simultaneously, the two knelt on the blanket, undressing one another as their breathing came heavier. Clouse felt an urge to look around in case someone might have made their way into the hotel for a free peep show, but his attention was entirely on Jane, and paranoia had left his mind with time.

He gently laid Jane on the blanket, kissing her deeply while he kicked off his boots. At this moment in their lives nothing could be more perfect, and perhaps it never would be again.

As the couple made love in the grand atrium, their passionate moans echoing throughout the hotel, a light along the sixth floor switched on as a shadow crossed the room, finally coming to a stop behind the room's drawn curtains.

Everything around the newly engaged couple seemed much more at ease lately. They could enjoy the children, their own company, and now the idea of a life together. With Clouse's tragic events almost a year behind him, it was time to move on and start over.

Time for a new life.

Life without haunting memories of tragic death.

Memories that might finally stay buried.

And perhaps, some that would not.

0-595-23260-4

Printed in the United States
70502LV00007B/13

9 780595 232604